A HOE LOT OF TROUBLE

A NINA QUINN MYSTERY

HEATHER WEBBER

AVON BOOKS
An Imprint of HarperCollins*Publishers*

This is a work of fiction. Names, characters, places, and incidents are products of the author's imagination or are used fictitiously and are not to be construed as real. Any resemblance to actual events, locales, organizations, or persons, living or dead, is entirely coincidental.

AVON BOOKS
An Imprint of HarperCollins*Publishers*
10 East 53rd Street
New York, New York 10022-5299

Copyright © 2004 by Heather Webber
ISBN: 0-06-072347-5
www.avonmystery.com

First Avon Books paperback printing: July 2004

Avon Trademark Reg. U.S. Pat. Off. and in Other Countries, Marca Registrada, Hecho en U.S.A.
HarperCollins® is a registered trademark of HarperCollins Publishers Inc.

Printed in the U.S.A.

10 9 8 7 6 5 4 3 2 1

For my family,
for their love and support
(and for inspiring an occasional murderous
thought or two)

All my love

Acknowledgments

My many, many thanks to my writing buddies, Shelley Galloway, Cathy Liggett, Hilda Lindner Knepp, and my long distance buddy Laura Bradford, for their keen eyes and amazing ability to decipher my ramblings.

Thanks as well to my agent Jacky Sach of BookEnds LLC for believing in me, and to Sarah Durand for making me a part of the Avon family.

A HOE LOT OF TROUBLE

One

Thou shall not stuff pictures of thy husband down the garbage disposal.

I made a mental note to add this to my list of personal commandments. I'd put it right after "Thou shalt not eat more than two pints of ice cream in one night" and just before "Thou shalt never wear the correct size jeans." Priorities and all.

I opened the cabinet under the sink and stared at the root of my problem. My newest commandment wasn't a result of sudden regret at the loss of the photos. Instead it came from the fact that by stuffing pictures of the two-timing weasel down the disposal I had caused the sink to clog.

Little Kodak bits of my husband's head floated around the sink's stainless steel basin. I found an odd sense of peace seeing Kevin Quinn drowning—even one-dimensionally—but I couldn't risk Riley seeing the pieces. I fished them out and shoved them in the trash can.

I stared at the stack of prints I'd yet to destroy and picked up the top one. It had been taken soon after I met Kevin. I'd been twenty-one and fresh out of college when Officer Kevin Quinn pulled me over for speeding. Being somewhat desperate—since I'd already gotten two tickets in the previous six months—I faked being sick. I still remember with startling clarity the mad dash I'd made toward the tree line, where I'd given a fair imitation of that *Exorcist* girl—without the head spinning, of course.

Officer Kevin let me off, but later that night showed up at the off-campus apartment I'd shared with my cousin Ana with a pot of chicken soup.

Looking back, I should've taken the ticket.

We looked so disgustingly happy in the picture I was holding.

Kevin, the weasel, hadn't changed much in the last eight years, at least physically. He was still one sexy piece o' man. Six foot, three inches. Short, jet-black wavy hair. Clear green eyes. And a smile that made my knees go all spongy.

He'd been eight years older than me, a widower with a seven-year-old son and a boatload of baggage, but when he looked at me with those vivid green bedroom eyes, smiled that mischievous smile—I'd never had a prayer of escaping, heart intact.

Okay, I admit it. I hadn't wanted to—until recently.

I looked down at my younger, naïve self. My mother liked to think all her kids looked like movie stars. According to Mom, my younger sister Maria was the spitting image of Grace Kelly. My older brother Peter? George Clooney. And amazingly, there *was* some resemblance in a slightly out-of-focus way.

Mom, however, never specified who I looked like—she just kept telling me I had a face for the movies. Which left me wondering if I had more in common with that *Exorcist* girl than just that incident with Kevin.

But I didn't think so. Or at least I hoped not.

Unlike my sister, I'd never be movie-star gorgeous. She was French baguette where I leaned toward . . . pumpernickel. But I'd never minded. My heart-shaped face had its own unique charm I've grown fond of during our twenty-nine years of cohabitation.

As I looked at the picture, I realized I hadn't changed much since I met Kevin either. My shoulder-length brown hair was still styled in that same nondescript bob. My lips were still too full, my smile too wide. Though they could pass for brown most of the time, my eyes remained a dark muddy green, but nowadays they had tiny lines creasing their corners.

Kevin had said I was beautiful.

And I'd believed him.

Until two days ago.

Sighing, I split the photo in two. Tucking my half into my robe pocket, I dunked Kevin's half into the full sink, enjoying it almost as much as I would dipping a Krispy Kreme into hot chocolate. As I tried to figure out what to do about the sink full of water, the phone rang.

I checked the clock. It was early.

"Hello?" I said with an edge to my voice that was sure to frighten any telemarketers.

"Nina?"

Didn't sound like a telemarketer, and although the female voice sounded oddly familiar, I couldn't place it.

"Yes." My tone still warned that I was in no mood to buy a time-share in Costa Rica.

"It's Bridget," she said. "Tim and I got your message and your card. Thank you."

My mouth dropped open. I'd called and left a message on her machine the other day, but I hadn't expected her to call me back. Not for a while, at any rate. Not with all she had going on.

I wrapped the phone cord around my finger. "I was so sorry to hear about Joe."

Bridget's father-in-law, Joe Sandowski—"Farmer Joe," as I used to affectionately call him—was found dead in one of his cornfields early last week. Ordinarily the death of a man as old as Joe wouldn't raise a plucked eyebrow, but apparently, according to the local paper, there had been *something* (which was never specified, and left inquiring minds wanting to know) found at the scene that indicated his death had been anything but natural.

"Thanks," Bridget said. "We're sorry too."

An irrepressible sadness tightened my throat. Although I hadn't seen Joe Sandowski in years, he'd played a pivotal role in my life. His love for the outdoors had rubbed off on me to the point where I'd gone to college for landscape design.

Soon after graduating I had opened my own run-of-the-mill landscaping business, which, through a quirky twist of fate, two years ago had morphed into what it was now: Taken by Surprise, Garden Designs. TBS was one of a kind in this area of Ohio, in the country really. We specialized in surprise garden makeovers. In and out in a day, hard work mixed with more than a little chaos, and in the end, a very happy customer.

My job was extremely gratifying, fun and rewarding. And I'd have none of it if it weren't for Farmer Joe.

I'd wanted to go to his funeral, to pay my respects to a man who'd shaped my life—even if he hadn't known it—but the paper had specified a private ceremony and I hadn't wanted to intrude. I sent one of Hallmark's finest to Bridget and Tim instead—a poor substitute, I know, but what else could I do?

"Nina, do you think we could get together?"

"I-uh—"

Bridget Sandowski had been my friend since she'd shared her purple grapes with me in kindergarten. We'd been joined at the hip until she met Tim, her future husband, our freshman year of high school. Even then, we'd remained close. It wasn't until she and Tim went off to Stanford that we started to lose touch with each other. However, it was one of those friendships that was set in stone, despite the fact that we didn't see each other more than twice a year. At most.

"Of course. Has something happened? Is this about Joe's death?"

There was a slight hesitation before she spoke. "Nina, I'd rather not discuss it on the phone."

Maybe Bridget thought I'd have inside information about Joe's case since I happened to be married to Freedom's lead homicide investigator. Unfortunately, my inside track with the police department had been roadblocked when I kicked Kevin out of the house. And I didn't think my landscaping skills would do her any good at this time in her life.

My curiosity piqued, I said, "Lucky for you it's my day off. When and where do you want to meet?"

"As soon as possible. And anywhere is fine."

I eyed the soggy picture of Kevin and the water dripping off my counter. "I have a few things to take care of here, but I can meet you at Gus's, say eleven?"

"I'll be there."

I hung up the phone, not sure what to make of Bridget's tone. Something in it raised the hairs on the back of my neck.

I tucked the rest of the photos back into my junk drawer and took a sponge to the water pooling on the countertop. As I devised nefarious ways to be rid of the rest of Kevin's images, I suddenly remembered I already had plans for a late breakfast with my best bud, Analise Bertoli—who also happened to be my first cousin on my father's dysfunctional side of the family.

Ana and I'd been close since we were eighteen—which was when my Aunt Rosetta left my Uncle Sal after she caught Uncle Sal playing more than Marco Polo with the pool boy. She'd packed up Ana and my cousin Victor and moved them out of California, back to Ohio, and in with us.

That summer still conjured up nightmares on occasion.

To escape the madhouse, I'd snagged an off-campus apartment and Ana moved in with me. I like to think that move saved my sanity. Ana's, however, was still in question.

I winced as I punched in her cell phone number. She wasn't going to be happy.

She answered on the first ring. "Ana Bertoli, glorified babysitter."

"One of those days, huh?"

"Nina, my life is one of those days. What's up?"

I bit my bottom lip, talked around it. "I need to cancel breakfast."

"What? Huh?" She made static noises. "Don't think I heard you right." More fake static. Her phone was going to be a slobbery mess. Hope she didn't get electrocuted.

When she paused for breath, I said, "I'm sorry. Bridget Sandowski called, said she needs to see me. She sounded weird."

"As in, she's-hitting-the-bottle-at-eight-in-the-morning weird, or just-plain-strange weird?"

"Plain strange weird, unlike you. Tell me you're drinking coffee."

"I'm not saying a word." She laughed, sort of an evil sounding *moo-ha-ha*. "Self-incrimination and all."

I heard a buzz of voices in the background, lots of phones ringing. Ana's a probation officer. Her desk sat smack-dab in the middle of the county's municipal building between four courtrooms and the local lockup. On a quiet day it was a madhouse. Today it sounded like a nightmare.

I picked a chunk of Kevin's cheating smile from the sink, tossed it in the trash. "Let's just hope they're not drug testing today."

Ana ignored me and said, "Who am I going to whine about my love life to?"

"*Your* love life? What about mine?"

"Me. Me. Me," she mocked, but I heard the smile in her voice.

I laughed at how pathetic I must've sounded these last

few days. The details of the Big Boxer Blowout could wait until later.

"Lunch tomorrow?" I offered.

"I won't hold my breath."

"Smart a—"

She cut in. "Buh-bye."

I hung up, smiling. Neuroses aside, Ana always knew how to cheer me up.

I supposed I should plunge. Get it over with. But the sway of the tail on the cat clock Riley had given me years ago reminded me that I had yet to see him this morning. At this rate he was going to miss his bus.

Ignoring the sink for the time being, I yelled, "Riley!" at the top of my lungs. Anything less was ignored.

"Ri-ley!"

I took a peek out the window, and sure enough my neighbor Mr. Cabrera had craned his head in the direction of our house. The walls of our house were notoriously thin, and what was heard during any given week usually provided Mr. Cabrera with enough gossip to get him through the neighborhood's weekly cribbage game.

My house sat in an established nook of Freedom, Ohio, affectionately nicknamed "the Mill." As in gossip mill. Unlike its booming surroundings, this neighborhood had been settled decades ago, and most of its occupants regularly received AARP mailings and insurance pamphlets with Alex Trebek on the envelope. I'd inherited the house from my aunt Chi-Chi just after Kevin and I married, which was why I was able to start up my own landscaping business without falling too seriously into debt.

Gossip here was a way of life. The Mill, located smack dab between Cincinnati and Dayton, was a throwback to a simpler way of life. A place where people sat on their stoops every night, took their neighborhood watch duties seriously, and jumped at every opportunity to pass on information gathered in over-the-fence chats.

At times, it was endearing. But knowing the whole neighborhood would soon hear of my marriage woes . . . Well, that was just annoying.

I started up the stairs armed with a dish towel. In my maternal cache of weapons, this one meant business. "Riley Michael . . ."

I paused outside his room. Bass thumped, vibrating the floor beneath my bare feet, but no music sounded through the closed door. I knocked. No answer.

My hand trembled as I set it on the knob and I cursed my cowardice six ways to Sunday. I'm not big on confrontations, not with surly teenagers and not with the state of his room—which I'm quite sure must have at least five health code violations.

The smell was the first thing to assault my senses as I slowly pushed open Riley's door. The pungency of teenage-male sweat, mixed with a slight odor of musk, hung over the room.

The utter chaos was the next thing to knock me down a notch. But this time only my sense of style was wounded. Decorated in what could only be called by interior designers as "early adolescence," the room was strewn with clothes from wall to wall. I couldn't be sure, because it had been so long since I had seen it, but I thought the rug was shaggy green. I looked down to check, but saw a cup with what I hoped had dried chocolate milk in it and decided I really didn't need to know.

Posters hung on every available inch of wall space. His art tastes varied: half-naked women, ball players, rock stars. But it seemed, at least to my quick perusal, that the babes outnumbered the others. Not really surprising, considering his age.

I refused to look at the glass tank gracing the wall to the

right of his bed. What was in that tank was scarier than the cup on the floor. A chill danced up my spine as heebie-jeebies made me want to run for the door.

I had met Riley eight years ago, when he was seven. Back then, he was a four-foot-odd pudge, his blue eyes rounded with hurt and a healthy dose of scorn. I'd like to say our bond had grown over the years, but another one of my commandments was not to delude myself. I had no trouble with out-and-out lying, but self-delusion was a definite no-no.

"Ry!" I shouted. No response.

His long lean body stretched facedown across the twin bed, his feet dangling over the edge. There was a hole in the toe of his left sock, I noticed, as his foot tapped a furious beat through the air.

Gone now was his pudge, replaced with sinewy muscle. In another year or so girls would be tripping over their feet to get his attention.

I *thwapped* him on the back of his thigh with my dish towel.

When he spotted me, he hastily shoved the magazine he'd been reading under his pillow.

Hmmm.

I saw nothing new in the blue depths of his eyes as he looked at me. Just scorn, an emotion I thought I had steeled myself against years ago. Today, however, it brought a fresh slice of pain. I had kicked Kevin out of the house. Eventually Riley would join his father. Swallowing a sudden lump in my throat, I pushed that thought out of my mind. One thing at a time.

Slowly he reached up and lowered his left earphone. "Yeah?" He ran a hand over his hair to smooth it into place.

His hair was normally a wavy brown. This week it was black with bleached stripes. A sign of maturation, in his opinion. A sign of idiocy, in mine.

"School. You need to eat." When addressing a teenager,

you needed to speak in short concise sentences. Anything less was not absorbed.

"Not hungry," he mumbled.

I *thwapped* him again with the dish towel. He raised his gaze to meet mine. Anger replaced scorn. I was actually grateful for the change, but his behavior grated on my already stretched-to-the-point-of-no-return nerves. *I will not fight. I will not fight*, I repeated until I felt my anger turn from boil to simmer.

Reaching up, he slid the headphones down around his neck.

I crossed my arms over my chest. "A banana?"

"I'm not a damn baby, Nina."

I dismissed the urge to tighten the headphone cord around his throat. What *would* Child Services say? "I didn't say I was going to mash it and spoonfeed you."

"I told you: I'm. Not. Hungry."

"Fine!"

"Fine."

"Fine!"

His dark lashes lowered. "You think I'm stupid."

I sighed. It was going to be one of *those* days, not just for Ana but for me too. "I do not think you're stupid, Riley."

"Yes, Nina, you do. You think I don't know what's going on with you and Dad?"

My stomach twisted, nausea coming sudden and swift. He was definitely smarter than I had given him credit for, but I had *never* thought him dumb. Kevin and I had tried to disguise his absence with a lame-o story of him being under cover. Riley had obviously seen right through our little sham.

"That's our business."

"No, it isn't."

He had mastered the art of condescension. I looked deep

into his unreadable eyes. "Your father and I are having some problems," I admitted.

"Did he cheat?"

The words hit me with force. I stumbled backward, a knot of something sour eating away at my stomach. My voice had gone AWOL, leaving me with nothing to reiterate that it was none of his fifteen-year-old business.

His lower lip jutted out. "Thought so."

I realized with a start that I'd been played. Riley'd been on a fishing expedition and I'd wriggled right up to the hook and impaled myself. Damn, I hated when that happened.

He waved a hand toward the door, dismissing me. "You can go."

Grrr.

Replacing the headphones, he turned his back to me. Carefully, I backtracked out of the room, supremely proud of myself for not slamming the door.

I paused outside his room. The notion that I should apologize nagged at me. *Why?* For caring if he starved? For wanting to keep his father's and my business to ourselves? The floor stopped vibrating, and I pushed away from the wall before Riley could come out and accuse me of spying on him.

Since I tended to clean when stressed, I headed for the laundry room to throw in a quick load of wash. As I stepped over the threshold, I stopped short. This was where it had all begun two days ago—the beginning to the end of my marriage.

Lipstick on his boxers—a shade that wasn't mine, seeing as how I hadn't worn lipstick since the seventh grade. His betrayal was so cliché I wanted to laugh. But I couldn't. It still hurt.

I left the laundry in the hamper.

Back in the kitchen, I broke a cardinal commandment by calling the office on my day off.

My secretary, Tamara Oliver, answered on the first ring. "Taken by Surprise, this is Tam."

Despite the mess my life was in, I couldn't help the shimmer of pride I felt. My company, Taken by Surprise, Garden Designs, had started as a lark and spread like wildfire. It was just about the only thing going well in my world right now. "It's Nina."

"It's your day off," Tam reminded, humor lacing her words.

I ignored her unsubtle dig. "How are things?" When I didn't get an immediate answer, I got nervous. "Tam?"

Her heavy sigh echoed across the line. "A hoe is missing."

"Another one?!" This was the third in two weeks.

"And a shovel. And a rake." I heard the wince in her voice as she continued. "And a wheelbarrow."

"What! From the storage unit?"

"No. From Kit's truck."

Kit was my head landscaping contractor and site foreman, and he was one of my closest friends.

"But he doesn't know when the things were taken. Last he saw them was at the Johansen site on Sunday. I hate to repeat it, but he said the truck hadn't been broken into."

I read between the lines: One of my employees had sticky fingers. Not really surprising, since I tended to hire people with questionable backgrounds. I was a sucker for the well-executed sob story.

"Should I file a report with the police?"

I drummed my fingertips on the counter. "No. I want to look into it first."

"All-righty."

I heard Riley on the stairs and told Tam I'd check in later.

As I hung up the phone, Riley came in wearing a red shirt with baggy, oversized army green pants, but I said nothing. I learned a long time ago not to argue with his choice in clothes. He had his father's fashion sense, and there was little I could do about it.

"Sink's full up."

I glanced at the water and caught one of Kevin's eyes staring back at me. Dashing to the sink, I blocked Riley's view as I picked the piece of photo out of the water and shoved it in the pocket of my robe.

"Disposal's blocked."

"Want me to plunge it?"

Shocked at this altruistic side of Riley I'd never seen before, I think I gaped at him. Finally, I found my voice. "Naw. I can do it."

"Fine." He plopped his backpack on the counter and grabbed his lunch money off the top of the microwave. Crossing over to the fridge, he removed the orange juice carton from the top shelf. He raised it to his lips.

"Don't you—"

He took a swig, replaced the carton, and turned to give me a sly "what're you going to do about it" smile. I fought the urge to scream at him. It was what he wanted—to get a rise out of me. He lived to taunt me. To him I was the embodiment of evil stepmothers—someone to be hated at all costs.

I smiled oh-so sweetly. "Have a nice day."

He swung his backpack over his shoulder. "Oh, Nina?"

"Yes, Ry?" This situation demanded my best behavior.

"Xena's missing."

I jumped onto the nearest chair and said, "Please tell me you're talking about the TV character."

"Sorry."

Funny, he didn't sound sorry at all.

"Then tell me you're joking," I seethed through clenched teeth.

"Nope. Been gone since last night."

"Dammit, Riley, why didn't you tell me last night?" My voice slowly rose to a pitch only dogs could hear.

He scrunched his nose in a manner that would be charming if he wasn't purposely making me suffer. "Didn't want to worry you."

"Riley—"

Ignoring the warning in my voice, he strutted out the door.

Maybe he was kidding. You know, just playing a prank . . . Biting my lip I thought back to the last time Riley played a practical joke. And couldn't remember one. Gulp.

Swallowing my fear, I scanned the kitchen floor, keeping my eyes peeled for a four-foot-long boa. Unfortunately, I had to get ready to meet with Bridget and I couldn't very well stay on the chair all day. Could I? While I debated canceling breakfast with Bridget so I wouldn't have to climb down from my safety zone, my gaze swept over the kitchen's nooks and crannies.

As I stared at the pot rack, a movement at the kitchen window caught my eye.

The chair wobbled beneath me as I turned quickly, fearing a sneak snake attack. My scream split the air as I spied a face peering in at me through the glass.

The chair gave one final shake and heaved me onto the tile floor.

Two

"Miz Quinn, you really oughta lock that back door." Mr. Cabrera helped me to my feet. He'd dashed into the house as soon as he'd seen my graceless free fall.

I tightened the sash on my robe, dusted myself off. When *was* the last time I'd washed the kitchen floor? "You really shouldn't peek in your neighbors' windows." I'd long ago given up on trying to get the old man to call me Nina. You'd think with all his spying we could at least be on a first-name basis.

"Seriously. There's been some burglaries lately."

He was right, but I wasn't about to own up to it. "The window, Mr. Cabrera?"

The baggy sleeve of his shirt, a fluorescent orange button-down covered in bright green bananas, flapped as he waved his hand. "Just checking to see if you were home."

Teeth clenched, I said, "Something wrong with my doorbell?"

The wrinkles on his face jiggled as he shrugged. He slapped a piece of paper on the counter.

I picked it up, saw a column of numbers. "What's this?"

"A bill."

"For what?"

"For the damage Riley caused in that overgrown steel

trap that takes him to school. Two hostas and a bed of New Guinea impatiens . . ." He snapped his fingers. "Gone, just like that."

Huh? "The bus? Why give this bill to me?"

He shook his head. A lock of snowy hair slid onto his forehead. "Riley didn't take the bus."

"He didn't?"

"Gray van, oversized tires, rust spots the size of New Mexico."

Didn't sound the least bit familiar.

"Kid wearing a dog collar driving."

"What?!"

"Maybe you oughta pay better attention, Miz Quinn."

I bit my tongue. Hard.

"Thanks for the visit, Mr. Cabrera." Herding him to the back door, I held up the bill. "I'll look into this."

"Be sure that you do."

I fairly shoved him out the door. He turned to look at me. "You don't happen to have a minute, do you, Miz Quinn? I'd like your opinion on something I'm planning out in the backyard."

My jaw dropped open in shock before suspicion snapped it closed. Mr. Cabrera was a natural-born gardener who needed no help whatsoever. Over the years I've tried to get him to work for me, but he's old and still clinging to his ancient delusions about men not working for women.

His asking for my advice about *anything*, but especially gardening, had me on the defensive. Warning sirens blared in my head, but curiosity got the better of me. "Uh, sure."

I ran back to the kitchen, used an I Love Lucy magnet to attach the bill to the fridge, and followed him out the back door.

The dew soaked grass squished between my bare toes. I was still trying to piece together what he was up to when he said, "I'm looking to make myself an oasis of sorts. A getaway."

I squinted as the sun reflected off his shirt, nearly blinding me. "A getaway?" This from a man who loved to be in the middle of it all?

"Someplace I can relax, unwind."

I winced as I stepped on a rock. Mr. Cabrera wasn't the relaxing kind, not in the least. *What* was he up to?

He spun, his arms waving, bright green bananas flapping at me. "I thought maybe you could help me plan something out." He nodded knowingly and smiled, his dentures nearly slipping out. "It's best to stay busy during these trying times."

I should have known that's what this was about! This little field trip into his backyard was Mr. Cabrera's own special way of prying information out of me to pass on at his weekly cribbage game.

He wanted the dirt on mine and Kevin's falling out, the sneaky, sneaky man.

I smiled brightly, refusing to give in. "What kind of scale did you have in mind, Mr. Cabrera? Something small, hammocklike? Or your own personal pagoda?"

His smile dissolved into a grim line. "Nothing too fancy," he muttered. "Something peaceful. I'm thinking of learning some yoga. A man needs to be at peace with himself."

I rubbed my temples, fighting off a headache.

His eyebrows snapped together, forming one long, thick snowy line across his forehead. "I'd like some shade, too. Some privacy. A man also needs his privacy."

My eyebrows jumped up. He was definitely feeding me a line. I just wasn't quite sure about what.

"A hammock'd be okay, I guess," he said.

We'd stopped smack-dab in the middle of his backyard. There wasn't a single tree in this area and I really didn't care for the look of a freestanding hammock. "Then we'd need to move farther back," I said, "near the trees . . ." I started back toward the woods that served as a boundary for all the yards on this side of the street.

"No!"

Stopping in my tracks, I turned to face him. "No?"

His arms were flying out every which way. "It has to be here. Right here."

I sighed. "Why? There's no shade here. Or any privacy."

"I've been reading up on that Feng Shui stuff. It needs to be right here." He stomped. "Right. Here."

I knew very little about Feng Shui, so I couldn't dispute for certain what he was telling me, but I had the sneaky feeling he was making it all up.

He rubbed his hands together. "Whatcha got for me? I'd like to get started right away."

I tightened my robe. It was useless to point out to him how long it took me to perfect my designs, how many hours I spent poring over each detail. The draw of TBS was how quickly the job could be done. In and out in a day. Designs had to be relatively simple, yet stunning and dramatic. It wasn't as easy as it looked. Many, many hours went into coordinating and planning, not just inside the office, but with various contractors and craftsmen.

However, Mr. Cabrera wanted instant gratification, and I wanted out of there, so I gave it to him. I'd recently designed something similar to what he was looking for, so I used that.

"You could have a gazebo built, maybe with benches inside, or maybe that hammock, although that might take up a lot of room, leaving you with none for your *yoga*."

One bushy white eyebrow snaked up as he apparently tried to decide if I was mocking him.

I pushed on before he figured it out. "It'll have a roof, so that will provide shade. You can trellis or lattice the walls, or leave them open and plant some ivy or other vines that are winter hardy to fill in spaces and gaps. In the warmer months you can have flower boxes or hanging baskets too. You can add a path—gravel or flagstone—and have some shrubs around it . . ."

He was rubbing his chin and nodding thoughtfully. "That might do."

"Some quick-growing evergreens will help with the priva—"

"No! No trees."

"Ohh-kay."

"I'll go get me some lumber from that new Home Depot and start today."

The man was full of surprises this morning. I felt the need to warn him. "This is a big job, Mr. Cabrera, especially if you're doing it on your own—which I don't recommend."

"I've got the wherewithal. And the time."

"What about Margaret? What's she have to say about this?" Margaret was his latest in a long line of 'women friends.' He'd long since told me he was too old to have girlfriends.

He kicked at the grass. "Nothin'."

I gasped. "Oh no! She didn't die, did she?" I hadn't heard, but I'd been out of the gossip loop for a few days.

"No!" he snapped.

I winced. "Sorry."

"But she heard the rumors."

Everyone had heard the rumors. Seemed Mr. Cabrera never settled down and remarried because the majority of his 'women friends' kept dying on him. All of natural causes, or so the autopsies said. That didn't stop people from gossiping, though. Or from thinking Mr. Cabrera was one jinxed man.

"I'm sorry."

He waved the apology off, and we started walking back

toward our houses. He turned to me with a glint in his eye. "I haven't seen the detective in a few days."

So we were back to the fact-finding mission, were we? As I made a beeline toward my backdoor I didn't mention that I hadn't seen him either. "I'll give him your best," I said.

"You do that."

I pulled open the backdoor, wiped my feet on the mat.

"Oh, Miz Quinn?"

I sighed. I should have known I wouldn't escape his questions that easily. "Yeah?"

"Uh . . . thanks. For your help."

The man was actually blushing. I smiled. "You're welcome."

Closing the door, I made sure I flipped the deadbolt. I'd have to have a talk with Riley soon about leaving the doors unlocked. This wasn't the first time.

As I passed the kitchen window, I saw Mr. Cabrera out in the middle of his backyard coloring the area for his gazebo with orange marking paint. As he looked left and right to guide his markings, my mouth dropped open.

An oasis—what a fool I'd been!

It all made sense now. He didn't want a serenity zone. He wanted spy central. A gazebo smack-dab in the middle of his backyard would give him an unfettered view of the backyards of everyone on the block.

I had to laugh. I should've known. I really, really should have known. I shook my head. There was nothing to be done about it now, except maybe keep my blinds closed. Once Mr. Cabrera got an idea in his head, he went at it full steam ahead.

I checked the clock, sucked in a breath. I was running seriously late. The sink was still full of water, but it would have to wait a bit more.

After talking with Tam that morning, I decided I wanted to check on the missing hoes before meeting with Bridget.

Kit, my foreman, was heading up a mini makeover today over at Ursula Krauss's new landominium. I'd just pop over and check things out without being too suspicious about it.

Yeah, that was me. Nina Colette Unsuspicious Ceceri Quinn.

On full snake alert, I tiptoed through the living room and rushed up the stairs. I paused at the top as the magazine Riley shoved under his pillow called to me. But there was, quite possibly, a reptile on the loose in his room. My cowardice won out over my inquisitiveness, and I ignored my impulse to snoop.

I debated for about two minutes on what to wear, before realizing I didn't really have a choice. All I owned were T-shirts and jeans—oh, and my all-purpose black dress. Not that it mattered. Not really. It's just that I hadn't seen Bridget, a Stanford-educated lawyer, in a while, and I didn't want her to think I'd gone all schlumpy, with my cracked, almost nonexistant nails, sun-freckled face, dull brown hair cut at the Clip and Curl, and my laid-back wardrobe.

But since I hadn't worn makeup in years, I decided the risk of conjunctivitis from tainted mascara was too great and ditched the idea completely.

My thoughts once again turned to Bridget and her reason for calling. She'd sounded so serious on the phone.

I scrubbed my face and pulled my hair back into a ponytail. Shimmying into my favorite pair of jeans, I topped the outfit off with a white V-necked T-shirt.

Bridget's wanting to get together had to be about her father-in-law's death, and I suspected it had a great deal to do with my relationship with Kevin. Unfortunately Kevin had kept everything about Farmer Joe's murder hush-hush, despite my constant nagging and quizzing.

Kevin's closed-mouth attitude should have been an obvious tip-off that our marriage was in trouble, since he had used me as a sounding board for years. Only I'd been oblivious. Nothing like a big neon orange SUSPICIOUS BEHAVIOR sign dangling above his tight lips to give a girl a clue.

I admit I'm naturally, uh, *curious*. But Joe's death stirred up more than the usual amount of interest I had in Kevin's cases. It baffled me that anyone could harm the old man. Tim's dad was one of those people who kept his door open for everyone and an extra spot at the dinner table—a table I'd eaten many meals at during my teen years. Sure, Farmer Joe had been crankier than a newborn baby, yet he'd been just as lovable in his cantankerous kind of way. Truly a man with no enemies.

I guess I simply needed to wait and see, which irritated me to no end since I wasn't a big fan of patience.

Opening the door of my bedroom, I peered into the hall. No signs of snake activity. I tippy-toed downstairs and into the washroom. The hamper beckoned, and I threw in a quick wash while whistling "Puff the Magic Dragon" to keep my mind off Kevin.

From the utility closet, I grabbed, as protection from Xena, Riley's hockey stick and a pair of knee-high rubber boots I used for work. Appropriately armed, I ran back upstairs. The sink still needed plunging, but my curiosity over that magazine Riley had shoved under his pillow couldn't be quenched. Something was up with him, and I was determined to find out what it was. After all, it was my evil stepmotherly duty to snoop, right? However, as I reached the landing at the top of the steps, I heard a car door slam. Running into my bedroom, I peeked out the window, swore under my breath.

The unmarked assigned to Kevin sat in the driveway, parked next to my ancient Corolla. *Oh no, not now.* I hadn't seen him for two days. Two whole days my anger had had time to fester.

My knuckles turned white as I gripped the hockey stick with undue force. The front door slammed.

I checked the drawer of Kevin's nightstand. Locked. It was a good thing. I had the feeling that if Kevin gave me any crap, I'd be tempted to grab the off-duty gun he kept in there and shoot him. The mental picture made me smile. Oh, I wouldn't shoot to kill. I'd aim for more . . . *strategic* points. Points south.

"Nina!" he yelled up the stairs. "I'm here. Is everything ready?"

This was just like Kevin. He didn't even know I was home. He just *assumed* I'd be waiting for him. I hated that about him. For all he knew I could be next door having a cup of lemonade with Mr. Cabrera. Not that I'd ever done so at nine in the morning before, but that was beside the point.

I straightened my shoulders and walked calmly downstairs.

"What the hell? Why on earth are you wearing goulashes and carrying a hockey stick?"

Better to hit you over the head with, my pretty.

"Xena's loose."

He roared with laughter.

"It's not funny!"

"That snake wouldn't hurt anything."

Unlike myself. I itched to erase his cocky smile. I flexed my fingers, loosening them, so I wouldn't be tempted to take a swing. "What are you doing here?"

"Didn't Riley tell you I was coming? I told him I had to go out of town on a case and asked him to have you pack up some clothes for me."

I rolled my eyes. Imbecile. "Well, he didn't believe you. He knows."

"You sure?"

I glared.

Kevin dragged a hand over his face. "I'll deal with it."

Sure he would. Sighing, I said, "This isn't a good time for me, Kevin. I have things to do." I could only imagine what he'd say if I actually admitted I was about to snoop in his son's room.

"Like what? It's your day off." He walked into the kitchen. "Sink's full up."

My throat tightened. It was the same thing Riley had said.

Kevin took off his suit coat and rolled up his sleeves. "Did you try plunging it?"

"No."

His shoulder holster crisscrossed his muscled back. His gun nestled under his left arm. Shaking his head at my apparent lack of attempting the obvious, he picked up the plunger I had set out. "Weird things are happening in this town. Take the call I responded to this morning . . ."

I snatched the plunger out of his hand. "What do you think you're doing?"

"What?"

"You can't come in here and start plunging sinks." I jabbed him with the plunger, leaving a big wet ring on his shirt. "You can't come in without knocking. You can't come in and start telling me about your calls. You can't."

"Why not?"

"You. Don't. Live. Here. Anymore." I was becoming crankier by the second, especially after I felt moisture stinging my eyes.

Something swept across his features. Some emotion I couldn't identify. He backed away from the sink.

His voice was tight as he spoke. "I thought you might be interested in the call, is all. Especially since it involves a family you've been bugging me about for over a week."

I shouldn't ask. I knew I shouldn't. Not after my little speech, but my curiosity begged for conclusion. Coquettishly, I tipped my head. "Who?"

"The Sandowskis . . ."

"Oh no! What happened?"

He leaned against the counter. "Seems someone heard shots fired at the old farmhouse. Went there, but Mrs. Sandowski said she hadn't heard anything, but something was off. I'm sure she was lying. I just don't know why."

I backed up, using the counter for support. Lena Sandowski. Bridget's mother-in-law. I didn't think Bridget's out-of-the-blue call was coincidental. What was going on? Had Kevin said gunshots? Why hadn't I paid better attention?

"You don't think she had anything to do with . . ."

"I can't tell you that."

Oh yes, his newfound confidentiality rule.

"Nina?"

I looked up, caught an unexpected concerned look on Kevin's face. "You okay?"

"Fine."

"You don't look fine."

I dropped my gaze to look at myself. I had a plunger in one hand, a hockey stick in the other, and I was wearing muck-covered rubber boots in the kitchen. My stepson hated me, there was a snake loose in the house, and I was on the verge of divorce. I was definitely not fine.

"I'm fine."

"Fine."

Didn't I already have this conversation this morning?

"Look, Nina, about what happened, with the boxers . . ."

Shaking my head, I held up the plunger, stopping him. I didn't want to hear it. It was too much for me to handle right now. "I think you should go. Come back when no one's home to get your things."

"This is still my house too, Nina. You can't tell me what to do."

"Oh no?" I said softly. Too softly. When my voice dropped that low, it was a sign of danger, and he knew it.

Kevin snapped his mouth closed. "I'll be back later, then."

He started for the door. I followed him to make sure he really went.

On the front porch, he turned to face me. He opened his mouth, closed it again. He seemed to be struggling to find something to say.

Peering around him, I saw his partner in the car. Ginger Barlow. His lover. I held onto the hockey stick so tightly my knuckles turned white.

"Go," I said hoarsely.

He took a step out. Stopped. Again he faced me. "Nina . . ."

Taking a deep breath, I said, "Come for dinner on Thursday. Riley has the night off from work and we can talk to him then. I don't want to do it by myself."

"You won't need to."

"I better not have to. And don't bring Rosemary with you."

"Ginger," he corrected. "Her name is Ginger."

As if I didn't know. "Whatever."

He turned and walked away.

I closed the door and leaned against it, fighting for composure. *Damn him.*

Wishing I had time to wallow in my self-pity with a box of Nilla Wafers and some chocolate milk, I ditched the plunger and ran up the stairs, huffing more than a bit. I'd gotten more exercise that morning than I'd had all year.

I paused in the hall outside Riley's room. I knew I shouldn't go in, especially with a snake on the loose, but that magazine, and Riley's odd behavior, ate at me. It was probably some skin magazine, but I needed to be sure.

With a turn of the knob, the door swung open. Peeking

in, I scanned the floor. Chills danced up and down my spine and I shivered. Who knew what lurked beneath all the junk on the floor?

Sure enough, the tank to the right of his bed was empty. A part of me had hoped Riley made up the story of Xena's escape so I'd stay out of his room, knowing I'd be curious about that magazine. Unfortunately, he'd underestimated my nosiness. And my ability to appropriately equip myself.

Using the hockey stick to clear a path, I crept to the bed. I lifted the pillow. Nothing. Maybe he took it with him, I reasoned. *Maybe not*, my inner voice said. Slipping my hand beneath the mattress, I felt for paper. Chances of Xena being under there were slim, so I felt reasonably confident as I slid my hand back and forth.

Finally, I hit something solid. Grasping it, I slowly pulled the magazine out, fully expecting to see a half-naked woman staring at me. After I glanced at the cover, I wished it *were* a half-naked woman staring at me. Even a fully naked-woman would be better than this.

My stomach turned. The barrel of a sawed-off shotgun greeted me from the pages of *Gun Pride*. What the hell was he up to? *Gun Pride* was a small magazine which mostly sold to militia-type groups. There'd been a big report on the news about magazines just like this not all that long ago, about how these groups liked to recruit teenagers for their cause. Had they gotten to Riley? How else could he have gotten hold of something like this?

What to do? I needed to talk to him about this, didn't I? But that meant he'd know I snooped. Not that our relationship could get much worse, but still.

Blowing out a deep breath, I replaced the magazine under the mattress. I'd talk to Kevin and see what he thought. Maybe it was normal male adolescent fascination. *Maybe not*, my inner voice warned. I told the voice to shut up and hurried out of Riley's room.

I checked the hallway. All clear. If Xena wasn't found soon, we'd just have to move, no two ways around it.

Checking the clock, I cursed my inability to be punctual.

The phone rang and I hurried to answer it, nearly tripping on the plunger as I rushed down the stairs, thinking it might be Tam reporting more missing hoes.

It wasn't.

"Nina, what's wrong?" my mother asked.

I wasn't in the mood to have her pry so I inserted a light lilt into my voice. "Nothing, Mom."

What was it about mothers and their ability to know when something was wrong—and why were stepmothers excluded from this gift?

"I don't believe you."

How did I argue with her when she was right?

I could hear her breathing, but she remained silent. "I'm fine," I finally said. Hopping on one foot, I tugged off one boot, then the other.

"You're lying to your mother. Tonio," she called out to my father, "your daughter is lying to me!" To me, she said, "This is what carousing with that cousin of yours will do."

"You're not fooling me. You love Ana."

She sniffed. "Nina, the apple and the tree, my darling."

I groaned. My mother had had an ongoing feud with my Aunt Rosetta from the day she'd moved in with us and proved to be a better cook, housekeeper, mother, than Celeste Madeline Chambeau Ceceri.

"Now, tell me no lies," she demanded.

"Nothing to tell at all."

I could hear muted whisperings, then my father came on the line.

"Don't lie to your mother, Nina."

"Yes, Daddy." Static crackled in my ear as the phone was passed back to my mother. I slipped on a pair of Keds, hoping the canvas was snakeproof.

"Now what's wrong?" my mother asked once again.

I could picture my father being hauled out of his favorite chair, dragged to the phone, then dismissed. I had to smile. My mother had been in the military in a former life. I was sure of it.

"Nothing's wrong, Mom. I'm fine." I stressed the word fine. It seemed to be the word of the day.

"Hmmph."

"Gotta run."

"Why?"

I didn't want to tell her about my meeting with Bridget or I'd never get off the phone. I looked around for an excuse, found one in the murky water pooled in the sink. "I have to fix the sink."

"What's wrong with the sink?"

"It's clogged." She didn't need the sordid details. "I have to go."

"Wait!"

"What?"

"Your fitting is next week. Write it down or you'll forget."

I didn't write it down. I wanted to forget. "I will."

"Do it now. You have Tuesdays off so there's no reason to cancel." She paused for effect. "Again."

I mimicked writing noises using the counter and the pads of my fingertips since my nails were practically nonexistent. "There," I lied.

"Your sister's counting on you. You're her matron of honor and you're the only one of her girls who hasn't gotten her dress yet."

Her girls. She sounded like a pimp.

I had hoped if I delayed long enough, I'd miss the deadline and get kicked out of Maria's wedding altogether, but it was looking more and more like I'd be hogtied and carried to the bridal shop if I didn't get there on my own.

"You'll be there?"

"Mom!"

"Okay, okay."

We said our good-byes just as the annoying cat clock Riley had given me one Mother's Day meowed ten times. Crap. The sink would have to wait. I was late.

Three

Mrs. Ursula Krauss lived in a brand spanking new landominium not all that far from the Mill. Landominiums were growing in popularity in the area. Basically, a landominium was a run-of-the-mill condo, but the owner also owned a small patch of land too.

I drove down a bumpy side road faster than my little Corolla liked to go. The clock on my dashboard blinked at me accusingly. I was pushing it, time-wise.

The nearer I got to Mrs. Krauss's, the more my muscles tensed. It had nothing to do with the missing equipment and everything to do with Mrs. Krauss.

"Brickhouse Krauss," as we used to call her back in the tenth grade at St. Valentine's. She used to torture her students by assigning long tedious essays on subjects like "The Relevance of the Middle English Translation of *The Canterbury Tales* to Modern Society."

I shuddered at the memory.

Mrs. Krauss's evil personality lurked behind a benevolent Mrs. Claus (as in Santa's wife) kind of face. The "Brickhouse" came from her shape. Not an hourglass to be seen—Mrs. Krauss had been a thick rectangle with hands, feet, and face sticking out. Sort of like a female German Spongebob with spiky white hair.

We'd never gotten along. It was only because of Mrs. Krauss's daughter, Claudia, that TBS was doing this "mini" in the first place.

As I've mentioned, I'm a sucker for a sob story, and Claudia had a doozy.

With a flip of my blinker, I turned into the complex of landominiums, condominiums, and town houses, noticing the boring landscaping.

Seemed the bigger the complexes around here, the more the builder scrimped on landscaping.

I rolled past a man-made pond, wishing there were benches or even a dock to pretty it up. There wasn't even the standard fountain, for goodness' sake.

I turned left and pulled to a stop behind Kit's truck. All my employees drove white Ford F-250s, each with a discreet sign on the door that said TBS. Another TBS pickup was parked in front of his, and Stanley Mack's green Dodge was parked in front of that, its tailgate open.

Stanley was one of the contractors I often used. His carpentry skills were unparalleled. I'd hired him for this job to construct an arched arbor, and I was eager to see how it turned out.

Hammering echoed as I walked up the front path and skirted the perimeter of Mrs. Krauss's condo, er, lando.

I paused at the corner, hid behind the brick façade. Everything looked to be well under way.

For the most part, TBS focused on full garden transformations, productions that took months of planning and coordinating. However, about six times a month, we fit "minis" into the schedule. A smaller version of a full TBS makeover, a mini usually had only one or two landscaping elements and was perfect for people with smaller yards or who wanted to focus on just one problem area.

For the most part, after designing the mini, I left the actual completion of the project to Kit Pipe, my foreman and head landscaping contractor.

I saw him now, hard at work wrestling pond liner into a six-foot-wide, freshly dug hole. Kit had been my very first employee, long before TBS had ever seen the light of day. Over the years we'd become close friends, and I trusted him completely. I didn't think for a minute he was involved in the thefts of my garden equipment.

He paused in the wrestling, took off his hat and wiped the top of his head with his forearm.

I squinted, the glare from the sun bouncing off his bald head, highlighting the skull tattoo on his scalp, before he replaced his hat.

Behind him, Coby Fowler, one of my part-timers, was helping Stanley Mack assemble the arbor.

I smiled, already able to envision my design coming to life. It was going to be fabulous. I almost hated to waste it on Brickhouse Krauss.

"Nina!"

I jumped, cursing under my breath as Claudia Krauss came up behind me. "Hey, Claudia."

Bouncing on the balls of her feet, she beamed at me. "Everything's going so well, Nina. Thank you so much for doing this. I know it can't be easy, with your hard feelings for Mamma and all."

I wouldn't have done it at all except I'd felt sorry for Claudia. She was due to be married in December and her mother had been threatening to move in with the newlyweds.

"That's in the past," I said, hoping the words rang true.

"Ever since she moved in here after Dad died, a garden is all she's talked about." Her curly reddish blonde hair bounced as she talked. "She's been so lonely since he's been gone. Maybe this will give her something to do." A scared look came into her bright blue eyes. "We really, really want her to love this garden, Nina."

"She will," I assured her, even though with Mrs. Krauss you could never be sure about anything.

Claudia pulled me toward the backyard. Kit looked up, the brim of his hat shading his eyes. He didn't seem the least bit surprised to see me.

Panic laced Claudia's tone as she said, "Your design did have flowers, right? I don't see any flowers."

"Deanna's bringing them later. The yard is too small to have everyone working here at once."

"Oh, thank God. Mamma loves flowers. I don't think she could have a garden without flowers."

Her cell phone rang, and she scurried away to answer it.

Kit lumbered over, all six-foot-five, 250 well-muscled pounds of him. "Hey, boss. Whatcha doing here?" he asked, though by the glint in his eye he knew darn well why I was there.

I hedged. "Just thought I'd stop by and check on things."

A smile curled up one corner of his mouth. "A *hoe* lot of things?"

"Ha-ha." I pulled him aside. Thankfully, he went willingly or I wouldn't have been able to budge him. "You notice anything else missing?"

"Not since this morning."

"Any idea what's going on?"

His eyes narrowed. Long ago he'd had them lined with black ink. He looked scarier than a pit full of vipers, but it was all for show. "Yeah," he said, folding his massive arms across his chest. "Someone's stealing the equipment."

I rolled my eyes. "You're a big help."

"That's why you pay me the big bucks," he said, walking away.

I moseyed over to Stan and Coby and managed to say hello and admire their handiwork before Claudia came rushing toward me, nearly knocking me over. "That was Mamma! She's sick of the flea market and wants to come home. My Aunt Elna is trying to stall, but I don't know for how much longer. Two, maybe three hours if there's traffic on I-75."

Kit turned to me, a look of panic in his eyes. "Since you're here, boss, why don't you stay and help out?"

Normally, I would, but I was already late meeting with Bridget, and I knew Kit was capable of pulling it all to-gether. "Sorry, I can't. I've got a *hoe* lot of things to do."

"Smart-ass," he grumbled.

I smiled. "Call in reinforcements, Marty or Jean-Claude."

He was already reaching for his cell. I said my good-byes and rushed out of there.

Guilt nagged. I should have stayed.

But seeing Mrs. Krauss again just wasn't something I wanted to do.

Ever.

Gus's was a small diner in the heart of the Mill that had been there forever and then some. And I suspected the grease ac-cumulation on the walls was older than my twenty-nine years, not that anyone would complain and risk Gus's wrath.

The stools lining the horseshoe-shaped counter were filled, and my gaze skipped over wobbly tables, balding heads and poofy blue hairdos, looking for Bridget. I found her in the back near the rotary pay phone that hadn't worked since 1976, her head bent over a laptop.

Squeezing my way between the tightly packed tables, I stepped over canes that acted as speed bumps, wiggled past aluminum walkers while smiling and waving at familiar faces. A lock of Bridget's white blonde chin-length bob covered most of her face, but I could see clearly that she hadn't broken the habit of biting pen caps.

"Excuse me. So sorry," I said as the small leather back-pack I used as a purse nearly tore the toupee off Mr. Goldbine's wrinkled head. Always good-humored, he grinned toothlessly at me and patted my rear as I passed.

Funny how men never change, I thought, shaking my head.

A gnarled hand snaked out, gripped my wrist like an iron shackle. "Nina Quinn, I need your help."

"Hi, Mrs. Daasch. What is it this time?" Mrs. Daasch never missed an opportunity to pry gardening tips from me.

Now that she had my attention, she peeled her fingers, one by one, from my wrist.

"It's my potted impatiens, Nina."

She said this as though she were speaking to a doctor. I looked over Mrs. Daasch's over-permed head. Bridget hadn't seen me yet. "What's wrong with them?"

"Scrawny! Limper than—" She glanced sideways at Mr. Daasch, who was busy staring into the depths of his coffee mug. "Well, limp."

Much more than I ever needed to know. "Are they in the shade? You know impatiens love their shade."

Mrs. Daasch clutched her chest. "I'm no amateur, Nina Quinn."

I smiled. "Hmmm. Watering every day?"

"Every single."

"How about drainage? Could be root rot."

Her rheumy eyes brightened at that. "I bet you're right! I just bought new pots."

"Some gravel, old stones, or terra-cotta chips at the bottom of the pot should do the trick."

She patted my hand. "You have a good lunch, Nina Quinn. Thank you for your help."

I scooted away before she thought of something else. "Bridget," I called out.

Her head snapped up and she quickly closed the lid of her laptop before struggling to her feet, a wide smile blooming on her face.

I stopped mid-stride, my feet nearly going out from under me. My eyes widened. My jaw hit the floor.

Bridget put one arm behind her head, the other on her hip and posed, model-style, showing off her very pregnant tummy.

I clapped out of sheer instinct and about thirty weathered, puckered faces turned our way. I couldn't take my eyes off her rounded stomach. "You didn't tell me!"

The patrons in the diner began clapping too, calling out their congratulations. Bridget bowed, offered her thanks.

"Are you going to stand there all day?" she asked me.

"I might. I'm in shock. I'm just so happy for you! I know how hard you tried . . ." I felt myself getting teary eyed. Just what I needed. If I started crying now I might not ever stop.

She pulled me into a hug, planted noisy kisses on both my cheeks.

It was strange, our relationship. We could go months and months without seeing each other, yet the second we were together again, time fell away.

She had snagged a triangular booth, built for two—three if you were *really* friendly—tucked into the farthest corner of the room. I slid in, ignoring the cracks and tears in the padded vinyl bench.

"You didn't tell me," I said again.

"I wanted to surprise you. Besides we didn't tell anyone until after that tortuous first trimester. Not after all we've been through."

We had to raise our voices to be heard over all the noise. Between Gus cursing in the kitchen and the hearing aids of most of the customers apparently needing their batteries replaced, the room was buzzing.

"I'm so happy for you, Bridget. I really am." She and her husband Tim had been trying to conceive for years. Procedure after procedure netted nothing but heartache and growing mountains of debt. They'd finally turned to IVF, in vitro fertilization, about two years ago, and gotten good news—until Bridget miscarried at eight weeks. She'd had several more pregnancies after that, all ending the same tragic way. No doctor could tell her why, or even offer any hope.

"I know. Can you believe we weren't even trying?" Her ice blue eyes shone. "One day I wasn't feeling well . . ."

"A miracle."

Her eyes clouded, teared up. Her gaze dropped to the table's surface, decoupaged with old newspapers.

"Bridget?"

"Yes, a miracle," she murmured, tucking her laptop into a leather satchel at her feet.

"Are you okay?"

She waved my concern away. "Fine. Fine, really. I just get emotional sometimes." A quivery smile played on her lips. "How're you? Kevin? Riley? I keep hearing wonderful things about your business—you must be thrilled with its success."

I pasted on my brightest, happiest, fakest smile and hoped it fooled her. "Everything's wonderful." I skipped right over Kevin and Riley and zoomed in on my work. "Business is growing so fast I can't keep up with it."

"That's so great. You know, I'd love for you to come up with a baby-friendly design for us. Something Tim and I could work on ourselves. He loves those do-it-yourself shows—it's one of the reasons we bought our fixer-upper in the first place. We'd pay you, of course."

"Nonsense! I'd love to do it as a gift for the baby. I can probably stop by later this week, take some measurements."

Her face brightened. "Wonderful! Oh, I can't wait to see what you come up with. Everything's going so well for you. I couldn't be happier with your success. And your family too . . ."

This subject needed to be redirected before she could ask

anything specific about Kevin. I didn't need to drag her down with my worries. "So, Tim must be beside himself about the baby."

"Oh, he is!" She leaned in, as much as her belly would allow. "Honestly, Nina, I don't know if we'd still be together if it weren't for this baby." Her blonde hair swung as she shook her head. "With everything we went through we had grown so far apart. We couldn't share our grief with each other and it pushed a wedge between us. Add the fighting about the bills on top of that . . ."

"But everything's better now, right?" I interrupted, trying in vain to keep the conversation upbeat.

She smiled. "The truth?"

I nodded.

"It's better. Not great, but better." Her lower lip trembled. "He hasn't touched me in months. Says he's afraid of hurting the baby."

I reached across the table, took her hand. "I can understand that. After everything . . ."

"I can too, I suppose. But it just hurts, y'know?"

Oh, I knew. But I didn't think she needed to hear about my problems right now. "So, how far along are you?"

"About seven months."

My gaze zipped to her stomach. "Is it twins?" I said in shock. Already her stomach protruded right below her breasts. My secretary Tam was six months pregnant and barely showing.

She threw a napkin at me. "I don't care if I gain a hundred pounds. I'm going to enjoy every second of this pregnancy."

"And you should. You look wonderful. I'm so happy for you."

Bridget's dad was Polish through and through, but her mother was a mix of Swedish and Norwegian. As a result, Bridget was a tall, big-boned girl with the most delicate, finest, beautiful features you could ever imagine. Her pale skin fairly exuded good health and happiness, yet sadness clouded her crystal-clear baby blues.

"I'm so glad you had the day off. I needed someone to talk to so bad. I knew I could count on you."

"Always."

My stomach rumbled and I looked around for Gertie, Gus's daughter and also sole waitress, who was sixty if a day. She was far on the other side of the room, chatting it up with the Molari brothers. The help here was notoriously slow, but the food was oh-so worth it. "We might be here awhile."

"I'm in no rush," she said, looking past me, staring at something over my shoulder, a mutinous expression on her face.

The smell of sausage and sautéed peppers hovered as I swiveled, following her gaze. "What?"

"Look at that baby, sitting there all alone. Why, someone could just walk by and take him."

I looked at the little guy, wedged with a safety belt into a wooden booster seat, his grandmother, Dottie Laredo, not two feet away, gabbing it up with Mrs. Casperian. Besides that fact, the kidnapper would have to deal with a maze of approximately ten canes and three walkers before making it to the door. Not a chance.

I looked back at Bridget, narrowed my eyes. "You okay?"

She gave a shake to her head. "Sorry. I just don't understand people some times. I'd never do that to my child. Where were we? Oh yes, being here awhile. No, I don't mind."

I barely had time to think about the emotional scars she must be carrying before she said, "With Tim out of work, I've been putting in extra hours and I'm grateful for some free time."

"Tim's out of work? I didn't know."

She sighed. "Remember that big death-penalty case he

tried up in Columbus about six months ago? The one he lost?"

I nodded. I'd followed the story in the paper.

"His firm fired him."

"Oh no."

Quite honestly, I'd been glad Tim, a defense attorney, lost the case. His client had been the worst kind of bad—rotten to the core—and was now serving out his remaining days on death row. Good riddance to bad rubbish, as my mother always said. I did feel bad for Tim, though.

"He's been out looking, getting a nibble here and there. But most of his offers have come from out of state. And we hadn't wanted to move, not with the baby, and my job going so well . . ."

My heart went out to her. As an environmental lawyer, Bridget worked her tail off, most of it pro bono. Now with a baby coming and Tim's unemployment—

"And with Tim's dad being sick—we couldn't just up and lea—"

I gasped, covering my mouth. My appetite vanished. "Oh, God, Bridget, you must think I'm the worst person in the world. I'd totally blanked on Joe's death. I saw your wonderful belly and everything else went right out of my head."

She smiled. "It's okay."

"No, it's not. Really, it's not. How's Tim holding up? Mrs. Sandowski? You?"

She shook her head, picked up her empty water glass, looked around. Gertie was still yapping with the eligible, octogenarian Molaris.

"Orange juice okay?" I asked Bridget.

"Great, but—"

I pried the glass from her hand, made my way behind the horseshoe counter, smiled at Gus, who was flipping pancakes, and filled the glass with juice from the tap with the oranges on it and shimmied my way back to our table.

Bridget laughed, sipped her juice. "I've missed you."

"Same here. So, tell me about Joe. What happened to him, and what happened at the farm this morning?"

Her blue eyes blinked, owl-like. "How did you know?"

"Kevin. He mentioned something happened there."

Her eyes darkened. "What did he say?"

"Not much. There was a report of some gunshots. Apparently Tim's mom didn't know anything." I left out the part where Kevin said he was sure Mrs. Sandowski had been lying. I didn't think Bridget would take too well to that. "What's going on? Does this have something to do with Joe's death?"

She shifted in her seat, clearly uncomfortable. "I don't know where to begin."

"At the beginning?" I suggested. I hoped that didn't come out as insensitive as it sounded to my ears. It was that whole impatience thing again. Mix it with my curiosity and it was almost always a caustic combination.

"About a month ago someone poisoned the sheeps' water."

"What? Are you sure?"

She nodded, motioning with her juice glass. "One died and the other two are still under the care of a vet. Startzky's Rat Poison."

"Oh God."

"Whoever did it left the box next to the trough, like they wanted it to be found. Taunting us, almost."

"Do you still have the box?" I'd lived with a cop long enough to learn a thing or two. Maybe fingerprints could still be retrieved.

"No. We passed it on to the police when it happened. Nothing came of it."

"No fingerprints?"

"Not that I know of. No one ever said."

I pressed on, being my usual nosy self. "What else has happened?"

"Threatening phone calls in the middle of the night, death threats in the mail, and someone started a fire in the west field. Luckily a passerby noticed before it could do any real damage."

"Do you have any idea why?" Because it sure as hell didn't make sense to me.

"The land."

I remembered Sandowski's Farm quite well. It was nothing to brag about. Multiple acres of fields and crops. Mostly corn and some soy if I recalled correctly. They had a few cows, some sheep, and oodles of chickens.

"I don't understand."

Placing her elbows on the table, Bridget leaned forward, her blue eyes searching. "You've heard of Vista View?"

"Sure." I was lucky enough to have a few clients in the subdivision of half-million- to million-dollar homes nestled snugly together between their ritzy country club, private golf course, tennis courts, and pool. For me, Vista View meant big profits and more publicity than I knew what to do with. "Congressman Chanson lives there, along with dozens of other movers and shakers."

Off a main road, Vista View houses were set back, rising like monoliths against the horizon. The subdivision itself never held much appeal to me. If I were going to own a half-million-dollar house, it would be in the middle of nowhere, surrounded by nothing but nature. In Vista View, if you sneezed, your neighbor blessed you.

"What does Vista View have to do with Tim's family?"

"It's having traffic problems. I'm sure you know Vista View is a shortcut from Liberty Avenue to Millson."

"I use it all the time. It's always backed up, especially at rush hour." Most of my work was in that direction. With all the developments popping up on the acres and acres of old farmland to the north, my business was booming. "But what does traffic in Vista View have to do with Sandowski's Farm?"

"Vista View wants to become gated. Residents only. Guards at the gate, the whole shebang."

"I hadn't heard." Already I mourned the loss of my short-cut and dreaded the added minutes of commute time along one of the most congested roads in town.

"They haven't gone public with the announcement yet."

"Why?"

She clasped her hands together, looking very lawyerly. "They're having a bit of trouble. In order to become gated, a road must be paved from Liberty Avenue to Millson."

"So why doesn't the town build it?"

"Because there's a farm in the way."

I did some mental geography. "Ahh. Sandowski's Farm?"

"Exactly. Tim's mom and dad were offered a small fortune to move, but refused."

"How much and why not?" I hadn't thought of it before, but Sandowski's Farm had to be worth a small fortune. I'd heard a story of one farmer who sold his land for eight million so a shopping mall could be built for the new suburban-ites. Although the Sandowskis didn't own nearly as much land, the asking price would still be up there, considering its prime location.

"About three million dollars," she said solemnly, "and because it's their home. Sandowski's Farm has been in Tim's father's family for nearly one hundred and fifty years. It's Tim's heritage. There's no way they would have sold, not for any amount. And they shouldn't. If every farmer sold out to make way for new office plazas, think of all the valuable resources that would be lost." Her almost-white eyebrows dipped as she frowned. "It just makes me sick to think of all that beautiful farmland paved over."

"So you think someone took to using terror tactics to get them to leave?"

She nodded. "The list of people who want them out is endless. All the residents of Vista View; developers who would give their eyeteeth for the land that would bracket the new road; and Congressman Chanson had visited them himself to plead his case."

"You think a congressman would kill sheep?"

"I think he would do a lot of things to get what he wants."

I crossed my arms, suddenly cold. "Kevin said something about shots fired this morning. What was that about?"

"Jumper, Tim's mom's cocker spaniel. He lost a leg to a bullet, but he'll be okay."

My eyes widened in shock. "Why didn't you tell the police?"

"Tim and I went to the police when the sheep were poisoned. They made a report and told us it was probably teenage misfits. We went back when the death threats arrived. Again, they did nothing." She took a deep breath. "You haven't heard the worst of it yet."

I leaned forward, intrigued by her expression. It was a mix of sadness, of anger. "What?"

"Nina, someone killed Joe."

Four

For crying out loud, I'd forgotten again! What kind of person *was* I? So wrapped up in the story of the sheep and land, I'd forgotten that Farmer Joe had been murdered. I gasped. "My God. You don't think a congressman . . ."

She cut me off before I could finish the thought. "As you know, Joe had cancer."

I nodded. It had been why she and Tim had moved back down to the Cincinnati area from Columbus a few months back, buying an old run-down Victorian near the city.

"It was end-stage, but he wouldn't let it keep him down. He was so very weak, but still wanted to run the farm as best he could." She paused, then continued, her voice shaky as she said, "When Tim's mom found him out by the foot of his tractor in the middle of the cornfield, it looked like his heart had just given out. He was already gone by the time the paramedics arrived. They took him straight to the mortuary."

"But that doesn't make sense if it was murder—the medical examiner would have been called in."

Sarcasm oozed from her lips. "Apparently they didn't know."

"But how—"

She interrupted. "That night . . ." Her gaze dropped to her hands, where it studied her short, trimmed nails. "Tim's mom couldn't bear to leave the mortuary. So Tim and I went back to the farm, took care of the animals. When Tim went out to move the tractor back into the barn, he noticed there was a nearly empty thermos of coffee in the cab."

The enormity of her statement didn't escape me. Besides me, Joe was the only other person I knew who didn't drink coffee.

"Since Joe hated coffee, there's no way he would have drunk it . . . unless someone forced him."

"Maybe it was Mrs. Sandowski's?"

"It wasn't; we asked her about it. Finding the coffee made us suspicious enough to turn it over to the police immediately. We also had a few drops of the contents analyzed." She sighed. "We found out a few days later that it was laced with cyanide."

"Well, that proves something, doesn't it?" I said.

"To us." Bridget ran her finger along a scratch in the tabletop. "But not to the police."

"Why not?"

"They're waiting for the contents to be verified by their own lab—the one we used wasn't certified, so the analysis is virtually useless."

"I can't . . . I just can't believe it. You really think Joe drank the coffee?"

"I think someone forced him to, yes. The cancer had taxed his strength. He'd become so weak . . . There's no way he would have been able to defend himself." Pushing a hand through her blonde hair, she said, "The sheep, the threats . . . If we hadn't found that thermos, I would have kept believing Joe died naturally."

"Why wasn't the ME called right away? Didn't the paramedics notice something was off?"

"Maybe they did." Revulsion laced her tone. Her features

hardened. "Maybe they were told they'd be having a pickup that day. Maybe they were told to bring Joe to the mortuary, no questions asked."

This conversation was getting creepier by the second. "A cover-up?"

"Paramedics are employees of the county. And Congressman Chanson can pull a lot of weight, since he lives here. He is a powerful adversary."

I couldn't seem to close my mouth. I stared. I gaped. It wasn't pretty, I was sure.

"I know it seems unreal. And sure, I could be wrong about the paramedics. Joe's skin tone *was* poor. The cancer had spread from his lungs to his liver. He really needed to be on oxygen, but refused." She looked at me. "You remember how stubborn he was?"

I nodded.

She exhaled. "The liver damage had turned him a slight yellow color—jaundice—and his low oxygen levels caused his nails and lips to have a bluish tint. But that doesn't explain why his death is being swept under the rug."

"What do you mean?"

"You said in your card that you'd read about Joe's death in the paper? When was that?"

I thought back, trying to remember. "Last week? Monday? No. Tuesday."

"Right. And have you read anything since?"

Come to think of it, there had been no further mention of Joe's death. Not in the newspaper or on the TV. "No."

"It's being kept quiet."

I thought of Kevin and his silence on the subject. Maybe it had had nothing to do with the end of our marriage. Maybe he was under orders to keep things to himself.

"That does seem odd."

"Then yesterday . . ." Her fists clenched. "Yesterday I got a call from Freedom PD. Seems the thermos has been lost en route to the lab. Apparently someone just up and stole it while the driver made a stop. Or so the police say." Sarcasm dripped from her words. "Please excuse me if I don't believe them."

My stomach rolled. I could see where the paramedics might have made a mistake. And maybe the media just wasn't all that interested in the death of an old farmer, murder or not, but this . . . This was too big to discount. There was too much coincidence. And too much coincidence usually meant something hinky was going on.

"What about an autopsy?"

She shook her head. "Joe was cremated before we knew about the thermos. It's what he told Tim he wanted."

Shock rippled through me. "I'll give you Kevin's number. You and Tim should talk to him about all this."

"I wish I could, Nina. But we don't trust anyone who works for this town. I mean, I have faith that Kevin's an honorable person, after all, you wouldn't have married him otherwise—"

I thought maybe I was going to be sick right then and there.

"—but I don't think I can convince Tim to trust anyone right now. And honestly, I shouldn't even be talking to you about it, but I just can't keep it in anymore. Tim refuses to discuss it and his mom just doesn't want to think about it. I feel like I'm going crazy, not being able to talk about it. You're the only one I can trust with this, Nina. I know you can keep a secret." She leaned in. "You will keep this secret, right?"

"Of course. But you really need the police involved, Bridget. Mrs. Sandowski, Tim even, could be in danger."

"I'm well aware of that, but with the attitude of the cops we don't know what to do. We thought about hiring a private investigator, but Tim and his mom are wary, and frankly, we don't have enough money for a long, drawn-out investigation."

My mind skipped to my bank account and realized I didn't have enough to float a decent-sized loan. Most of my money was tied up in Taken by Surprise. But surely there had to be some way.

I opened my mouth to say so, and couldn't believe what I heard come out. "Let me look into it."

Her mouth widened in a dramatic *O* as her face drained of color. "What? No—"

I held up a hand to cut her off. "Tim and Mrs. Sandowski know me, know they can trust me. With my business as a cover, I can nose into things without being obvious. Not to mention my close connection to the investigation through Kevin." Who *was* this person talking? I was too hyped up to linger on the fact that Kevin and I weren't exactly on speaking terms.

Bridget's knuckles had gone white, her fists were clenched so tightly. "I don't know." Her hair swooshed as she shook her head. "No. Absolutely no."

"Just let me try. We need to find out who's doing this, before someone takes potshots at you, too."

"I can't let you take on that responsibility!"

"I'll be careful. And if I get in over my head, I'll back out and take out a loan if I have to, so a PI can be hired."

Tears filled her eyes. "I really don't want you to get involved, Nina. It's dangerous."

I reached out and clasped her hand. "I *am* involved."

She sighed. "I don't know . . ."

"Just let me talk to Tim's mom. Let her decide."

Resigned, she said, "I'll let you talk to her. That's all I can promise, but I can almost guarantee she'll say no."

"It's worth a shot." I looked over at Gertie. Still flirting. I sighed. "Should we go now?"

Bridget didn't look all that gung ho. "I suppose."

I tossed a five-dollar bill on the table to cover the cost of the OJ and helped lever Bridget to her feet.

"It's going to be okay, Bridget," I said as she laid a hand on the table to steady herself. Once again I was amazed at the changes her pregnancy had brought on.

She shook her head, waddled ahead of me. "I don't have a good feeling about this. Not at all."

Five

I followed Bridget as we took the side roads to Sandowski's Farm, avoiding Vista View altogether.

At a four-way stop, I examined a ragged fingernail, picked its jagged edges. I wanted to turn around, go home. I had no business whatsoever looking into a murder. I was in way over my head, knew it, and yet still felt compelled to help. What was it with me?

I lost sight of Bridget's late-model Jeep for a moment as I crested a hill. Not that it mattered. I knew where the farm was, had been there many, many times during my teen years, when I used to tag along after Bridget and Tim because I had nothing better to do and no one else to do it with.

I slowed for a yellow light at the corner of Millson and Liberty. Up ahead, behind the do-it-yourself car wash, I could see the roofline of Sandowski's Farm.

Stores crowded each corner of the intersection. A supermarket, a pharmacy, a Mickey D's, and a gas station. My eyes swept it all in, remembering it as it was ten, fifteen years ago, when there was nothing here but open fields, wandering cows, and an endless blue sky.

As I passed the gas station, I did a double take. I caught the profiles of Kevin and Ginger sitting in the gas station's parking lot, the nose of their unmarked pointed in the direction of Sandowski's Farm. Clearly they were doing a little surveillance. I'd have paid to see Kevin's face when he realized just who Mrs. Sandowski's visitor was.

Gravel spit under my tires as I turned into the driveway, rolled to a stop. Though I must've passed this way a thousand times, I hadn't taken a good look at the place in years. Gone was the freshly painted picturesque farmhouse I remembered. Weeds choked the yard, the walkway. Bushy shrub branches thrust here, there, everywhere. Bricks were missing from the steps leading up to the door and the screen door hung by only one hinge. Clearly the Sandowskis had fallen on hard times in the last few years.

I imagined a couple million would come in handy for the family right about now. It went beyond my reasoning why they hadn't taken the money.

Bridget climbed out of her Jeep. After closing the door of my truck, I made sure Kevin got a good view of my face. I almost laughed as I imagined his mouth agape in shock.

Aside from my wanting to help the Sandowskis—and I did, don't get me wrong—I had to admit I was going to enjoy sticking my nose into Kevin's investigation. My interference was going to make Kevin's hair stand on end. Not quite the punishment I was aiming for—unless he was attached to the electric chair—but it would do. For now.

Farmer Joe's meticulous landscaping had been allowed to run wild, with overgrown flower beds chock full of weeds and his shaped hedges growing every which way.

Weeds choked the cracked brick pathway leading up to the door. The designer in me already had ideas to transform the yard back to what it used to be.

I shook my head to clear my thoughts. I needed to remember why I was here.

Taking hold of the door handle, Bridget jumped back in surprise as the screen door fell off its frame, landed with a soft *whoosh* in one of the overgrown Japanese yews that flanked the steps.

At closer inspection, I realized the house itself was quite beautiful. Run-down but beautiful. A classic Federal style and shape: a white brick square box with symmetrical lines and incredible detail on the paneled doors and moldings. It was too bad it was in such disrepair.

"You okay?"

Shakily, she nodded. "Nina, I really don't think this is a good idea."

I offered a reassuring smile. "So I've heard."

Sighing, she knocked once, entered.

Before stepping over the threshold, I turned to face the street, blew Kevin a kiss.

The scent of baking bread filled the air, and my stomach rumbled to life. Mrs. Sandowski's homemade bread was heaven on earth.

It took a moment for me to adjust from the sun to the dim lighting. Colored spots danced in front of my eyes.

Bridget cleared her throat. "Mom?"

I smiled. Bridget had started calling Mrs. Sandowski "Mom" long before she and Tim married. My eyesight slowly adjusted. The living room, where we were standing, was spotless. I doubted there was a speck of dust on any piece of furniture, and certainly no trace of soot in the large stone fireplace. I checked the soles of my Keds to make sure they were clean.

"Mom?" Bridget called out, slightly louder than before. Under her breath, she muttered, "Man, it's hot in here."

Hot was an understatement. Even with the windows open and a prehistoric ceiling fan droning above, hell had nothing on this place.

"I'm back here," Mrs. Sandowski yelled from the kitchen.

I followed Bridget down a short hallway into the sun-filled kitchen. I felt my breath catch as memories assailed me. I had spent many a happy hour in this kitchen, back when I had thought my own family was just too weird to be associated with. Oh, the wallpaper had faded and the linoleum had cracked, but it was as though I had just stepped back in time. The only thing different was the gallons and gallons of jug water bottles stacked against the rear wall.

Mrs. Sandowski sat at a pea green kitchen table, shucking corn, a window fan providing her little relief from the intense heat. She looked older, now with more gray than brown hair, but her eyes were the same. Sparkling hazel. Keen. Piercing. Alert. They narrowed as she looked at me.

"I'll be darned. Nina Ceceri! Is that you?"

She jumped up, moving much quicker than I would have thought she could. She had to be at least seventy.

Before I knew it I was engulfed in a big hug. She smelled of baking bread and Ivory soap. I smiled as she pulled away. "It's Nina Quinn now."

"Yes, yes, that's right." She waved to her head. "I'm old. The memory goes." The twinkle in her eye told me she was teasing.

"Nonsense."

She smiled. "My oh my, you're a sight for these old eyes."

"You look wonderful, Mrs. Sandowski."

She patted her hair, then slid her hands down her still slim figure. "Well, you know, I try."

My voice shook slightly as I said, "I'm so very sorry about Joe."

Her smile faltered. "So am I, Nina. So am I. But he's at peace now. I have to keep reminding myself of that." Clapping her hands, she said, "No melancholy today. I'm too happy to see you after all this time." She turned to Bridget, tsked lovingly. "Why didn't you tell me you were bringing Nina? I would've set out lunch, or tea, or something."

"I didn't know. It just sort of came up. And actually, I can't stay all that long." She lowered herself into a chair, stretched out her long legs, rested her hands on her belly. Dark circles under her eyes were beginning to glow beneath her translucent skin. "I have an appointment in an hour."

"You should be resting, honey," Mrs. Sandowski said, rubbing a hand over Bridget's hair. "It's not good for the baby, you working so hard."

With great effort, Bridget shifted. "We're fine. Really, we are. You know I wouldn't take any risks."

Mrs. Sandowski clucked. "I know. I just hate seeing you working yourself to the bone."

Strands of pale blonde hair fell forward onto Bridget's face. She pushed them back behind her ears. "I hope you don't mind us stopping in."

"Not at all, honey." To me, she said, "Sit, sit." She pulled out a chair for me. "Catch me up with you. You're in landscaping now, right?"

I smiled, thinking about Taken by Surprise until I remembered those damn hoes. "It's not your traditional landscape company."

Her wrinkled face puckered. "Oh?"

"It started that way until a client offered me an absurd amount of money to be done with her job in a day. She wanted to surprise her husband while he was out of town."

"And you did it?"

"Do I look like someone who'd turn down an absurd amount of money?" I laughed before I realized who I was speaking to—someone who *had* turned down an absurd amount of money.

My discomfort eased, though, as Mrs. Sandowski laughed.

I pressed on, talking fast to cover my nervousness. "I realized there was a whole market out there for garden makeovers. One client became two, then three. A local paper did a story on us, then the local news, and now I have to turn people away."

"Do you enjoy it?"

"I love it. I try to do as much hands-on as I can, but between consultation and design meetings, it's tough."

"Joe always loved puttering around those gardens out there with you."

"I loved it too."

She tsked. "He hated that he couldn't take care of the garden once he became ill."

A thick lump of sorrow lodged in my throat. It was hard to talk around it. "I wish I had known. I'd have been glad to help out. Actually, I'd still like to help. Maybe get things back to the way they were. Make Joe proud."

Bridget sniffled.

Mrs. Sandowski's eyes filled with tears. "I'd really like that," she said.

"So would I."

We sat in silence for a long minute before she picked up another ear of corn. She smiled at us. "So what brings you here? A trip down memory lane?"

"Uh," I stammered, looking at Bridget. "Not quite."

Bridget stiffened. "How's Jumper?"

Mrs. Sandowski's smile faltered. "Better," she said warily. "Doc said he'd be home in a few days."

Bridget cleared her throat. "That's why Nina's here, Mom."

Hazel eyes narrowed into thin slits. "Tell me you did not tell her about this."

I felt her anger as much as saw it and was glad that I wasn't at the receiving end. Still, I felt guilty for having caused such feelings in the first place.

"Nina wants to help. And we need help. You and I both know it."

She shook her head. "We can do this on our own. You shouldn't have involved Nina in this. It's none of her concern."

Bridget paled.

I leaned forward, trying not to feel hurt that Mrs. Sandowski didn't want me around. "It was my idea, Mrs. Sandowski. Don't be angry with Bridget."

Mrs. Sandowski picked up an ear of corn and ripped it open, revealing a golden yellow cob. Honestly, how could she continue to work in the stifling heat?

As sweat trickled down my hairline, I said, "I know that you didn't want any outsiders helping, but you're in over your head. What happened with Jumper this morning proves it."

"No offense, Nina, but it's private."

Bridget flashed me an I-told-you-so look, then slowly wobbled to her feet. "I'm going to head out now and let the two of you hash this out."

Bridget promised she'd check in with me soon, despite having to prepare for an upcoming trial, and gave me her business card with all her numbers on it. She mentioned something about dinner Friday night with her and Tim as she kissed my cheek, then Mrs. Sandowski's. Teetering toward the door, she said over her shoulder, "Don't say I didn't warn you."

A moment later, the front door opened then closed and an engine sputtered to life.

Mrs. Sandowski continued to shuck corn.

Now, sitting here, just the two of us, I felt a hundred times a fool. What to do? What to say? Had I really volunteered to become embroiled in this mess? Unfortunately, it seemed as though I was already too involved to back out, that I didn't have a choice in the matter, even if I wanted to.

I leaned forward, propping my elbows on the table. "You have to trust someone, sometime, Mrs. Sandowski. Why not me? I have connections through my husband."

"Ah, yes. Detective Quinn." She said this as though she had some serious doubts about Kevin's character. Not that I blamed her. I now had serious doubts about his character too.

Grabbing an ear of corn, I ripped it open. "My point is I have access to certain information. And I can use my business as a cover while asking around about this land, and who's most interested in it. But most of all, you know me. I'd never do anything to hurt this family. I hate what's happening to all of you. And I hate that nothing's been done about it."

Lines creased her forehead as her brows dipped. "You're serious?"

I set my shucked ear with the others in a bowl near the edge of the table. "Completely."

She sighed heavily. "I don't know what you can do to help, Nina."

Corn silk clung to the table. "I'm not sure, either, but it's better than nothing being done at all, right?"

"Perhaps."

Feeling as though I'd just stumbled, flailing, over one hurdle, I pressed on, hoping to keep her talking. "When did all this start?"

Mrs. Sandowski rubbed her hands together. They were dark from the sun and dotted with liver spots. "I'd say three, four months ago. That's when we were approached by a developer about selling our land."

"Which developer?"

She picked at the strands of yellow corn silk left behind by the shucking and now covering the table. "Demming. John Demming."

Demming was a popular builder. His billboards dotted Freedom's landscape, and I thought I recalled seeing ads for his homes on TV.

"He offered us three million dollars for our house and land. Joe and I said no." Her voice cracked when she said her husband's name.

I picked another ear of corn from the pile. Softly, I said, "May I ask why?"

She shrugged, a delicate movement that said volumes. "This house was built by Timmy's great-great grandfather. I've lived here near all my life, since I married Joe at sixteen. Timmy was born in the upstairs bedroom. It's our *home*. I know it's not much to look at, but it's ours. The memories are here."

I could understand her reluctance, but three million dollars? "What happened then?"

"A few days after Demming's offer, the congressman came."

"Chanson?"

"Yes. He's a charming man, easy on the eyes, if you know what I mean, but he's arrogant."

I liked arrogant in a man. I've chalked it up to genetic defect and written it off as something I could never change. An arrogant man had confidence, was sure of himself, secure. He wasn't a pushover, and I'm sure Chanson tried every which way to get Mrs. Sandowski to sell.

"Pushy?" I'd seen Chanson on TV and he played the role of politician perfectly. Smooth, suave, amiable to a fault. He had to have some flaw, somewhere. But was he capable of murder?

"Not overly."

Well, there blew that theory.

"He has a way about him that makes you want to bend to his will. That if you don't, you're in the wrong."

"Do you think he has something to do with what's been happening here?" I dropped the gleaming golden corn on her teetering pile.

"Hard to say. He has a lot of money behind him, and he lives over there in that Vista View, so he has a stake in what happens too. I just don't know." She inhaled deeply. "He came armed with an offer of four point five million—

money from a group of investors from Vista View, himself included. I said no and told him never to come back. So far, he hasn't."

She bandied about the huge sums as though they were pocket change. *Millions.* I couldn't imagine it.

"Demming came back and upped *his* offer," she said as calm as can be. "He doesn't understand about this being a home, a legacy. He thinks money can buy anything."

Glancing at the entryway, I thought it could certainly buy a new screen door, but I kept my mouth shut.

"I tried explaining to him that money wasn't everything, that it didn't buy happiness. That's when Demming offered five million."

Five million! "And you turned it down?" I said incredulously.

She shrugged, half smiled. "This house makes us happy. This is what's important to us, not padding our bank account." Swiping her hand across the table, she gathered all the corn silk into a paper bag at her feet.

She kept saying "our" and "us" as if Farmer Joe would come strolling in from the fields at any moment. It broke my heart and at the same time made me uneasy.

She glanced at me. "It was after that last refusal when the calls started."

"What were they like? Just hang-ups?"

Wiping her hands down her apron, she said, "No. Heavy breathing, then hanging up."

"Nothing was ever said?"

"No. It was always the same."

I bit my lip. "Did you try Star 69 or Caller ID?"

She shifted in her seat and began twisting her wedding ring. I looked down at my own hands, at the diamond band that seemed heavier each day.

"I tried that Star 69, but the number was unavailable."

"What about Caller ID?"

"Too expensive."

Frustrated, I picked at my nails. I had a niggling suspicion that she was holding something back from me, that she still wasn't entirely comfortable talking about her family's problems to an outsider. "Do you still get calls?" I asked.

She shook her head. "No. The calls stopped about a week after they started, and we were so relieved, but then the letters started showing up."

"Bridget mentioned them. What were they like?"

"They looked phony," she said, her voice a bit tight. "Like something copied right out of a movie. The letters were cut out of newspapers and magazines and glued onto a piece of paper, then the page was photocopied. That's what we got," she said with a frown. "The photocopied version."

"What did the notes say?"

"They always said the same thing."

"Which was?" I prompted, almost out of patience.

"'Sell the land or face the consequences,'" she said, monotone.

Pretty blunt. "Consequences" was a fairly fancy word, so I figured whoever was sending the letters was educated, although I'd been wrong before.

I leaned in, hating the concern that wrinkled her brow. "And the police?"

"Were no help whatsoever. We let it be, figuring it would blow over once whoever this was figured out we weren't going nowhere." She paused a moment. "Bridget tell you about the sheep and the fire?"

"Yes. I'm sorry."

"At first we didn't want to involve Timmy and Bridget in our troubles, but with the sheep we knew we needed help. Unfortunately there wasn't much they could do either. Especially after they went to the police and nothing was done. The sheep were the first real sign that we were in for the long haul. We're afraid to drink our water. We still have well water. Who knows what someone may have dumped in there?"

That explained the bottled spring water. My blood pressure rose. This was why I'd volunteered to look into this. Whoever was terrorizing this family needed to be caught. And I just hoped I could be of some help.

I had a few ideas where to begin: an old friend at the fire department, meeting with Chanson, maybe Demming . . .

"I feel like we're prisoners in our own home. It's horrible."

Again, the "we're" and "our." I shifted, uncomfortable. A buzzer sounded and Mrs. Sandowski rose. She removed a bread tin from the oven and placed it on the stovetop. After pressing her fingers into the dough to test it, she turned off the oven.

"Smells good," I said, hoping she couldn't hear the rumbling of my tummy.

"You can take it with you."

"I couldn't."

"Nonsense. I have a dozen more in the freezer."

I brushed away that feeling of stealing from the poor. "Then, thank you."

She wiped her hands on a dish towel and sat down. "Do you really think you can help us?"

"I'm not sure if I *can* help, but I can try. Something has to be done."

She tugged on her plain gold wedding band. Her grief creased her forehead, tugged at the lines at her mouth. I looked up at the clock. It seemed as though I had been in the farmhouse for hours. I'd been there twenty minutes.

"Where would you start? What would you do?"

A piece of corn silk clung to the end of the table. I picked it off. A hint of worry lined her eyes and maybe a bit of fear as I said, "I need to talk to Congressman Chanson, and Demming too. The paramedics, maybe, and some friends at the police station. I might even talk with a few of the residents of Vista View—they know my name through my business, so I might be able to get them to talk to me. I'll see what I can find out."

She reached out, grabbed my hand, gave it a squeeze. "Thank you for helping. As much as I hate to admit it, Bridget is right. We do need help, but I just don't trust the police. Don't go to them, all right? And if they question you, you won't tell them about any of this, will you?"

I thought of Kevin and those boxers. Frankly, at the moment I never wanted to speak with him again. But if I found myself in over my head, it was nice to know I could go to him. "Not if I don't have to."

"Promise me."

Her gaze burned into me. With the pads of my fingers, I wiped the perspiration from my upper lip. "I promise," I said with reluctance.

"Please be careful."

"I will."

"And don't be worrying if you don't find anything. I have a feeling this will all be over soon."

As I drove away from the farm, a loaf of freshly baked bread and a half dozen ears of corn seat-belted in next to me, I couldn't help wondering what Mrs. Sandowski had meant by her last comment. Did she know something?

Feeling a little lost, I wondered what I had gotten myself into.

Scanning the floor as I entered the house, I grabbed the hockey stick from against the wall. Still no sign of Xena, but I wasn't going to walk around unarmed.

After finally plunging the sink and changing out of sweat-dampened jeans and into a pair of khaki shorts, I sat on the sofa, wondering where to begin my informal investigation. Chanson seemed my best bet. As a congressman and a resident of Vista View, he'd have a good overview of the whole situation.

I allowed my head to fall back against the cushion. I kept the hockey stick tightly gripped while my thoughts flitted from Xena to Bridget to Kevin to Riley, and to—of all things—my missing hoes.

The rumble of my stomach drowned out most of my coherent thoughts, so I gave up on trying to figure things out and went in search of lunch. I hadn't eaten all day and was beginning to get a bit dizzy.

Out the window I could see Mr. Cabrera carrying lumber into his backyard. "So it begins," I murmured under my breath.

From the fridge, I grabbed a Diet Coke. My stomach continued to yell at me. I was opening the drawer to grab a knife to cut into Mrs. Sandowski's bread when I saw the light blinking on the answering machine. Three messages. I figured they were all from my mother, but I decided to check. The first was from Kevin. No hello, just a tired, "What do you think you're doing?"

The kitchen echoed with my laughter. The next message, though, erased all my good humor. "This is Robert MacKenna. I'm the vice principal at Freedom High. I need to speak to you about your son, Riley. If you could call me at your earliest convenience I would appreciate it."

My mouth went dry as he read off the number. I made a quick grab for a pencil and copied it down. *Oh, Riley, Riley.*

The third message was a lot of heavy breathing and a hang-up. It shouldn't have bothered me, but it did. It was too coincidental and I didn't believe in coincidences—it's another one of my personal commandments.

My appetite vanished. I rewrapped the bread. And keeping a tight hold on the hockey stick, I checked the locks on all the doors.

Six

As I drove to the high school to meet with Vice Principal MacKenna, I tried to ignore the memory of the hang-up phone call. It was probably just a wrong number.

Probably.

Definitely.

This wasn't merely an example of self-delusion—it really wasn't. I was flat-out lying to myself.

After I had arranged to meet with Riley's vice principal, I had called Kevin. After dodging his questions regarding the Sandowskis, I told him about the call from the school and mentioned the magazine under Riley's mattress. Kevin hadn't seemed overly concerned, but agreed to meet the vice principal with me.

Flipping on my blinker, I turned right into the high school's parking lot.

It must have been between bells because the halls were filled with teens. I spied the office and was walking toward it when someone grabbed my arm.

Whirling, I came face to face with a very angry Riley. His hand dropped as soon as I turned around.

"What are you doing here?" he whispered, looking stricken.

I stepped back. "I have an appointment to see your vice principal."

"Why?"

He seemed nervous, continually looking over his left shoulder. Following his gaze, I saw a group of boys huddled near a row of lockers.

Troublemakers. Not smash-your-mailbox troublemakers, but the real deal: drugs, stealing cars, shoplifting . . . You could tell by just looking at them. What was Riley doing?

I tried to control my temper, to not lash out and shake him until he came to his senses. I swayed slightly, a bit dizzy. "I don't know why he called me. Is there something I should know?"

"No."

My right eyebrow rose. My eyebrows were, as I liked to say, my built-in bullshit meters. The more crap I heard, the higher they arched.

"Who are those boys?"

"Friends of mine."

"Since when?"

"Since whenever."

I stared at him. Blinked. "Those weren't the clothes you had on when you left this morning."

Gone was the red and green, replaced now with black from head to toe.

The bell rang.

"Hey, man, you coming?"

That from a boy wearing a charming metal-studded black leather coat and spiked dog collar. His lip was pierced and his hair was black with blonde polka dots. Very original. Now I knew where Riley's latest hairstyle had come from.

Riley caught my gaze and muttered something under his breath I couldn't understand. He swiveled and walked away without answering me. My stomach twisted as he blended in with the group of troublemakers and disappeared down a corridor.

I let him go.

A second later, I stepped into the office.

"I'm Nina Quinn," I said to the secretary, trying to keep the snap out of my voice.

"Mr. MacKenna is running a bit behind, Mrs. Quinn. If you'll have a seat." She gestured to a bench against the wall.

"You haven't seen my . . . er, husband yet, have you?" I nearly choked on "husband."

"Oh, I forgot to tell you that Detective Quinn called and said he couldn't make it."

I was going to kill him with my bare hands.

"Did he say why?" I asked, my tone sugary sweet.

"I'm sorry." She shook her head. "No."

I slumped into a chair. Heat rose up my throat, dampened my armpits. I silently fumed. At Riley for getting involved with kids who were no good, at Kevin for leaving me to do what was rightfully his dirty work.

How was I going to handle it all? And for that matter would I even get the chance to try?

If I was smart, I'd start pulling away from Riley, not become more entwined with him. My heart was already broken from his father leaving. It was going to shatter when he left too.

But I couldn't distance myself. Riley needed me. More now than ever. And distancing myself seemed so cold because, unfortunately for me, I loved the little bugger. Dammit.

I knew one thing for sure. I didn't want to meet with the vice principal alone. To the secretary, I said, "I'll be right back." She nodded as I pulled open the door.

In the hallway, I fished my cell phone from my backpack, punched in familiar numbers.

Ana answered on the first ring. "Ana Bertoli, underpaid and overworked."

"Still one of those days?"

"You need to ask?"

"Guess not. Hey," my gaze swept down the long hallway, past the trophy case and the standard artwork covering the white cinder-block walls, "do you have a few minutes? I mean, if you don't have the time it's okay, I know you're busy and all, probably on the lookout for those probationers out there running loose, needing your guidance."

Swaying a bit, I leaned against the wall. The municipal center was just five minutes from here. Knowing the way Ana drove, she could be here in three.

"What's wrong? You're rambling. I know something's wrong if you're rambling."

"I need backup. Riley's in some sort of trouble and there's this meeting with his vice principal and Kevin bailed on me."

"You're there now?"

"Standing in the hallway looking at some really bad self-portraits."

"I'll be right there."

Before I could even say thanks, the phone went dead. Reluctantly, I dragged myself back inside the office.

"Mrs. Quinn?" The secretary was waiting for me. She gestured to follow her down a carpeted hallway. "Mr. MacKenna's ready for you."

"Thanks. I'm, uh, expecting someone. Could you point the way when she gets here?"

"Sure thing," she said over her shoulder as she led me along.

My legs went spongy as I dutifully followed. Incomplete thoughts swirled. I pressed a hand against the wall to steady myself when a wave of dizziness nearly knocked me down.

I readjusted my backpack straps on my shoulders and took a deep breath, willing air into my lungs. The door at the end of the hallway stood open. I walked in, feeling the tension of my day rising like tsunami.

"Mrs. Quinn? I'm Robert MacKenna."

I heard the door close behind me as the secretary stepped out.

"It's nice to meet you," I murmured politely. I was lying through my teeth. I didn't want to be here. I knew what he was going to say, and I didn't want to hear it. I didn't want to have to defend myself, my actions.

"Have a seat." He motioned to a chair opposite him.

I sat.

Silence ensued. Was this some form of vice principal torture?

Finally, I looked up from studying my shoelaces.

His eyes were a light blue. There wasn't anything too unusual about the color, but what he was able to portray with just a glance was highly extraordinary.

Sympathy. Empathy. Concern.

Completely different from Kevin's heated, passionate looks that had made my knees quake when I first met him. But there was something similar to Kevin in this man's gaze. An underlying current ready to zap me from my seat and into his arms. I shifted my gaze to look out the window.

My imagination was running wild, I reasoned. It was on overload. Robert MacKenna wasn't even my type. He was too all-American for me. I've always been drawn to the bad boys.

His hair was too blonde and cut too precisely over his ears for my tastes. He wore a suit and tie that looked as though it had been designed—and made—in the sixties, and when he came around the desk to sit in the chair next to mine, I noticed he wore—of all things—cowboy boots!

I needed some sleep, was all. About a week's worth.

Pointing to a coffee pot on a small table near the window, he asked, "Coffee?"

I noticed he wore a wedding band. I didn't know why I noticed—okay, maybe I looked for one. So sue me. But that settled whatever my overactive imagination had planned. He was off-limits. Not that I wanted him. I didn't. I was on the rebound. That's all this, this . . . reaction was about. I was trying to figure out if I was still appealing to the opposite sex. Speaking of sex, the lack of it might also be the cause of my raging hormon—

My temples began to throb, and I shook my head, clearing my thoughts. I would *not* go there.

I tugged at my V-necked collar. It had to be ninety degrees in his office. Didn't anyone have air-conditioning anymore?

"Coffee?" he said again.

I bet he was thinking he knew why Riley was so screwed up. Where was Ana when I needed her?

"No thank you. What's going on?"

He crossed one leg over the other, pulling his foot up onto his knee. The boots looked like they were made of snakeskin. My eyebrow arched, studying them. I instantly liked them better.

"Mrs. Quinn," he began.

That name grated on my nerves. *Mrs. Quinn. Detective Quinn's wife. Nina Quinn, Nina Quinn, Nina Quinn.* Blech! "Please, call me Nina." My voice rang through my ears.

"Okay, *Nina.* I'm very concerned about Riley."

Oh, *he's* very concerned about Riley. I wondered what he'd say if I told him about the gun magazine under Riley's mattress. Then I'd like to see how *concerned* he was.

"Is that so?"

My voice had an edge to it I couldn't identify. It sounded . . . snippy. Which caused immediate alarm. I'm never snippy. Perhaps sarcastic or smart-mouthed, but never snippy. My sister Maria was snippy. She could snip about anything. From the smell of strawberries to the shade of platinum on her three-carat engagement ring. Snip, snip, snip.

"Mrs. Quinn?"

"Nina," I snapped.

Snip, snap.

The room whirled. Spots danced before my eyes.

"It's okay." MacKenna stood at my elbow.

What was okay? Why was there suddenly two of him? And why did he sound muted, echoey? My ears rang, and I blinked to clear my double vision.

"Close your eyes," he said, snippy-like.

No, my inner voice whispered. Not snippy, commanding.

One of these days I was going to see someone about that inner voice.

My eyelids fluttered closed. I felt his cool hand curve around the back of my neck. With gentle pressure, he pushed. I opened my eyes and was surprised to find that I was staring at the floor.

Keds vs. snakeskin-kick-ass-cowboy boots.

Those boots were definitely growing on me. I was going to have to ask him where he got them once I could find my voice again. Maybe he had hunted the snake himself . . . A girl could hope.

His hand rested reassuringly on my shoulder. "It's okay."

I pressed my forehead on my knobby knees. The dancing spots faded.

"Get Mr. Quinn on the phone," I heard him say into the intercom.

I swayed as I jerked up my head. "No! No, no."

MacKenna grinned. "Cancel Mr. Quinn."

He pressed a glass of water into my hand. I drank slowly.

"When was the last time you ate?"

I tried to think, but the gurgling of my stomach was so loud it made it hard. "I had a Snickers last night at nine."

He gave me that look a parent gives a child when the parent knows something's bad for the child, and the child knows it's bad for the child, but the child does it anyway.

My God, I was rambling to myself. The water felt cool as I took another sip.

"It's satisfying," I muttered, using the candy bar's motto.

"It's unhealthy. You ought to eat three regular meals every day. And lots of fruit."

"Yes, Doctor."

Opening a desk drawer, he rummaged around inside. Finally, he pulled out an Almond Joy. Sliding it across the desk, he said, "Emergency supply." He smiled at me, fine lines appearing around his eyes.

"Is this a test? After that lecture you just gave me about healthy foods, you expect me to eat that candy bar?" I asked, a teasing lilt to my voice. I was *not* flirting. I wasn't. Honest.

Liar.

"Do as I say, not as I do. Unless, of course, you don't want it." He reached across his desk for the Almond Joy.

I slapped his hand and grabbed the candy bar.

He smiled a knowing grin as I tore open the package.

Ahh. Heaven.

He was kind enough not to stare at me as I inhaled the two sections of the Almond Joy in three seconds flat. The back of my hand served as a napkin. *Quite a first impression, Nina.*

"About Riley," I said, suddenly mortified by my behavior.

The vice principal smiled as if he knew why I had suddenly changed the subject, then his expression turned serious.

A loud knock echoed and the door flew open. Ana stood there, doubled over, panting, her C cups heaving beneath a white camisole and linen suit coat. Her long dark hair fell forward as she gasped for breath.

I jumped up, helped her over to a chair. "Mr. MacKenna,

this is Analise Bertoli, my cousin." I opened my mouth to explain that I hadn't wanted to take this meeting alone, but decided he really didn't need to know I was a big wuss.

MacKenna poured Ana a cup of water. His eyebrows dipped. "Are you okay?"

"Fine, fine," she said in between gulps of air. "Need to bump up those trips to the gym."

"Water?" MacKenna held out a cup.

She glanced up at him, her eyes going wide as paper plates as she got a good look. "Thanks." Turning to me, she wiggled her eyebrows.

"Married," I mouthed.

"Damn," she said into the cup as she took a sip.

To a puzzled MacKenna, I said, "Ana's here because Kevin couldn't make it. I hope you don't mind."

"Not at all."

Ana looked around. "Whoa. This is like déjà vu."

A half smile playing on his lips, MacKenna leaned back in his chair. "Spend a lot of time in the principal's office did you, Ms. Bertoli?"

"Too much. You know, if you're free sometime, I could share—"

I kicked her shin beneath her linen skirt.

"Ow!"

"Married," I mouthed again.

Rubbing her shin, she frowned. "Testy. And after I rushed over here and everything."

I swallowed hard over a sudden lump in my throat. "Thanks for coming."

Forgiven in a blink of her brown eyes, she took my hand. "Now what's this all about? Riley's in trouble? That new hair color affecting his brain cells?"

MacKenna leaned over his desk, his hands clasped. "Since the start of the fourth quarter, my staff has noted changes in Riley. He has become uncooperative, mouthy, and his grades pale in comparison to last semester."

Here it comes . . .

"Is there anything going on at home that our counselors should be aware of?"

I *knew* it was coming.

Of course Riley's change in attitude was about Kevin and me. It's always the parents. It couldn't just be normal adolescent rebellion. It had to be my fault. His father's.

I grit my teeth. "There's been some tension."

Ana snorted. "What?" she said at my perturbed stare.

MacKenna pressed on. "Involving Riley?"

Resentment swelled. I didn't want to have to admit my marital problems to this stranger.

"Tangentially." Was that really a word? I wasn't sure, but it sounded good.

His eyebrows arched as his eyes widened. I wondered if he had the same bullshit meter I had.

"Marital?"

Marital, I mimicked silently. I didn't want to do this, to have this conversation. But he *had* given me his candy bar.

Ana answered for me. "Nina and Kevin are divorcing."

It sounded so final coming from Ana's lips, that it stole my breath for a second.

"Ahh." MacKenna nodded.

I felt compelled to clarify. "As of yet Riley is unaware of that fact."

Why I was talking like a high-priced lawyer, I had no idea. Being around Bridget that morning must have worn off on me.

"But there must be fighting, tension, stress in the household . . ."

"No."

"Nope," Ana agreed.

There hadn't been. Kevin and I hardly ever saw each other. Which could explain the divorce. Well that and Ginger Snap—er, Barlow.

Lines creased his forehead. "No fighting?"

"No. Well," I amended, "one huge blowout two days ago, but Riley was at school."

"So he is unaware of any problems."

The vision of a worm impaling itself on a hook entered my thoughts. "That's not quite true."

"Mrs. Qu—" He paused, caught himself. "*Nina*, you're going to have to give me some details."

I took a deep breath, and dipped a shoulder in a sort of half shrug. "He knows his father cheated on me. I think he can tell the end is near."

"I see."

Ana piped in. "But this all happened recently? His slipping grades?" When MacKenna nodded, Ana continued. "Then Nina and Kevin can't be a part of that as there was no trouble until the boxers."

"The boxers?" he asked.

I shook my head. "No need to go there."

"I'm inclined to agree," he said, and I didn't know whether he was talking about the boxers or Riley's attitude until he added, "that this behavior doesn't stem from Riley's home life."

I thought about the boy with the polka-dotted hair and lip ring. "Perhaps it's those punks he's hanging out with."

He twirled his wedding ring. "The Skinz."

"The Skinz?" Ana repeated. "Sounds like something you'd find in the contraceptive aisle."

It really had been too long since Ana'd had a date. I scooted to the edge of my seat and said, "Who, or what, exactly, are the Skinz?"

His blue eyes narrowed. "Trouble."

* * *

I left MacKenna's office sensing panic taking over my life. It seemed as though everything was out of control. Riley, Kevin . . . Farmer Joe.

"Oh ho ho!" Ana exclaimed as the office door closed behind her.

"Oh ho ho what?"

"Are you blind? Mr. Hubba Hubba MacKenna has the hots for you."

I blinked. "Are you delusional? The man is married. Gold band. Left hand."

She rolled her eyes, wagged her finger at me. "Didn't you see the way he looked at you?"

I hadn't noticed him looking at me at all. Of course, the way I was looking at him . . . *that* was a different story. "You're seeing things. He's just a nice man who cares about the kids here."

In a know-it-all voice, she said, "Don't say I didn't tell you."

"You're certifiable."

She let that pass. "What are you gonna do about Riley?"

"I don't know. Thanks for coming, though. I didn't want to do that alone."

"You're welcome." Glancing at her Wizard of Oz watch, she said, "I've got to get back. I've got a meeting in five minutes."

"You got plans for tonight?" I asked.

"Are you mocking my love life?"

I smiled at her defensive tone. "Just trying to live vicariously through my older, wiser cousin."

"By a month and day! And actually, yes, I do have plans. My final fitting for my bridesmaid dress is tonight. Have you seen yours yet?"

"No." I stopped, mid-stride. "What's that smile?"

"Nothing. Not a thing. I just think that Maria might secretly hate you."

"That bad?"

Her eyebrows arched as she nodded.

Great. Maybe an ugly dress was my punishment for missing all my appointments with the seamstress. "I'm still trying to get out of the wedding."

"Your mother would have an apoplectic fit and die on the spot."

I groaned. "I know."

"I'm serious. You should have seen her after Maria told her that she'd invited my mother to the wedding."

Shading my eyes against the sun, I smiled. "I heard the paramedics got an earful."

"That they did."

In the parking lot, the sun lit up the auburn highlights in her long dark hair, making me think I should see a stylist about getting some myself. I dismissed the thought almost as fast as it had popped into my head. Much too much work.

Ana's heels tapped rapidly against the pavement as she made a beeline for her car. "Hey," she called out. "How did the meeting with Bridget go?"

I cringed, having forgotten for a moment what I'd gotten myself into. It would take forever to explain to Ana. "I'll tell you all about it at lunch tomorrow."

She rolled down the window, started the engine. "Just so you know, I'm still not holding my breath."

I winced as she backed up, slammed on the brakes. The car jerked forward as she switched gears. She stuck her hand out the window and waved as the car swerved, squealing, around the corner.

"Nina?" a very male voice said over my shoulder.

I spun in surprise, my hand flying to my pounding heart. My eyes widened as I took in the man standing casually near my car.

I squinted. "Michael Novak! I haven't seen you in ages."

Kevin's former patrol partner was the last person I had expected to see in the school parking lot.

Michael grinned and patted the protruding stomach under his uniform. "I've changed a bit."

He was paunchy where once slim, balding where once hairy, but his face was the same. Crinkly, smiling eyes and a wide warm smile.

"You look great. What are you doing here? Has there been trouble?" I immediately thought of Riley.

"New assignment. School resource officer."

A school cop. I wondered what he did to deserve this torture.

"You always did like kids." I tried to make his new job sound like a good one when in fact, it sounded like hell on earth. But that was me. Just my oh-so humble opinion. I blinked. I was rambling to myself again. Sugar high from that Almond Joy. Had to be. I cleared my throat. "Hey, what do you know about the Skinz?"

His eyes clouded, then cleared. He hooked a thumb in his pocket. His chest puffed. "Those guys? They're harmless."

"Do you really think so?"

"Would I lie to you, Nina?"

My right eyebrow inched up. "I guess not."

What the hell was going on?

Seven

I stopped at my office after leaving the high school. Tam frowned as I opened the door, the cowbell ringing out my arrival.

"Don't start," I warned.

"Wouldn't dream of it." She straightened an already straight stack of papers on her desk. "However, you are aware that today is your day off?"

Here it comes.

"A day for rest. For relaxation. Take a long walk through the woods. Soak in a bath until you look like a raisin. Sleep in. Read a good book. You're not good to any of us if you're cranky and overworked. I only say this—"

"Because I care," we both said at the same time.

"Thank you," I said. "I know you care, Tam, but honestly, there's no way I can relax today, and this thing with the hoes is bothering me."

"Kit mentioned you stopped by the site this morning when he called in for reinforcements. Find out anything?"

"Not a thing. Could I possibly see the work log for Sunday, and all the other days tools have gone missing?"

She nudged her blotter into alignment with the edge of her desk. She sat flanked by two huge potted palms, a queen in her oversized rattan throne chair. "It's on your desk."

I bit my lip to stop the smile. "You knew I'd be in."

"Of course."

Clients often commented that Tam was an exact replica of Queen Elizabeth. I had to agree. Beyond the hairstyle and regal bearing, she even had the haughty tone down pat. It wasn't the words—just the cultured way she spoke them. It tended to freak me out, since Tam had just turned thirty and was six months pregnant.

"I hate that you knew that."

She ran her hand over her belly. "I know."

Smiling, I paused at my office door. My nameplate winked at me. NINA QUINN, PRESIDENT. Quinn. I needed to decide whether or not to keep that name. Soon.

Sure enough, a stack of files sat on my desk. Each paper corner matched perfectly to the one below it. The pile sat at a precise right angle to my stained blotter.

I slumped back on my chair. I picked up a file and leafed through it. I had six employees. Three full-time, three part-time. Occasionally, I'd hire an extra hand or two in a pinch. Hey, what the IRS didn't know wouldn't hurt them.

After sifting though all the work logs, I thought I had a place to begin. Well, three of them.

Jean-Claude Reaux, Marty Johnson, and Coby Fowler. All had worked the sites where tools had gone missing.

All had police records.

Eenie, meenie, miny, moe.

I dropped the last log on my desk, setting it purposely askew in Tam's sea of neatness.

The metal drawer of my desk creaked as I pulled it open. A small notebook was pressed into the corner of the drawer, right where "Tornado Tam" always set it when she blew through my office on my days off.

I ripped off a piece of paper and tapped a pen on my blotter, not sure what to do about the missing hoes.

If I called in my three suspects, sat them down and asked

oh-so surreptitiously about the theft, they were bound to get their shorts in a twist. Over the years I've discovered that people with arrest records got a bit touchy when faced with an accusation, however subtle it is.

I bit my lip. Checked my calendar. I had a few ideas on how to go about this, and I wasn't above setting a trap. Mrs. Bobbi Smythe-Weston had planned a backyard makeover for Friday while her husband was off at an all-day conference, morning till night. I'd fiddle with the schedule a bit to make sure all three worked that day.

I scratched out a few notes to myself, folded the paper and shoved it in my pocket. I dropped the notebook back in the drawer and purposely mussed the pens, paper clips, and rubber bands while I was at it.

I looked up as Tam knocked once sharply before coming into my office. She wrung her hands, wouldn't look me in the eye.

I'd seen that stance before. "Not another hoe!"

She tipped her head. "No. Not precisely."

"Then what?"

"I just took the trash out . . ."

Not surprising, since Tam seemed to empty the trash barrels at fifteen-minute intervals. "And?"

"That missing wheelbarrow?"

"Yeah?"

"It's leaning next to the Dumpster out back."

I came out of my seat. "Are we sure it hasn't been there all along?"

"Nina, it wasn't there fifteen minutes ago."

I pulled into a parking spot in the visitor lot of Station 6, the oldest firehouse in the county.

An early heat wave had my clothes sticking to me, my hair in humidity hell, and my mood sinking fast. It was May—where was spring?

I crossed the lot, thinking about that damn wheelbarrow. Upon closer checking, Tam and I also found one of the missing hoes and a shovel behind the Dumpster too.

Who steals things just to return them two days later? A thief with a conscience? Or maybe—and this was much more plausible—my thief simply didn't want to risk jail time if caught with the items. Whoever took the tools had to have known their disappearance would be noted, and that I'd come looking.

I shook my head, determined not to think about it for the time being.

A stream of soapy water licked at my Keds. The tall muscular firefighter washing down the firehouse's driveway turned off the hose's nozzle as I approached. His eyes traipsed over me, head to toe and back again.

"Is Dave in?"

"Kitchen duty," he said, apparently finding nothing about me to sustain his interest as he hooked a thumb toward the stairs just inside the engine bay.

A girl's ego could seriously get wounded.

The metal stairs leading up to the second floor creaked under my weight. The air smelled heavily of ash and gasoline—not entirely unpleasant. I looked around at the staff hurrying about—fixing this, cleaning that.

I pushed open the door at the top of the steps. Air-conditioning slapped me in my face. Ahhh. I peeked at the large rec room. No one was around. Pots clattered behind slatted swinging doors. I pushed on one and it opened into a large informal eat-in area, the remnants of a late lunch—or early dinner—still out on the countertop.

I smiled. "I never thought I'd see the day. Dave Mein doing dishes."

He turned, a look of surprise taking over his face as recognition hit. "Nina Bo-bina!"

I groaned. "Please. Not the Bo-bina."

He swiped soapy hands down his dark blue T-shirt. I accepted his bear hug, losing my breath as he swung me around.

"How the hell are you? How's Peter?"

Dave had been my brother Peter's best friend since Pee Wee football. Their high-school years had been spent tormenting my sister Maria and me. And then they went off to college and became respectable.

"Great. He just bought a partnership at an established pediatrician's office."

"Good for him. He never answers my e-mails."

"Mine either."

"A girl?"

"Undoubtedly more than one."

His gaze hiked over me, though not in a make-me-squirm kind of way. "Still the same. What's it been? Ten years?"

"I saw you at the Easter parade not a month ago."

"Everyone saw me. I was riding the truck."

"You waved to me."

"Hell." He laughed. "I waved to everyone. How's Kevin these days?"

"Quite well, I'm sure."

"Shit. That doesn't sound good."

"Let's not talk about it."

"You look hungry. You hungry?"

The smell of barbecued hot dogs tempted me. "I could eat."

He gathered up a plate, some potato salad, an almost charred hot dog, and handed it to me. I dug in.

A metal folding chair scraped against the floor as he pulled it out for me. I sat, the metal cool on the backs of my thighs.

"What brings you here?" he said, sitting next to me. "I assume you came to see me, but I have a feeling it isn't to catch up on old times."

I looked around the kitchen, stalling. I hated being here, asking old friends favors. I put my fork down. "I'm here about Joe Sandowski."

He dragged a hand over his angular face. "Why?"

"Do you know who drove the run to his house the day he died?"

He let out a deep and ragged sigh. "Why, Nina? What does any of that have to do with you?"

No longer hungry, I pushed my plate away. Luckily, I'd done some serious damage to that hot dog before this conversation turned my stomach. "I'm a family friend trying to get all the facts."

"Nina, you know I'd do anything for you . . ."

"But you're not talking."

"I can't."

"Says who?"

His dark lashes fluttered closed. "Shit."

"You did the run, didn't you?" When he didn't answer, I pressed. "Were you told you'd be making a run to the farm that day?"

He slapped his hands on the table, the veins bulging. "What? No!"

"Then why can't you talk to me? Why the secrecy?"

"You need to stay out of it, Nina."

"When have you ever known me to back away from a challenge, Dave? I'll get the information one way or another."

He shook his head.

"So, you're not going to help?" I batted my eyelashes all innocent-like. "It's just me, little Nina Bo-bina."

He winced. "That's low."

"I know."

He looked around the kitchen. In a whisper he said, "Give me your number. I'll call when I get a minute." His chair squeaked as he rose.

My thighs made suction noises as I stood. I pushed a Taken by Surprise card into his hand with my home number on the back.

"I called you once, y'know," he said, glancing at my card. "To surprise Mish. But you've moved up in the world. I couldn't afford you."

I smiled. "Call again. Have Tam put you right through to me. We'll work something out."

Grinning, he looked about twelve. "Hey, remember when Peter and I put snakes in yours and Maria's beds? Wasn't that fun?"

"Heaven on earth, Dave."

I walked out of the station, ready to head home to a hot bath and a good book. I knew I still had to talk to Riley, but it could wait until after I soaked some of this day away.

I'd just slid behind the wheel when my cell phone chirped. "'Lo?"

"Nina, it's Kit."

The engine turned over on the second try. I pulled out of the lot, turned toward home. "Job go well?"

"We've got a problem, Nina. I need you to come back to the Krauss house."

I heard a long string of angry German in the background.

"*Now*, Nina," he said in a voice I'd never heard before. He actually sounded scared.

Cursing, I banged a U-ey.

"I never did like you," Mrs. Krauss said to me. "Now look what you've done to my yard." She clucked like a big hen. A big, fat brick-shaped hen.

I clenched my teeth and was an inch away from telling her exactly how I felt about *her*, but Kit's restraining hand on my arm stopped me.

Claudia's tear-filled eyes shimmered in the sunlight.

"Don't be mad at Nina, Mamma. This was my idea. I thought you'd like it."

"What on earth would give you that idea?"

Claudia blinked. "*You* did."

"I would never!"

I took a step back, out of the way of a wayward punch should one be thrown.

"The way you go on and on and on—"

Mrs. Krauss's head snapped to look at her daughter, one thick eyebrow raised up, nearly touching her spiked white hair.

"I mean," Claudia cleared her throat, "the way you reminisce about the old gardens . . ."

As they battled on, I looked around. The garden really had turned out beautifully.

My design arched out from the back porch, the arbor standing proud at the top of the curve. Deanna had planted clematis at its base. By the end of summer, the arbor would be covered in big, beautiful bluish-purple blooms.

A rounded bench was nestled in tall ornamental grass, overlooking the new goldfish pond filled with oxygenating grasses and water lily leaves.

The tri-level border of the curve had a pink theme. The tall, daisylike pink blooms of American Dream stood proud in the background, the medium height of Bath's Pink filled the middle, and dusky pink begonias looked stunning against the dark mulch.

The sound of trickling water from the pond seemed to echo as the Krausses paused for breath.

I wished I'd thought to borrow one of Kevin's Kevlar vests as I said, "Mrs. Krauss, maybe you just need some time to adjust to the chan—"

"Ich bin krank!"

I didn't even want to know.

"Oh, Mamma!" Claudia cried.

"I want it out! All of it!"

"Mamma!"

I wanted out too. Peeking over my shoulder, I saw that Kit was already beating a hasty retreat. Coward.

I swallowed. Hard. "I'm sure you don't, Mrs. Krauss. Claudia spent a lot of time, effort, and expense to make this yard special for you."

"I thought you wanted a garden, Mamma."

She clucked again. I could sense her softening. If a slight drooping of her rigid shoulders was softening.

"I don't know how to care for this, Claudia. Not one bit." With a hitch in her voice, she added, "Your father took care of such things."

For crying out loud! The last person I wanted to feel sorry for was Brickhouse Krauss. But that catch in her voice hit a little too close to home these days.

Damn it all!

Glancing over at Claudia, I remembered her telling me how lonely her mother had been. My jaw dropped as a thought came to me.

"Maybe I can help," I said.

"The last person I need help from is you."

"Mamma! Don't be so rude!"

I pushed on, even though my every instinct was to dunk Mrs. Krauss's head into the pond. "The help isn't from me, really."

She brightened. "Oh?"

"I have this neighbor, a very sweet man who likes to feel needed since he retired. He's excellent with flowers and such, and could teach you everything you would need to know."

"A retired gentleman, you say?" Her thick eyebrows arched up.

I nodded. I almost—*almost*—felt bad for siccing Mrs. Krauss on Mr. Cabrera, but anything that would delay his spy shelter and help heal his broken heart had to be a good thing.

"Shall I have him call you?"

"How tall is he?"

"Oh, five nine or so."

"Hair?"

"Full head of shocking white."

She clucked. "Yes, you give him my address. Have him come by around eleven tomorrow. I will fix a nice brunch."

"I'll see what I can do."

"It's the least you can do after what you've done here."

"Mamma . . ."

I backtracked out of the yard. Yeah, so I forgot to mention to Mrs. Krauss that women friends of Mr. Cabrera's tended to, uh, expire.

I was willing to take that risk.

All in the name of Mr. Cabrera's happiness, of course.

Eight

I woke the next morning determined to actually make progress on Farmer Joe's murder. How, I had no idea.

Keeping my eyes peeled for Xena, I did some light housecleaning and ushered a reluctant, surly Riley off to school at seven, making sure he stepped onto the bus this time. He had been late getting home from his job bagging groceries at Kroger the night before, and I'd barely had time to say hello before he disappeared into his room. So much for the grand inquisition I had planned.

After leaving Mrs. Krauss's yesterday, I'd called Congressman Chanson's office pretending I was interested in making a donation to his campaign. I had an appointment with him at nine. Amazing how money talked.

Mrs. Sandowski's voice tumbled through my head. *Easy on the eyes, if you know what I mean.* I'd never met Chanson personally, but felt as though I knew him from all his face time on TV. He *was* easy on the eyes—in a Lawrence Welk sort of way, not a Brad Pitt kind of way. Thank God. I could only handle so much active testosterone. I was still humiliated over the way I had ogled Vice Principal MacKenna in his office the day before.

I popped over to Mr. Cabrera's and, er, persuaded him

(okay, so I used a little blackmail) to help Mrs. Krauss with her garden. I had just enough time left over to answer a few e-mails at work before heading over to meet with the congressman.

The telephone book listed Chanson's headquarters in a mini-mall near Vista View. I was early so I decided to take a spin through the subdivision and see if I could scare up a clue as to who was behind the shenanigans at Sandowski's Farm.

Construction on a gatehouse had begun, the first few bricks having been laid. Confidence that Mrs. Sandowski would soon be evacuating her farm?

I drove through the maze of side streets, stopping occasionally to check in on the jobs I had done. These yards had been a particular challenge, not just because of the high quality the homeowners expected, but because the houses were packed together like sardines. Not a lot of elbow room.

The houses stood two and three stories high. Elaborate masonry played a key role in the style of most of the homes. Every now and again, a house veered from the popular colonial style: a Spanish villa on one corner, a Mediterranean-style beach house on another.

I drove out of the subdivision shaking my head. I just didn't see the appeal. But then again, I'd always been a little slow on the uptake.

Finding a parking spot in the mini-mall wasn't too difficult. I parked in front of Domino's and walked two storefronts down, to where a large sign proclaimed CONGRESSMAN CHANSON HQ in bold letters.

Not one for modesty, was he?

I straightened the skirt of my all-purpose dress and smoothed my hair. I hoped I passed for an extremely wealthy woman who had oodles of money to throw around at will.

I donned an air of confidence and strode into the office. Workers had gathered at a table nearby stuffing envelopes.

The receptionist looked up at me, a phony smile plastered on her face.

I smiled brightly, talked through my nose. "I'm here to see Congressman Chanson. He's expecting me." My voice sounded as though I had gone to a prep school on the East Coast instead of St. Valentine's Parochial School.

"Ms. Quinn?"

"Yes."

"The congressman is awaiting you."

Awaiting me? It sounded so quaint, I almost wished I had a few hundred thou to bandy about.

She led me into a small office in the back, where another receptionist, a buxom blond with mile-high legs, sat behind a slab of marble designed as a desk.

I hated her instantly.

And I hated that I was so callous and judgmental, so I tried, really tried, to find something to like about her. I studied her bloodred fingernails, her full lips, her perfectly plucked eyebrows, her made-for-earrings earlobes. Nothing. I couldn't find a damn thing.

"Please have a seat, Ms. Quinn."

Her voice was a high-pitched nasal whine. *That* I liked! Made her somewhat human.

I sat in a nearby chair and crossed my legs. I figured people with scads of money wouldn't lower themselves to flip through the array of magazines on the glass coffee table before me, so I eyed them with disinterest and studied my fingernails. They were chipped and cracked and not at all the nails a high-society woman would have. Folding my fingers into a fist, I shoved them under my thighs.

Ten minutes went by, then twenty. I started to fidget. My pantyhose itched. I hated pantyhose. The last time I had worn pantyhose was my wedding. I was a more natural type of girl. What you saw was what you got, except in this case, where I was trying to be someone I wasn't. Using my toe of my low-heeled pump, I surreptitiously scratched the back of my calf.

Big-busted, blonde, and beautiful looked up.

I froze in mid-scratch and pretended to find interest in a Thomas Kinkade painting on the wall.

Blowing out a breath, I looked at my watch. Could Congressman Chanson afford to keep big spenders waiting? Or was that his ploy? Keep them waiting and maybe they'll think he doesn't need them . . . Then the investor would woo *him*, wanting to become one of an inner circle.

What a sham. I hated politics.

Finally, just when I thought I was going to have to slip into the ladies' room and forcibly remove my nylons, the door to the congressman's office opened.

Two men came out, one patting the other on the back.

"It will all be over soon," Chanson said.

I tried not to appear as if I was staring, but frankly, I think I gawked. "Easy on the eyes" was an understatement, and the TV did him no justice. Men had no right to be so, so, so utterly beautiful.

The shorter man walked out the door and Congressman Chanson took a step toward me, his hands tucked into his pockets as if he were a six-year-old boy with something to hide. He grinned a sheepish grin at me.

Oh, he definitely had something to hide.

"Ms. Quinn, I'm so sorry to keep you waiting."

Offering me a hand, he shook it while pulling me out of my seat. Impressive. Smooth. Practiced.

I smiled, saying nothing, afraid I'd be tempted to give away my imaginary money.

"Why don't you come into my office and we can chat?"

He placed his hand on my back and steered me into his office, which was luxuriously furnished. Not bad digs, if you asked me. Weren't politicians supposed to appear on the verge of bankruptcy so that people would bankroll their ambitions?

He guided me to a leather high-backed chair and sat down in a chair next to mine. Mahogany paneling encased the room. Oil portraits hung on the walls. The pile of the carpet seemed three inches deep. Even the air smelled rich.

"I really am sorry to have kept you waiting. An emergency came up that couldn't be avoided."

"I see."

He tipped his head. "I heard you want to make a donation to my campaign. May I ask why?"

His face was Botticelli perfect. He looked like an angel living in a man's body. A girl angel. It was disconcerting. Curly blond hair was styled just so, his cheeks rosy with what I would've sworn was blush if it had been on a woman, and he had the rosiest red lips I had ever seen. Snow White would have been jealous. Androgynous? I checked his hand. A large gold band glistened on the ring finger of his left hand. I wondered what kind of woman would marry such a perfect-looking man.

I hated to burst his bubble, but I decided to be as honest as I could. "I really don't have any money to give you."

His lips turned down, barely denting the skin around his mouth. Botox? "Then why did you want to see me, Ms. Quinn?" His voice had lost its charming edge.

"I came to see you about the Sandowskis."

Perfect morning-glory blue eyes narrowed. "Who?"

"Oh, come now." I *tsked*.

Part of his masked slipped. "I think perhaps you should leave."

"I think not."

He rose. "Then perhaps I should call security."

"Then perhaps I'll have to go to the press with this whole sordid mess. And if you aren't involved, your name will still be dragged through the mire with everyone else who has a stake in Vista View. What would your constituents say?"

"Who are you?"

I slid my card across the desk. "I'm a friend of the Sandowski family."

"I've heard of you," he said, looking up from the card. "My wife is enamored of the work you did on the Joneses' house. I, however, did not ask for a consultation with you, but seeing as though you're here, maybe we can set something up. My anniversary is in a few months . . ."

"Sorry. All booked up. About the Sandowskis . . ."

His eyes clouded, his lips thinned into a tight line. I wondered how often he was told no.

With an edge to his voice, he said, "What about them?"

Even in anger, his looks hadn't changed. A raging angel. There was something about him and his perfection that disgusted me on a vain level. No man should look that good. Or maybe it was on a subconscious level. I knew he wasn't what he portrayed himself to be. Nobody could be that charming, that boyish.

"I'd like some answers." I tried kindness. "Please."

"About what?"

"About Sandowski's Farm. About what's been happening there."

"I have no idea what you're talking about."

I stood. I didn't like him staring down at me.

"No?" I queried, arching an eyebrow. My meter was working on overdrive.

"No."

"What about Joe Sandowski's death?"

He scratched his chin. "What could I possibly have to do with his death?"

"I would think a murder investigation linking a congressman to a run-down farm would spark your constituent's interest, don't you? Enough bad PR and your next election is shot."

In a graceful move, he sat in his chair behind his desk. He leaned forward and folded his hands on top of each other.

"So maybe," I said, "you'd like to keep it all quiet, cover up Joe's murder as quickly as possible."

A hint of a smile played on his rose red lips. "I'm sure I have no idea of what you're speaking. I'd like to help you, Ms. Quinn, but I think you ought to go now."

"Are you trying to tell me that you don't want Mrs. Sandowski to sell?"

"I didn't say anything of the sort. I would love her to sell."

"Aha!"

His eyes widened into an amused expression. "I said sell, Ms. Quinn."

"And how far would you go, Congressman Chanson?"

"She'll sell eventually. Money always wins."

I scratched the back of my leg with my foot. I was beyond pretenses. "And if it doesn't?"

"It will."

He tapped my business card on the desktop. "I trust if you need to speak to me again, you'll know how to contact me." He slid my card across the desk, making his point clear. He wouldn't speak to me about this again unless I agreed to a TBS makeover for his wife.

I left the card on the edge of the desk. "Bribery, Congressman?"

Sparkling white teeth flashed in a wide smile. "It is the American way, Ms. Quinn." Pulling out a stack of papers I suspected were left on his desk as a diversionary tactic, he said, "Now if you don't mind, I'm a busy man."

Ana shrieked. "Are you out of your ever-loving mind?"

I sat across from her in a booth at the front of Gus's. We'd been sitting there since eleven, ordered at eleven thirty, and now it was twelve and we still hadn't been served. I'd just told her about my meeting with Bridget.

I winced. "Probably."

"This is serious. Joe Sandowski was murdered. This isn't some game of Clue."

"Hey, I was always good at Clue."

She dropped her head in her hands. "I don't like this. Not one bit. What's Bridget have to say about it?"

Ana and Bridget had met a few times over the years, at barbecues and the like. "About the same as you."

"Do you see a trend?"

"I've always been a rule breaker."

"I don't like it, Nina. Tell Kevin."

I pulled a face. "No."

She sighed. "I'm not gonna convince you to change your mind, am I?"

Thinking of Farmer Joe, I shook my head.

"Then I suggest we change the subject before I'm forced to smack some sense into you."

"Bridget's pregnant," I said.

Ana smiled, wide and bright. "Good for her. I know how bad she wanted a baby." She picked at the edge of the table, not quite looking me in the eye. "Does that, uh, mean Tim's not free yet?"

I placed a napkin on my lap—wishful thinking—and looked around for Gertie. "I really hope you're not holding out for him."

"A girl can dream."

"It's been *way* too long since you've had a date."

"Tell me about it." Her eyebrows dipped. "This single life is seriously getting old."

"It's not as if people don't ask you."

"I'm a probation officer, Nina. Cons will say anything."

I swiped at the table, brushing stale crumbs to the floor. "Even still."

Ana leaned back, her eyes wide. "I'm not that desperate. Yet. You think Tim has a brother?"

"He doesn't."

"Damn."

"I'm having dinner with Bridget and Tim on Friday night—wanna come?" It'd been a long time since I'd felt like a fifth wheel.

"Oh no. Not me."

"Why not?"

Her eyebrows knit together. "I'm sure I have something to do."

"Like what?"

She waved her hands. "I need to, uh . . ."

"Since you're so desperate, you can pretend it's a date."

She barked out a laugh. "With you?"

"Why not me?"

"Wrong chromosome makeup, Nina."

"I said *pretend*. Besides, what's wrong with me?"

"You're cranky these days. I hate dates with attitude."

"Me!?"

"Not that you don't have good reason."

Gertie appeared out of nowhere and slapped two plates on the table. I stared at my BLT, my appetite suddenly gone.

Softly, Ana said, "Okay. Spill. You never did tell me about the big confrontation. The last thing I knew you had found his boxers in the wash, smeared with lipstick."

I groaned, remembering.

"What happened?"

Lowering my head, I rubbed my temples, trying to head off a budding migraine while remembering my near faint-ing spell at the school. I needed to eat, so I forced myself to pick at my sandwich.

"That bad?"

"Worse," I answered.

She took a bite of her turkey club, then put it down on her plate. Somehow, she managed to wave Gertie over. "Gertie, can you please bring us two of your largest hot fudge sundaes? Extra whipped cream, and please don't be skimpy with the cherries."

This was why I loved Analise. She always knew exactly what I needed.

"I assume you waited until Ry was out of the house," she prompted.

"Yes, but I think old Mr. Cabrera heard everything."

"That nosy old buzzard is going to get himself in trouble one of these days if he keeps snooping in other people's business."

"He's harmless." I frowned. "I think." Besides, I think foisting Mrs. Krauss on him made up for anything he'd done to me.

"Did he deny it?"

She didn't need to clarify that the topic had switched from Mr. Cabrera back to Kevin in the bat of an eyelash. We had been close for so long that we had a kind of shorthand with each other.

"At first. Told me I was crazy, blah, blah, blah."

"Did he tell you who?"

Miraculously, Gertie came back in no time flat, giving me a pitying look. Great. The Mill had heard about Kevin and me. I piled my spoon high.

The chocolate did nothing, however, to soothe my rising anger as I told Ana about the Big Boxer Blowout. "He had the gall to tell me he had busted a massage parlor and he was the fake John."

"He doesn't work Vice!"

"I know. He said they were short a guy. I think he thinks that I'm dumb." I lifted my bangs. "Do I have sucker stamped on my forehead?"

Ana leaned in, squinting. "Yes."

"What?" I sputtered in righteous indignation.

"You have to admit you're gullible."

I took another bite of my ice cream. I couldn't really argue with her—she was right.

"Was it Ginger?" she asked softly.

My mouth dropped. I was sure it wasn't a pretty sight considering I had just spooned in a heap of ice cream. "How is it you knew and didn't tell me?"

"I suspected is all." She sighed, resting her spoon on the table. "What are you going to do?"

"I've already hired a lawyer."

"Have you talked to Riley?"

"Not yet."

"Do you know what you're going to say?"

"Not really."

We sat in silence for a minute.

"Any hope of reconciliation? Counseling?"

"Castration?"

She laughed. "It would solve all the problems, wouldn't it?"

I licked my spoon. "You know, Ana, I don't think it would."

She tilted her chin downward, waiting for me to continue. I searched for the words. "I just—" I just what? I tried again. "I'm just so angry." I thought about that whole weird thing with Riley's vice principal yesterday, shook my head. "I don't know what's real."

"Nothing comes easy, does it?"

"Not these days."

Eyes intent, she pointed her spoon at me. "Throw yourself into work. That'll keep you out of trouble."

"Speaking of work . . ."

"Uh-oh. I know that tone."

"Several tools are missing."

"Who made it to the shortlist this time?"

"Jean-Claude, Coby, and Marty." Ana, as their probation officer, would know best who had the stickiest fingers.

"Have you talked to them?"

"Didn't want to spook them."

"Hmmm. Good idea. I'm not sure, Nina. They're all good guys."

"With a penchant to steal."

"Only Coby was arrested for theft, and it was a college prank gone wrong. Which is why he got probation."

Like most of my other employees, Coby had come to me through Ana. He'd needed a good-paying job quickly, to re-pay his debt to his lawyer and the courts.

I had an idea, as unconventional as it was, of a way to catch my thief. "What are you doing tonight?" I asked her.

"I hesitate to ask why."

"Just be at my house at seven."

"How do you know I don't have a date? Stop that grin. I could."

"Do you?"

"No."

"Then it's settled."

Nine

After lunch with Ana, I headed home, despite my inner voice telling me I should go to the office. I told it to be quiet since TBS was in Tam's capable hands. Heck, she ran the place better than I did.

Unfortunately, as I set my backpack onto the kitchen counter, my mind was already skipping to the design consultation I had downtown at three o'clock.

Shaking my head, I tried to clear all thoughts. It was twelve forty-five now. I had an hour and a half to myself before I had to leave, and I fully intended to use it to relax. A good book. A hot bath. Something to get my mind off my crazy, messed-up life.

The blinking light on the answering machine caught my eye. I groaned. Do I or don't I? After a moment of deliberation, I gave in and pushed the PLAY button.

Two hang-up calls beeped at me before a message from Bridget: "Hey, Nina. I just left your house. I stopped by to see if you were free for lunch, but you weren't there, so maybe some other time?"

I deleted the hang-up calls, then called the telephone company to subscribe to Caller ID. The person behind the calls undoubtedly knew how to avoid detection, but it was worth a shot.

After turning on the radio in hopes that music would soothe the savage Xena to sleep—wherever she was, I hopped up to sit on the kitchen counter, where I was safe from slithering reptiles.

I worried my lip. The more I thought of it, the more I wondered if maybe Kevin and I couldn't reconcile. Perhaps I could forgive him over time.

Perhaps I was deluding myself, which broke a personal commandment.

I scanned the floor, feeling ridiculous. I'd had enough of keeping an eye peeled for Xena. Grabbing the Yellow Pages, I flipped the book open. I was going to put a stop to this once and for all.

I looked under the heading of Animal Rescue and found a listing for Pesky Pests. I didn't hesitate to call. Their voice mail told me they were out in the field and to leave my name and number. I did and hung up, feeling safer already, just knowing someone would be out soon to catch Xena.

Flipping off the radio, I grabbed the ever-present hockey stick and a package of raw cookie dough to munch on, and headed upstairs to change out of my all-purpose dress and into something more comfortable.

Feeling suddenly wary, I stopped at the top of the stairs. The hairs on the nape of my neck rose.

I couldn't deny that my instincts screamed that someone had been in the house. That someone might *still be* in the house. I took a deep breath, warding off impending panic.

Stuffing the cookie dough into the belt of my dress, I positioned the hockey stick defensively and crept down the hallway.

My heart beat wildly in my throat. My hands went clammy as they gripped the hockey stick. I kept my spine pressed to the wall and fought the urge to call Kevin.

A bead of sweat rolled down my temple. I tried not to breathe.

Ever so slowly, I inched my way down the hall. Stopping every few seconds to listen for noises only increased my anxiety.

With what felt like the grace of a pregnant hippo, I crossed the hallway and pressed my back against the opposite wall. Visions of the movie *Psycho* entered my thoughts as I stuck my head into the bathroom. I pushed the thoughts out resolutely. Thinking of serial killers at a time like this would do me no good at all.

After a quick scan, I headed farther down the hallway. Riley's door was closed. Slowly, I turned the knob, trying not to make any noise. I pushed the door open.

It looked like a bomb had gone off in his room—which was completely normal, so I turned my attention to my bedroom.

My lungs felt fit to burst. I exhaled, then inhaled deeply. My cheeks felt like they were on fire as I tiptoed down the hall armed with nothing more than a hockey stick and hot fudge sundae breath.

I swallowed hard and reached for the knob on my bedroom door just as a horn honked outside, scaring the crap out of me.

My blood sounded like a river rushing through my ears. I didn't even want to guess at my blood pressure.

I gripped the knob and suddenly felt it turning by its own volition. I yanked my hand back. My eyes widened and I flattened myself against the wall, holding my breath.

The door opened a crack, then wider still. All I saw was a tall image, arms full.

"Hi-yah!" I jumped away from the wall, swinging wildly with the hockey stick. I hit the person, once, twice, three times.

"Christ's sake, Nina!"

Kevin.

I swung again for sheer spite and was rewarded by a

sharp crack. He grabbed the hockey stick, and I let him yank it out of my hand.

"What the hell are you doing?" He tossed the stick aside.

Blood trickled from a cut on his forehead, but I felt no remorse.

"You scared the hell out of me! What are you doing here?"

"Packing!" He dabbed at his head. I saw a welt forming above his brow. Pride welled. I did good.

Clothes rested in a heap at his feet where he'd dropped them when I attacked. I recognized the shirt Riley had given him one Father's Day and a pair of boxers I had picked up for Valentine's Day a few years back. I steadily raised my gaze, not wanting to see any more.

"You scared the crap out of me," I whispered. "I didn't know you were here."

"I have my doubts about that." His voice mocked. His fingertips were red with blood as he dabbed at his gash.

"Where's your car? It wasn't in the driveway when I pulled in."

"Ginger dropped me off. I heard her honk a minute ago."

Ginger. My blood heated. Who named their child Ginger? It was a ridiculous name.

"Don't drip blood on my carpet."

"You nearly kill me with that damn hockey stick, and all you can think about is the rug?"

"You're right. Go ahead and drip." Under my breath, I added, "I've wanted new carpet for years now."

"Nina," he said on a sigh.

I leaned against the door frame, coming down from my adrenaline rush.

His eyes squinted in humor. "Is that cookie dough, or are you just happy to see me?"

Jokes. He was making jokes. I glared.

"Sorry," he mumbled. "Couldn't resist."

After an uncomfortable second, I said, "You still coming for supper tomorrow?"

He bent down to scoop up his clothes, saying nothing, which told me more than I wanted to know.

I clenched my fists. "You will be here."

He stood, looked square into my eyes. "I'll be here."

"Good."

The leg of one of his pairs of jeans dangled over his arm. I swallowed hard.

"But there is one thing I want to talk to you about before then."

The horn honked again. Kevin glanced toward the window.

"If this is about the Sandowskis there's nothing you can say or do to change my mind about helping them."

His eyes widened, then he shook his head. "I don't think I even want to know, Nina."

I noticed his shock, and a feeling of uncertainty replaced my earlier fear. "If not the Sandowskis, then what?"

"Riley."

"Is he okay? It's those boys he's hanging out with. Did he tell you about them?"

"He's fine, Nina. Those kids are harmless."

My left eyebrow rose. Uh-oh. "What is it that you aren't telling me about those kids? Ry's vice principal seems to think they're trouble."

"I've looked into it. They're fine."

My other eyebrow arched. This was definitely not good news. I let it pass for now.

"What about Riley, then?"

Another honk. Kevin went to the window, opened it, and called down to Ginger that he needed a few minutes. He turned back to me.

I pressed my lips together to keep from saying something snide.

"I think that, for now, Riley would be best staying here with you."

"With me?" A wash of joy mixed with utter devastation raced through me. The joy for myself, the devastation for Riley. This was not going to go over well. "You're his father."

"I know. I know. It's just that Ginger's place is kind of small."

Kevin was talking to the floor, which meant he was trying to hide something.

I crossed my arms. "Does Ginger want kids someday, Kev?"

"Never talked about it," he said to my low-heeled pumps.

"Really. I would think that would be something that would come up between two people so in love." I drew out the word love.

His head snapped up. "It hasn't come up."

My eyebrows were practically in my hairline.

"It couldn't be that 'Paprika' doesn't like kids, can it? I'd imagine a fifteen-year-old might cramp you two's lifestyle."

"Are you enjoying yourself?"

I looked up at him. At six foot three, he loomed over me, I once found his height appealing. Now it was just damned annoying. Poking my finger into his chest, I said, "On a certain level, yes, I'm enjoying seeing you blunder your way through this. I don't mind having Riley here. I'd rather have him here with me, but he's never going to understand this."

"Yes, he will."

"Kevin, Riley still feels like Leah abandoned him even though she *died*—how in the world do you think he's going to react to this news?" Riley's mother, Leah, had been killed when he was just four, a boating accident of some sort that no one ever talked about.

He grabbed my hand. "I'm not abandoning him."

"Like hell." I itched to pick up the hockey stick and finish him off.

"He's not going to think that. I'll explain everything."

I flung up my arms. "You're so blind." Shaking my head, I paced. "You tell me he's not up to his neck in some cockamamie group who're bound to get him into trouble, then you tell me he won't think you're abandoning him. You're nuts."

"There's nothing going on with Riley!"

An ache pulsed at my temples. "You'll be here tomorrow night," I ordered. "And you'll sit down, look him in the eyes, and tell him that there just isn't enough room in your life for him right now."

"It's not like that."

"That's a load of crap!"

"I'll see Riley," he countered. "I can still do things with him. On weekends and stuff. It's just not feasible for him to live with me right now."

"Feasible," I repeated, numb.

He brushed past me. "This isn't getting us anywhere. I'll be back tomorrow."

His footsteps echoed on the stairs, then out the front door.

I crept to the window, staying hidden behind the curtains. Kevin threw open the back door of his unmarked and tossed his clothes in. With one last glance at the house, he lowered his large body into the car and Ginger drove away.

I thought about the expression on his face as he'd looked up at the house. It had resembled guilt.

Good.

Ten

I had the worst habit of cleaning when I was nervous. I couldn't be a normal person and just twitch. Oh no, not Nina Colette Neurotic Ceceri Quinn. I had to pull out the dust rags and run them over furniture. I even vacuumed the living room, but I had to admit I had an ulterior motive in that case. I'd hoped to suck up a snake.

So much for my relaxation time. I'd already used half of it cleaning. And after my little talk with Kevin had turned my stomach, I didn't even eat my cookie dough.

Pesky Pests still hadn't returned my call from earlier. I was going to have to do something drastic if Xena didn't turn up soon. Like evacuate the premises. I had too much going on in my life to worry about that snake.

The phone rang and I jumped a mile. My nerves were shot. Between Farmer Joe and those hang-up calls . . . This couldn't go on much longer or I'd be forced to medicate myself.

I reached for the phone.

"Hey there, Nina, it's Tim Sandowski."

Smiling, I wrapped a finger around the phone cord. "How've you been? Congrats on the baby. That's such great news."

"Thanks." He paused. "I know Bridget saw you yesterday, got you involved in what's going on at the farm."

"I'm glad to help," I said, not quite sure I meant it anymore.

"That's why I'm calling. I don't think it's a good idea, you being involved."

Sounds like he'd been talking to Bridget.

"Do you think," he said, "you could hold off on looking into things for a while? Until we have a chance to talk in-depth about it? Bridget said something about dinner on Friday?"

I guess telling him about my meeting with Chanson was out. "I don't know, Tim," I hedged. "I've got a few things lined up."

"Can you reschedule?"

Why wasn't he more interested in what I was doing? "I can try," I said, with no intention of trying at all.

"Thanks, Nina. See you Friday."

Hmmph. I rested the telephone in its cradle, stared at it. Why was I beginning to feel like no one wanted my help?

My self-esteem could seriously get damaged.

Sighing, I trudged up the stairs.

Unfortunately, avoidance was another one of my habits. And I had avoided looking into the closet and seeing Kevin's stuff gone. I carried Pledge with me, lying to myself that I was just going to clean a bit. I still had half an hour to kill before I headed downtown.

Unfortunately, the room hadn't changed since Kevin had left almost an hour ago. Spots of blood still spattered the rug, the bed was still unmade. My jammies were tossed over my pillow, and a *Good Housekeeping* magazine lay on the floor where I had dropped it last night.

Then I stepped into the closet.

Most of his hangers were empty. He'd left a few things: a sweatshirt, a crew-neck sweater, a pair of pants I knew were too small for him.

A knot of tension wound in my stomach.

I opened his chest of drawers in the back of the walk-in closet. Most were empty. He'd left a plain white T-shirt, a pair of brown socks.

I picked up the T-shirt and brought it up to my nose. Inhaling deeply, I felt my throat tighten, my eyes pool, as his scent washed over me. I swallowed hard and dropped the shirt.

Slammed the drawer closed.

Flopping on the bed, I tried to get a grip on my emotions. I flung my arms over my head in dramatic desperation. I heard a crinkling sound. I sat up slowly.

Pressing my hands to the comforter, I searched for the source of the noise. Nothing. Maybe I had imagined it. I was beginning to feel paranoid. This afternoon with Kevin hadn't helped.

I was about to give up when I brushed my hand over my pj's. There. I heard it again. I lifted my long nightshirt and a piece of paper fluttered to the floor. Bending down, I picked it up. Pasted using cutouts of magazines and newspaper, it said:

Stay away from Sandowski's Farm or face the consequences.

I raced out of the room and down the stairs and into the kitchen. My legs wobbled. Someone had been in my house. Someone other than Kevin. That was why I had picked up on those strange vibes.

I heard a steady *thump*, a shovel against ground. Looking out my kitchen window, I spotted Mr. Cabrera clearing the area for his spy shack.

The humidity had swelled the wood of the backdoor and I had to give it a hard shove to get it open.

"Mr. Cabrera?" Maybe he'd seen something, heard something.

"Miz Quinn."

He continued to dig and I picked up a half moon to help. Working out some of my fear by fighting with the stubborn clay soil was just the thing I needed right now.

I didn't want to come right out with my questions, so I asked about Mrs. Krauss instead. I'd gone over bright and early that morning, before my meeting with Chanson, to ask for his help dealing with her. He'd balked, until I told him that technically he needed a permit to install a gazebo, a permit that could take *weeks,* except I knew a few people in the zoning department . . .

His eyes twinkled. "She's a fine form of a woman, she is. Good cook too."

Levering my foot on the half moon, I pushed into the ground. Thankfully, I'd stopped shaking. "She's certainly . . . unique."

He waggled his snowy brows. "They don't call her 'Brickhouse' for nothing."

I sputtered. "She told you about that?"

"Sure, sure. We had ourselves a nice long chat over brunch. She's agreed to be my bowling partner this week."

So the rumors hadn't reached her. Yet. "Well, good for you. And her health?" I asked, trying not to sound too hopeful.

His eyebrows snapped together. "Just fine, thank you very much."

I smiled as I grabbed a hunk of grass, tossed it in a wheelbarrow. "Mr. Cabrera," I said, my stomach knotting as I thought about that note I'd found, "did you happen to see anything unusual at my house today?"

"What are you trying to say? Are you saying I was spying on you? 'Cuz I wasn't."

The look on his face eased my agitation. I bit my lip to keep from laughing at his offended expression. "Oh, no. I know that you'd never pry into others' affairs," I said soothingly. "I was just wondering if maybe my friend stopped by. I was late and I think I missed the visit."

"Drive a small white car, tinted windows?"

I tried not to betray my eagerness. "I'm not sure."

"Gray van?"

I shrugged.

"Well then, don't know."

"Do you mean to say that those cars were at my house today?"

He rested on the shovel. "Ain't that what I said?"

Uh, no. "I misunderstood. Did you see anyone ring the bell?"

"I wasn't prying or nothing."

I worked my way along his line of marking paint with the half moon. "Oh, no, never."

"A man got out of the white car. Tallish."

"Hair color?"

"Had a hat on, he did. Kind of skulked."

A skulker. That sounded promising. "And the van?"

"Younger kid. That friend of Riley's."

"But why would he be here? Riley was in school."

Mr. Cabrera returned to his digging, turning over clumps of grass. "Not today he wasn't."

"You saw him?" A blister was starting to form on my palm. I should've worn my gloves.

"I told you I wasn't prying."

"Yeah, yeah."

"He was home. For a little while, anyhow. He came over and paid me what he owed for the flowers. Thought he was sick or somethin'. Looked kind of pale. But that might be because of his new 'do. What's up with that? Black with bleached stripes? He going for the skunk look?"

He'd definitely seen Riley. No mistaking *that* hair. Great. Just freakin' great. Now Riley was skipping school.

"Then of course there was Mr. Quinn and his lady fr—uh, partner."

I rolled my eyes. All hope that Mr. Cabrera hadn't heard mine and Kevin's big blow-up vanished. So I had a truant son, a skulker, a Skinz, an adulterer, and a ho.

"Anyone else?"

"Oh," he said. "I just remembered."

"Yeah?"

"That friend of yours stopped by. The one you had breakfast with yesterday at Gus's?"

Bridget. It amazed me how fast news traveled in this neighborhood.

"The one about to pop?"

I bit back a smile.

"She knocked, but you weren't home."

"What time was that?"

"Twelve thirty-seven. Not that I was prying."

Eleven

As I drove southbound on I-75, I kept one hand on the wheel and used the other to check my voice-mail messages from my cell.

Bridget had called.

My mother had called.

And there was yet another hang-up.

I decided not to take the hang-up personally, ignored my mother, and punched in Bridget's number while stopped at a red light on the Mitchell Avenue exit ramp.

I hadn't had time to digest what Mr. Cabrera had told me before heading out to my meeting, and now, hours later, I was still purposely smothering the fact that someone had been in my house.

I could smother with the best of them.

The TBS consultation had gone well, and since it hadn't been all that far from Bridget's, I thought I'd make good on my offer to take a look at Bridget's backyard.

No one answered the phone. I figured she was still at work and nixed the idea of calling there and disturbing her. She didn't need to be home for me to poke around.

There were no cars in Bridget's driveway as I rolled to a stop in front of the old Victorian, which was just as well. I wasn't exactly in the mood for a face-to-face lecture from Tim about me snooping into Farmer Joe's death.

Stay away from Sandowski's Farm or face the consequences.

I pushed the letter out of my thoughts. It was just a scare tactic, that's all. One that wouldn't work if I ignored it.

Taking a second, I looked at the house. When Bridget said fixer-upper, she wasn't kidding.

Victorian Vernacular, I thought they called this kind of house, found only in the Cincinnati area. It had seen better days. The front porch sagged, slate tiles were missing from the roof, and the whole brick façade looked like it could use another coat of mortar.

I grabbed my sketch pad, Polaroid, and measuring wheel and hopped out of the truck.

An old garage door hung limply on a detached two-car garage that looked older than the house but clearly wasn't original. Fading sunlight slipped through the cracks of the door and I could see a car inside.

For a brief second, I swore under my breath, cursing my bad luck, thinking it was Tim's car, and that he was home after all. Looking more closely, however, I saw a battered tarp pulled over the top of the car. And by the looks of the dust, no one had been in or out of that garage in years.

I let out a sigh of relief as I skirted the edge of the house, already thinking how nice a set of steps leading down into the sloping backyard would look.

My stomach rumbled, complaining loudly about missing dinner. I'd grab something with Ana later on, while we were playing stakeout.

The backyard was almost completely sheltered by woods. I wondered if Bridget and Tim had thought about fencing it in. Smiling, I sketched a small picket fence on my blank pad, imagining Bridget's baby running around.

Mosquitoes pestered me as I took a few snapshots. Heat bugs *teeeck-teeeck-teeeck*'d from the woods.

High thick grass threatened to trip me as I walked around the yard, already cordoning off sections in my head. An entertainment area, a play area, a grassy terrace maybe. I took a few measurements with my handy-dandy wheel and jotted them onto the pad.

I glanced up at the house and stepped back in surprise.

Had a curtain moved?

Was someone home after all? Why hadn't they come out?

I hadn't heard a car pull in, though, and no lights shone from inside.

I shook my head, taming my imagination. Just my eyes playing tricks on me. I jotted a few notes about the surrounding area and sketched in a rough vision.

Suddenly a twig snapped in the woods and my pencil skittered across the pad. The hairs on the back of my neck rose. Everything in me screamed that I wasn't alone, that someone was watching me.

My inner voice bellowed for me to get the hell out of there, and I was in no state to argue.

Eyes intent on the tall pines and shadowed dense underbrush, I crept backward toward the house, toward my truck, toward safety.

And bumped into something—someone—who hadn't been there a minute ago.

A scream escaped me, and everything I held went flying.

"Nina! Nina, it's okay!"

I gulped the thick evening air and maybe a mosquito or two—but at that point I didn't care—and focused on Bridget's laughing eyes.

"You scared the shit out of me!" My pulse pounded in my ears. My heart couldn't take this twice in one day.

Her shoulders shook and she started laughing. Deep belly laughs that had her big tummy shaking.

"I'm sorry," she said. At my skeptical look, she held up a hand. "No, I really am."

My eyebrows shot up, and I bent to gather up my stuff, still keeping a wary eye on those woods.

"I thought you heard me," she said, still chuckling.

"I didn't." I started for the driveway.

Bridget kept up. She wiped her eyes. "Really, I'm sorry."

"It's okay." I knew I bordered on rude, but I was still creeped. Seriously creeped.

Her Jeep sat in the driveway, its engine ticking.

She smiled. "What are you doing here, anyway?" she asked. "I stopped by your house earlier, but you weren't around."

"Yeah, I know. I got your message. I must have just missed you. It's been a crazy couple of days." I left out the particulars. I didn't need to be recounting them in the state I was in. "I happened to be in the area and thought I'd stop by and start my baby-friendly backyard design."

"Oh! I didn't think you'd get to it so soon."

I pulled open my truck door and tossed my stuff inside. "I should be able to have a plan drawn up for it and to you by the end of next week."

She patted her stomach. "We have time."

By the size of her, I didn't think so, but I kept my mouth shut. I didn't think that was the sort of thing pregnant women liked to hear.

"I missed you for lunch. How about supper? Tim will be home soon."

I was too spooked to think about food. "Maybe some other time? I've got plans with Ana tonight."

"Oh. Okay."

"We still on for Friday?" I asked.

"Absolutely." She leaned on my door. "But I have to warn you, Nina. Tim's dead set against having you involved in this mess."

"Something to look forward to."

She smiled brightly. "Forewarned is forearmed."

I wondered at her tone, all dark and dripping with things that creeped me even more.

Shivering despite the warm evening, I turned the key. "So noted."

Ana slurped her triple-thick shake.

"Why don't you just use the spoon?"

"I'm hoping to burn some calories this way."

I trained the binoculars on Coby Fowler as he loaded up the truck in front of Bonnie Freel's house. Bonnie, Ana, and I had gone to college together and still kept in touch.

I'd conjured up some ridiculous reason Coby needed to go out there at 7:30 to take measurements, all with Bonnie's permission, of course. This gave Coby complete access to a wide variety of my equipment from a loaded TBS truck with no one looking over his shoulder.

Ana purred. "He's so cute."

"He's a baby!"

"Babies are cute."

I sighed and shook my head. "We need to find you a date."

"I'm doing okay on my own."

"Hah!" Her divorce had been finalized for nearly a year, so by my calculations, she hadn't had a date since 1999.

"I am!"

"When was the last time you went out?"

Her lower lip jutted out.

"See."

"Well, find me someone."

"I don't think you want my choice of men."

"Look." Ana pointed out the window. "He's leaving."

Sure enough, Coby had hopped into his TBS truck.

"What, exactly, are we looking for?"

"Him stealing hoes."

"Oh." She abandoned her straw and reached for a spoon.
So much for the calorie burning. "All hoes seem present and
accounted for."

I bit my lip to keep from saying something about Ana's
college reputation.

"He's supposed to be bringing the truck back to the office," I said as he turned west on Old Freedom Trail. The office was east.

"Seems he's lost."

"Quite."

We followed him up side streets and down back roads and
over the county line. After twenty minutes of driving, he
pulled into a cracked asphalt driveway.

We both ducked low in our seats as we drove past. Ana
said, "You know this place?"

"No."

I eyed the one-story contemporary as I parked down the
block on the berm of an embankment. "Come on."

"What! You didn't say anything about fieldwork. I wore
heels. I have a skirt on."

"Take the heels off. Hike up the skirt." It was one of those
long, flowy flower-child skirts. Perfect for getting snagged
on broken branches.

"The things I do for you," she mumbled.

I switched off the overhead light and pushed open the
driver's side door of my Jurassic period Corolla.

Crickets chirped as Ana and I did a crouch walk toward
the small house, staying hidden in the overgrown patch of
weeds and shrubs along the property line. Coby stood at the
Ford, pulling tools out of the bed.

"Doesn't this look compromising?" Ana said in a loud
whisper.

"Shhh."

Coby knocked once on the door, talked to a shadowy figure behind the screen.

A mosquito buzzed my ear. Coby walked back to the truck, grabbed an electric hedge trimmer and went about finding a socket.

"What is he doing?" I mumbled aloud.

"Trimming?"

I shot Ana a look.

"You asked."

My legs stiffened as we continued to watch, the setting sun glowing orange in the western sky.

After half an hour of watching Coby tame an unruly boring hedge, Ana sighed. "My NTP index just reached ninety."

"NTP?" This was a new one to me.

"Like it? I just made it up."

Bits of dark hair had fallen out of her ponytail and stuck to her cheeks. "I don't know what it is. How can I like it?"

"Need To Pee."

I laughed. "Is it a one-to-one-hundred scale?"

"Yep."

"Then ninety is pretty high."

She pressed her knees together and rocked back on her bare heels. "Yep."

I looked back at Coby. Chances were he was just helping out a friend, but I couldn't be sure. I eyed some tall grass near a clump of old pine trees behind Ana.

"Oh no."

"Like you haven't done it before."

"I was six and lost in the woods."

"See? You still sound haunted by it. This will give you the chance to put it all behind you. Literally."

"Ha. Ha. But I have to go too bad to argue with you."

She rustled off into the deeper grass, half hidden behind

the trees. Coby had finished hedge trimming and pulled out a spade. He was dutifully edging the driveway.

I glanced in the direction Ana had gone. I cringed, spotting tell tale leaves of three. "Uh, Ana?" I whispered loudly.

"What?"

"You aren't, by any chance, allergic to poison ivy, are you?"

Ana jumped to her feet, shrieking like a banshee. Her skirt fell into place, but her undies were wrapped around her ankles.

Coby dropped the spade and ran full tilt toward us.

Ana continued to screech, hopping from foot to foot, looking just like some gypsy woman stomping grapes. Except for the screaming. I didn't think people screamed when they squished grapes.

There was no place to run, nowhere to hide. I slowly rose.

Coby stopped dead in his tracks. "Nina?"

Ana's shrieks had turned into whimpers, but she was still doing the jig, trying to get her undies off her feet. Finally, they were flung free, almost hitting Coby in the face.

I pressed my lips together. Tight.

Ana screeched when she spotted him.

Coby stared at the undies lying at his feet, with eyes the size of baseballs. "Ms. Bertoli?"

Ana's cheeks flamed. "Uh, hello, Coby." Shoulders back, chin high, she walked over to him and snatched up her panties. She shoved them in her pocket, turned and glared at me. "You owe me. So big."

Guilt nudged at me. I glanced at Coby. His slightly chubby cheeks glowed pink beneath pale peach fuzz.

"What are you doing here?" he asked.

"I, uh, we . . ." I cleared my throat. "What are *you* doing here, is more like it." Nothing like going on the offensive.

"You were supposed to take the truck and the tools back to the office."

He dug his toe into the ground. Out of the corner of my eye, I saw Ana scratch her leg. Then the other. It was all mental, I knew, since poison ivy didn't usually show up for hours, sometimes days, after exposure.

"I know, I'm sorry. You're not going to fire me, are you? My nana . . ."

An older woman's voice was carried on the evening air. "Coby?"

I looked across the expanse of lawn as "Nana" (I assumed), using a walker, hobbled toward us.

Ana glowered. "I hope you're proud of yourself."

I felt terrible.

Coby pleaded to Ana with his puppy-dog eyes. "Please don't say anything about my arrest. She doesn't know."

"What's going on, Coby?" Nana said, her voice sounding like nails on a chalkboard.

I couldn't help but wince. Coby seemed immune though, as he said, "Nana—"

I broke in. "This young man was fine enough to help us." I gestured down the road. "Our car has broken down . . . overheated or something."

"Might be the fan belt," Ana put in.

I rolled my eyes. "As I was saying, this young man was kind enough to offer to look."

The woman's keen eyes swept over me. "I heard screaming."

Ana suddenly found interest with her toenail polish.

"I, uh, I fell," I said.

Her eyebrows arched. Her gaze meandered to Ana. "Uh-hunh. What happened to your shoes?"

Ana looked up, all brown eyes and innocence. "Lost them?"

Coby put his arm around the woman. "Nana, it's okay. I'll help them out and be back in just a minute."

She nodded sharply, and pivoted with her walker, nearly taking my feet out from under me as she turned. I heard her murmur something about vixens, and couldn't help but feel an odd sense of pride that I could still be considered one.

We walked a few feet toward my car. Coby's head hung. How I ended up feeling in the wrong, I had no idea. To him, I said, "Just bring the truck back when you're done. I'll see you tomorrow."

A smile lit his face and he trotted back.

Ana shook her head, scratched her leg as she got into the car.

I turned the key and the engine rumbled to life. "Don't say it."

We drove in silence for, oh, ten seconds before Ana said, "That was awful."

I nodded. Maybe I should have just sat Jean-Claude, Coby, and Marty down in my office after all. This investigating on my own wasn't quite working out the way I thought it would.

"I feel awful," I said.

"You should." She sighed dramatically, leading up to a lecture, I was sure. But instead said, "Why didn't you tell me there was poison ivy back there?"

Leave it to Ana to know how to make me feel better. I laughed.

A smile tugged at her lips. "Seriously, though. Could we stop at CVS and get some calamine?"

Twelve

"You damn well don't have to drive me." Scorn oozed from Riley's voice.

It was much too early to be exposed to such venom. I yawned. Sleep had been hard to come by. Too many bits and pieces floating around in my head, causing a bad case of insomnia.

"I can damn well get there on my own."

Biting my tongue to keep from chastising him about his language, I stared out the window, my face a mask of serenity. I was going to make sure he got to school today. I was going to watch him walk into the building. No more skipping.

"I think I do need to drive you, Ry."

I caught his startled blink. I hadn't told him I knew he skipped school. I figured he had enough on his plate to worry about. But now I wanted him to know. I didn't want him to think he was getting away with anything.

"What's that supposed to mean?" Belligerence replaced startled.

I shrugged. "What do you think it means?"

Crossing his arms over his chest, he glared at me. "I can't believe Dad's doing this to me," he muttered.

I glowered at Riley. I was a good glowerer, but he was obviously immune to my powers. "Don't forget about supper tonight. Five o'clock. Your dad and I need to talk to you."

"Well, I need to talk to you too."

"You do?"

He shouldered his backpack as I parked in front of the high school. "I do have opinions."

Grrr. "I look forward to hearing them."

He glared.

"Have a good day," I sang as Riley hopped out of the car. "Stay out of trouble!"

Turning, he flashed me a grin. I knew that grin. It was the same one I used to give my parents before I deliberately disobeyed them.

What was he up to now?

I swung my Corolla in the direction of the office. Everyone was due to gather there at eight to go over the timeline of tomorrow's job, start to finish. Okay, that was the excuse we used. Truly, we never got much work done. That hour-long meeting before a big job had turned into the office's weekly happy hour. With donuts and coffee, of course.

Speaking of which, I pulled into the Kroger lot and ran in for two dozen Krispy Kremes.

Ana called this morning and apparently she was none the worse for wear. No sign of poison ivy, though she was sure little bumps were going to pop out any minute now. Not taking any chances, she was keeping a bottle of calamine on hand at all times.

As I drove down Knickerbocker, I wondered why Dave Mein, my fire-fighter friend, hadn't called. Chickened out? I just couldn't see it. He was one of those guys whose word was gold. He definitely knew something he wasn't keen on sharing, and my imagination was running wild.

Up ahead, red lights blinked at a railroad crossing. I rolled to a stop as a freight train rumbled past.

Knickerbocker wound its way through the industrial section of Freedom. Office rent was cheap in this area, with lots of vacancies, but the location did nothing for me. I had been willing to pay a bit more for a location my clients would adore.

I turned left onto Mockingbird, then right onto Jaybird Lane, zoned residential and business. I passed Mighty Tots Daycare and turned into the Taken by Surprise lot.

The office itself was a renovated ranch-style home. I'd paved the front yard, and turned the backyard into a showcase of my designs. I couldn't help but smile, despite the whole hoe issue and the mess I'd made out of things with Coby.

Kit Pipe was leaning against his Hummer, smoking a cigar, when I pulled into my usual parking space.

He took one box of donuts from me and plucked out a glazed. "You look like crap."

"I love the way you kiss up to the boss." I set my backpack on the ground. "I haven't been sleeping all that great lately."

A smile pulled at his lips. "Heard you were playing in the bushes last night."

"Coby has a big mouth."

"He thinks you and Ana have something kinky going on."

I had to smile. "Ana sat in poison ivy."

He laughed, his stocky frame doubling over. "Must have been a sight."

"Oh, it was."

"Coby clean?"

I sighed. "Appears so. He was just doing some yard work for his nana." The sun beamed off his bald head. The skull tattoo looked especially scary this morning. "Gut instinct, who do you think: Jean-Claude or Marty?"

He took a bite of donut, then a puff of cigar. I winced at the combination. "Not sure. Both are hard workers."

"You hear that the tools are showing up again?"

"No shit?" His ink-lined eyes narrowed.

If I didn't know him so well, I'd be shaking in my Keds.

"Maybe if I just wait long enough, all the equipment will show up again and I won't have to worry about it."

"And let it happen again some day?"

Damn, I hated when he was right.

"I just don't understand it. It's not like there's a black market for garden tools."

"What're you gonna do? Follow Marty and Jean-Claude too?"

I didn't like his tone. "You have a better idea?"

His furry eyebrows dipped. "Lie detector?"

"Yeah, I've got one of those in my office."

"Smart-ass."

"I'm gonna be taking the rest of the day off," I said.

He pinched the end of his cigar. "Why?"

I pulled my backpack onto my shoulder. "I need to see a cop about some Skinz, and a man about a house."

"You have yourself a good time." He smiled. He had the best smile.

"Hey, you still dating Daisy?"

His tone turned suspicious. "Why?"

"Ana's looking for a boyfriend."

His hands shot up. "Oh no."

"Why not? She was only your probation officer for a month, a long time ago."

He was saved from answering by the squeal of tires. A small red hatchback swerved into the lot, jolting to a stop in the spot next to mine.

Deanna Parks bounded out of the driver's seat, her blonde ponytail flying out behind her. "Look who I found hitchhiking."

Jean-Claude tumbled out when she opened his door, looking green around the gills. He fell to his knees and kissed the ground.

Deanna didn't seem to notice. "Sorry I'm late. Lucah didn't want to get dressed. I couldn't pass him off to the sitter fast enough." She popped the back of her hatchback and rummaged inside, mumbling all the while about her two-year-old and potty training. Seemed Lucah liked being naked. Typical man.

Deanna was one of the best landscape designers I'd ever met. The fact that she was a twenty-one-year-old single mother with zero college experience didn't bother me in the least.

I helped Jean-Claude to his feet. "You okay?"

"Never again."

Kit frowned. "Been there, man. What happened to your ride?"

"Ran out of gas about a mile down." Despite his French name, there wasn't even the hint of an accent. Light stubble covered his cheeks, his chin. His hair was rumpled, his eyelids heavy. He was a dead ringer for Hugh Grant—his mug shot, that is.

Deanna's voice rang out. "Some days I'm just so happy to see the sitter. I wish I could pay her more money. She deserves it, for putting up with Lucah all day."

She didn't even notice that no one was listening to her. To Jean-Claude, I said, "I'll take you to the gas station and drop you at your car after the meeting."

He nodded.

"Oh, Nina?" Deanna said.

"Huh?" Being around Deanna taxed my energy.

"Strangest thing." She tugged a shovel and a small hand cultivator out of her hatchback. "Found these in my car this morning. No idea how they got there. I mean, I didn't put them in there." She frowned. "At least I don't think I put them in there."

I hadn't even known the cultivator was missing.

"Oh, and this," she said, tugging out roll of chicken wire.

I shot a look at Kit, who shrugged.

"And this," she said. She pulled on box of decorative edging, left over from jobs gone by. "And this pickax too." She smiled brightly as she spotted the Krispy Kremes. "Oooh. Donuts!"

The Freedom police station held that stale smell of old coffee in its stagnant air. I didn't know how Kevin stood it, day in and day out.

"Hi, Russell. How're you?" I asked the aging desk sergeant.

"Just fine. Fine. You look great, Nina."

"Thanks." I looked like something the cat had spit up, but I didn't want to shatter his mirage by denying his words.

"Kevin's not around. He's not on today."

Thank heaven for small favors. "Actually I came to see Candy. She should be expecting me."

"Sure, sure. Go on back."

I followed a bench-lined hallway that opened into a large room, about fifty by fifty. Offices lined one wall. The rest of the room was filled with desks pushed together in small squares like children's desks in grade school.

A quick head count gave me five people in the room, most of them pecking away at computers or reading through files. I spotted Candy in a far corner on the phone. She looked up and waved me over.

Wearing a bright red pantsuit, she stood out—which I thought was her intention. She held up a finger while she finished her conversation. Finally, she hung up the phone.

"Well, Nina Quinn! I haven't seen you since . . ."

"A month ago at Kroger." What was it about people not remembering me?

She frowned. "Oh yeah, that's right," she said, laughing. "In front of the ice-cream case. Sit down, will ya?"

I sat.

"I'm not going to say you look good. You look like hell."

I knew Russell had been lying. "I'm okay."

"Like hell."

I sighed. It would be out soon, anyway. "By the way, I'd appreciate it if you didn't tell Kevin I stopped by."

Her eyes, lined with a dark blue, blinked. "That sounds like some serious trouble. What the hell happened?" she asked, scooting her chair next to mine.

I shrugged. Part of me wanted to tell her the whole sordid story, and the other part, the part that respected Kevin as an officer, knew that his reputation would be sullied if it got around that he was sleeping with his partner. "Let's not talk about it."

"Hell."

"I agree."

"If there's anything I can do," she said.

I waved her offer away. "I'm fine."

Candy Carradon was short, stocky. Imposing. Her black hair was swept off her face, giving her a stern look.

"What's up?" she asked.

I leaned forward. "I was wondering if you have any information on a group called the Skinz?" Candy had been working juvie for three years. I figured if anyone knew about these punks, she would.

She leaned back in her chair. "Nasty little buggers."

"You know them?"

"Of course I do. They've been tied to a dozen robberies, but we can never get enough evidence on them. They're smart. Too smart."

"Dangerous?"

"The potential is there. A few of the robberies have targeted gun shops. By our count, this group has thirty or forty guns stashed away."

My head swam. "Any ties to militia groups?" I was thinking about that *Gun Pride* magazine I'd found under Riley's mattress.

Candy shook her head. "Not that I've ever come across. But again, there's potential. They're not exactly white supremacists, but they haven't exactly been friendly to people of different races. By races I mean the whole gamut: Irish, Italian, Norwegian, Polish . . . the list goes on and on."

"Great."

"Why? Do you know something?"

"No. Riley's been hanging around this group lately."

"No kidding?"

I shook my head, my ponytail slapping me in my face.

"Nina," Candy said, leaning in. "You call me if you need me or have any more questions. Because if Riley's involved with these kids, he's in some serious trouble. You need to get him away from them."

Great. Just how was I going to do that?

Thirteen

I pounded on the front door of Ginger's town house. I took some pleasure in her bland landscaping. Usually a yard reflected its owner. There wasn't even a withering pot of marigolds to be seen. Just boring, cracked, chipped cement stairs.

The door finally swung open. Kevin cursed.

"Good to see you too."

"What are you doing here?" He shaded his eyes against the sun.

I swallowed hard. He was clad in a pair of old denim shorts, left unbuttoned and barely zipped. His chest was lightly tanned, broad and flat, his stomach, muscled and taut. I tore my gaze away from the little trail of hair that ran down from his belly button.

"I need to talk to you."

"You ever heard of a phone?"

I went to jab him in the chest, then thought it wiser if I didn't touch him. "I tried. You didn't answer."

"You could have paged me."

"Again, no answer," I snapped. Oh, no. I was turning into my sister, and hated it. I didn't want to be snappy, or snippy, for that matter.

He dragged a hand over his face. The gash above his eye

had scabbed over, the goose egg had begun to turn a pretty shade of purple. Stubble dotted his cheeks, his jaw. Clearly I had gotten him out of bed.

"Jesus, Nina, did you have to come here?"

"Oh, gee, sorry I'm intruding on your little love nest, but this is important."

"How'd you even know about this place?"

"Phone book."

He finally stepped out onto the small stoop, closing the door behind him. "What do you want?"

I sat down on the front step. "Riley."

"Can't you give the kid a break? He told me how you embarrassed him at school in front of his friends."

"I embarrassed him? Oh that's rich. And they aren't his friends. I know Riley. He wouldn't hang out with kids like those."

"Those kids are fine," he said tightly.

"Harmless?"

"Perfectly."

Reaching down, I grabbed one of the hairs on his calf and yanked. I knew from experience where to inflict pain.

"Ow!"

"You're such a liar. I don't know how long I've been blind to that, but I see it clearly now."

His face steeled. I had ticked him off. Okay, maybe I'd gone too far pulling out his leg hair, but damn, it felt good.

"A liar?" His voice was hard.

"Shall I count the ways?"

"That's personal, Nina. That has nothing to do with Riley."

He infuriated me. "You lied about the Skinz!"

"Did not."

I wished I had my hockey stick. "Those kids are trouble. I talked to Candy Carradon this morning. Seems she has a different viewpoint on those kids than you do."

"Your curiosity is going to get you into trouble one of these days."

"She said I should get Riley away from them as soon as possible. I'm sure my father would be happy to home school him."

"You'll do no such thing!"

"Why not?"

"Riley belongs in school. He's had enough turmoil in his world without you yanking him away from the only stability in his life."

"So you want me to leave him there to become more deeply enmeshed with a group who has nearly forty stolen guns in their possession?"

"That's not fact."

"So you knew!"

He stood up. "Stay out of this, Nina. I mean it." He stormed into the condo and slammed the door behind him.

The picture of maturity, I stuck out my tongue.

I stopped at home to grab a quick lunch and called Bridget at her office, but got her voice mail. I tried her cell and she answered on the third ring.

"Just wanted to check in," I said.

"Find anything?"

"A reluctant congressman and a scared paramedic. Not much to build a case on."

"Let's just drop it, Nina. Tim's not happy you're involved in all this. It's much too dangerous. We'll find the money for the PI sooner or later."

The last thing I wanted to do was give up. "I know how Tim feels, but I really think I'm getting somewhere. Give me a few more days, Bridget. If I don't come up with anything by then, I'll back off."

Her sigh echoed across the line. "Saturday, that's it."

"Tuesday."

"Sunday."

"Monday."

"Deal. Please be careful, Nina. I mean it."

"I will."

I told her about the plans I had to meet with the developer, Demming, later that afternoon, but I didn't mention the calls I'd gotten, or the note that had somehow found its way onto my bed. The less she knew about that sort of thing, the better.

"I'm looking forward to dinner tomorrow night with you and Kevin."

I bit my lip. Cringed. "Uh, bad news, there. He has to work. Ana's gonna tag along, if that's okay."

"That's fine. I haven't seen Ana in ages. But be sure to say hello to Kevin for us."

Righty-o. We said our good-byes after setting a time and place for dinner.

There was only one new message on my machine—from Pesky Pests. I called them back, but they were once again out in the field. I was beginning to think Xena had run, uh, slithered, away, but I still didn't relax my guard. It would be just like that snake to lull me into a false sense of security, then spring.

I hurried through lunch, eager to see what Demming had to say. Okay, not entirely true. My house just didn't feel like a home anymore. Sure, Xena terrified me, but she wasn't the only thing. At least with her I knew the enemy. Someone had come into my house yesterday. Someone had been in my bedroom. Had touched my jammies.

Even though I was ticked at Kevin, and didn't with 100 percent certainty trust him, I admit I entertained thoughts about letting him see the note and telling him about heavy breathing calls. He had more resources than I did. But telling him would not guarantee his silence, and I had promised Mrs. Sandowski I wouldn't involve the police. What's a girl to do?

I'd figure something out. Eventually.

I placed a call to an alarm company and arranged for someone to come out to show me the different alarms the company offered. Better to be safe than sorry, and although I knew any professional criminal would know how to by-pass most systems, it was worth a try.

The phone rang and I jumped. I reached for it, then let my arm fall to my side. I swallowed. The answering machine clicked on.

"Nina? This is Ma-ma. Don't forget Tuesday!"

Tuesday? Tuesday? Oh, the fitting. I pressed the delete button. As far as I was concerned, I had no plans for Tuesday.

I hurried the dishes, wiped my hands on my jeans, and had reached for my backpack when the phone rang again. I instinctively reached for it without thinking.

"Hello."

"Nina Quinn?"

"Yes?"

"This is Robert MacKenna, Riley's vice principal."

Dread built in my stomach.

"I was just wondering if you knew that he wasn't in school today."

"But I dropped him off there myself," I said inanely.

"I'm sorry. He didn't even make it to first period."

I banged my head against the kitchen wall. "Thanks for letting me know."

"He'll be punished for missing."

"What kind of punishment?"

"Detention. If it keeps up, we'll have to sit down with him and work out a probationary plan."

Great. Just great.

"Oh, and Nina?"

"Yeah?"

"In case you didn't know, it's morning detention. Six thirty to seven fifteen. The school board recently decided that making these kids get up so early adds a little oomph to their punishment."

"No flogging?"

He laughed. "No. Some parents complained."

A man with my sense of humor. I managed a smile as I pressed my eyes together to keep the moisture in.

"Any chance Mike Novak's in? Could I talk with him?"

"Hold on," MacKenna said. "I'll check."

A minute later he came back on the line. "Can't seem to find him."

"Thanks for trying."

I hung up, picked up the phone again. Knowing Riley had skipped again left me uneasy. I wanted more information about the Skinz.

A quick call to Candy Carradon left me with more questions. Seems she left work right after lunch to go to a conference somewhere out of state.

Funny how she hadn't mentioned that to me earlier when she asked me to call her if I had any questions.

What was going on?

Fourteen

John Demming had stood me up.

"He's out at a site," his receptionist said.

"We had an appointment."

She shrugged.

"Can you at least tell me what site?"

She worried her lip. John Demming had probably told her to tell me he was out, but I guessed he'd never told her not to tell me where. She didn't look like the brightest bulb on the Christmas tree, so I leaned in close, slipped my wedding band off my finger and slid it into my pocket.

"It's kind of important," I said.

"It is?"

Definitely, air made up most of what was in her head. She wiped a strand of dark brown hair out of her eyes and tucked it behind her ear. She was young, maybe nineteen.

I covered my eyes dramatically and tried desperately to scare up some tears. It wasn't too hard, considering the state of my life. I sniffled. "D-do you have a tis-sue?"

She reached in her desk and handed me a box. I plucked out a Puffs. "Th-thank you." I hiccupped.

Taking a deep breath, I started talking fast, hoping that John Demming was indeed married. "He was supposed to be here, and oh, I knew I shouldn't have trusted him when he told me he would leave his wife, then told me that he'd love me forever, then got me pregnant and he said he'd support us. Now me and little Johnny are gonna be kicked out on the street if he doesn't come up with the money he owes us for back child support." I sniffed again for effect.

"Men are slime," she said, coming around the desk. She put a comforting arm around my shoulder. She smelled like cigarettes.

"I know." I hiccupped again, blew my nose.

"He's at a development off Millson Road. Do you know where that is?"

"Yeah. I think," I said softly.

"Here," she said, tossing me a hard hat, "you'll need this."

I followed the receptionist's directions to the new subdivision. I took Vista View as a short cut. If I lived there I'd be a little ticked too, but as a driver, it was much easier than going around.

I turned onto Millson, and as I approached Sandowski's Farm, I slowed. Nothing looked unusual. The house was still falling down around itself.

I kept driving east on Millson, and about a half mile down from Sandowski's Farm, I turned left into the subdivision.

The streets were wide and tree lined. Electric reproductions of gaslights dotted the sidewalks at intervals of every third house. It looked to me as if the construction was completed in the neighborhood, but as I wended my way down the twisting streets, I saw the frames of new houses being erected.

I pulled up to the curb, parking in front of a beautifully landscaped house. The house itself looked new but lived in. My sympathies went out to its owners for all the construction noise and traffic.

My eyes swept the area for a clue as to where John Demming might be, since the whole street was lined with trucks that said JOHN DEMMING CONSTRUCTION on their sides.

The echo of hammering drew my eyes to the shell of a house across the street.

The clay dirt beneath my feet was hard, dusty. For early May it was damn hot. The sun beat down on my face and I shaded my eyes.

I climbed the ramp that had been built to get into the house. The hammering stopped, then started again. My T-shirt stuck to my back.

"Hello?" I called out. No answer. I stepped into the house. A maze of two by twelves closed in the part of the house where I stood. Obviously the living room. The house was still in the rough-in stage. No electrical wiring ran through the two-bys.

I glanced at the stairs. They looked like someone had haphazardly nailed plywood strips to risers. I tested one, found it held my weight, and climbed another one. There was no handrail. I put the hard hat on.

The hammering stopped. I took advantage of the momentary silence. "Hello?"

"Up here," a masculine voice called out.

Inching my way up the stairs—if that's truly what they could be called—I exhaled with relief when I finally reached the top.

It didn't take long to spot the man, since there were no walls blocking my view.

"Yes?" he asked, his tone clipped.

So much for a how-do-you-do. He was a big man, tall and wide. He looked fat, but I had the feeling that it was mostly muscle under the surface. He held a claw hammer in one hand and a nail in the other. A tool belt rested on his hips, dragging down his jeans just a bit. I kept my distance; he was scary. "I'm looking for John Demming."

"He ain't here." He turned and banged a nail into a stud.

Thanks for the tip. I watched as he crossed the room. I took a step back, but he stopped at a row of boxes stacked neatly along the wall. I craned my neck. There were several cardboard boxes filled with smaller boxes. Red, green, and orange lids proclaimed contents such as DRYWALL SCREWS and 1½-INCH NAILS. He reached a meaty hand in one and pulled out a handful of nails. He started hammering again.

There was a large box on the floor with a skull and crossbones stamped on its side under the name STARTZKY'S. I caught sight of some red box tops inside. Hadn't Bridget said the poison used to kill the sheep was Startzky's? Was this was the same stuff? I inched closer for a better look.

I bent to reach for a box when Big & Meaty stepped in front of me. "I said: He's. Not. Here."

Ohh-kay.

"Do you know where I might find him?"

"No."

Mr. Sociable he wasn't.

"You couldn't happen to tell me what he looks like?" It would certainly make my job easier.

He sneered. Honest to God, he did.

"All-righty. Thanks for your time." If I thought the stairs were scary walking up, they were downright terrifying going down. Having no pride, I actually shimmied down on my butt.

That cardboard carton with the skull and crossbones nagged at me. How could I get in to see for sure if it was in fact rat poison if I couldn't get a box?

I suppose . . .

Nah, I couldn't.

But, really, it wouldn't be breaking and entering if the house had no doors, right?

Sure.

With that settled in my delusional mind, I felt better. But when? Nighttime was obvious, but Ana I had plans to follow Marty tonight. Maybe I could squeeze it in afterward.

I took off my hard hat and wiped the beads of sweat off my forehead with the back of my hand. I eyed the other unfinished houses on the street. There was one, on the corner, that looked promising. Landscapers were out planting a row of boxwoods in the front yard, which meant the house was almost done . . . Maybe Demming had come out to give final approval?

Instead of an unsteady wooden ramp, the almost-finished house actually had real concrete stairs leading into it.

I left the hard hat on the steps and wiped my feet before entering. Air-conditioning blasted me in the face and I *ahhed*. Gleaming hardwood covered with a sheet of plastic lined the entryway. The rooms were carpeted in an inviting green and the woodwork was amazing. I ran my hand over the banister, inhaling that new-house smell which would likely give me cancer someday.

"Nice, isn't it?"

Startled by the voice, I jumped. Looking up the stairs, I saw a man at the top, clipboard in hand. "Yes, it is."

Slowly coming down the steps, he studied me intently. "Let me introduce myself. I'm John Demming. And you look incredibly familiar to me. Do I know you?"

"I don't think so." Was it possible he'd seen one of the stories on *Taken by Surprise*? I ponied up a smile. "But you're just the man I was looking for." He looked oddly familiar to me too, but I couldn't place him. As far as I knew, his ads and billboards never featured him at all.

"Really?"

Shoot! I thought fast. Why? Why would I be looking for him? If I came out and admitted who I was, then he might shoo me away and I'd never get answers. But if I lied and made up some crazy story, then I wouldn't be able to ask the kind of questions that might get me some answers. Tough decision.

"I'm looking to buy a house," I fibbed.

"Then you've come to the right place. But I have to tell you, it's not necessary to meet with me. You can get any information you need from the model home at the end of the street."

"Oh." I batted my eyelashes, trying to appear incompetent. "I didn't know."

"New to the area?"

"Uh, yes. Yes, I am."

He smiled, putting his hand on my arm. "I think you'll find *everything* you need in a Demming home."

The flirt! I couldn't believe it. "Really?"

"Quality workmanship," he said with pride. Then he lowered his voice a notch, and said, "Years of experience."

I nearly choked on the laughter I held in. He was actually rather cute in a grandfatherly, Bob Barker kind of way, if you liked that type, which I didn't. Demming's dark hair had grayed at the temples, his blue eyes looked to have lost some luster over the years.

"Let me show you around," he said.

I poured it on. "Sure, I'd love that." I managed not to cringe as he put his hand on the small of my back. "Do you build much around here?"

"About seventy percent of the new development."

"Isn't that a lot?"

He smiled. "I'm the best there is."

I giggled demurely. It was tough but I managed. He showed me the living room, dining room and den, pointing out all the selling features I might be interested in.

"This development looks nearly completed," I said as he finished his tour.

"All the houses in this particular area have been sold. But

I have new areas just beginning and some still in the design phase."

"Oh yeah?"

"Sure. People are selling their farms left and right. There's tons of land to be had around here—for the right price."

"A farm? That couldn't be too expensive."

"You'd be surprised."

"Come now." I set the bait, hoping he'd take it. "I drove past a farm on Millson coming here that was so beat up, a strong breeze could knock it down."

He laughed. "If it's the farm I'm thinking about, the price tag is in the seven figures."

Men were suckers for women who batted their eyelashes, I decided. He stepped right up to my bait without even thinking twice.

I widened my eyes, hoping I looked shocked. "That thing? It was nothing but some old bricks stuck together and some land that looked like it hadn't been tended to in years."

"It's not the house or the quality of the land."

"What else is there?"

"Location."

"It didn't seem all that appealing to me. Off the main street like that and all." I batted my eyelashes again. He led me into the living room and we sat on the hearth in front of a marble fireplace.

He put his hand on my knee. No wedding ring. *Gulp*. Did that mean he was married and just didn't wear a ring, or was he really single? No, he couldn't be single. His secretary played right into my little trap. She'd know if he were single. Wouldn't she? Then I remembered how ditzy she was. Anything was possible. She gave brunettes a bad name.

"Imagine that farm gone, that land razed and paved. A four lane road."

"Okay." I made a point of squeezing my eyes shut.

"Now imagine that land with developments on one side, businesses on the other."

"Umm-hmmm," I murmured.

"The development just isn't any ordinary development. Because it butts up against Vista View, it has the same types of houses."

"Vista View?" I said, playing dumb. I thought I played it quite well, actually. I was proud of myself. Ana would be dying of laughter if she could see me now.

"It's a very affluent neighborhood. Million-dollar homes."

I opened my eyes and oohed. "So you plan to copy it?"

"Darn right. I'll make many, many millions." There was a greedy gleam in his eye.

"So did you buy the farm?"

"Not yet."

"Why not?" I asked. "It sounds to me like it's a pot of gold. Others must have looked at it too."

"Won't do them any good." He slid his hand from my knee up to my thigh, squeezing.

Eww. He seemed to like my attention, though, so I forced a smile on my face. Actually, he seemed the type that would like anyone's attention. "Why not?"

"The owner won't sell."

"Not for seven figures?"

He shook his head. "But I'm working on it."

Fifteen

What to eat for supper? I was not in the least looking forward to dinner with Kevin. Just how was Riley going to take the news of our divorce? He had enough to worry about without adding a divorce to his problems, namely his school skipping and his association with the Skinz. It was enough to make a stepmother have an anxiety attack.

Needing to call Bridget, I dialed her work number. The secretary told me Bridget had gone home for the day, not feeling well.

I called her there, but a busy signal buzzed my ear.

Searching the cabinets for something to make for dinner, I came up empty. Pizzas were in order. Pepperoni. Kevin hated pepperoni.

I tried Bridget again. She answered on the second ring.

"Sorry about the busy signal," she said, sounding harried. "I was doing some online research—I didn't know my cell was off. What's new?"

I filled her in on Demming and finding the rat poison. She didn't seem all that surprised.

"In the back of my mind, I knew a developer had to be behind this. It's the only thing that makes sense."

"I'll need to get a box of that rat poison to be sure it was the same kind."

"And how do you plan on doing that?"

Tim's voice carried over the line from the background. "Doing what?"

Bridget shushed him. "Go ahead," she said to me.

"I'm going to go back to that house tonight, borrow a box."

"What?! No, you can't. It's illegal."

"It's completely open over there, Bridget. No harm will come of it."

She sighed. "Just be careful."

"I will."

I hung up, feeling as though I was finally getting somewhere, and it felt good.

Unfortunately, Kevin was due any minute now and I didn't know what on earth to do about him.

"Nina Colette Ceceri!"

My mother's voice could portray many things. When she was excited, it rose steadily till it was as shrill as a high-pitched whistle. When she was tired, it was a dull, plain monotone. When she was mad, it dropped an octave and she could easily sing baritone in a barbershop quartet. And when she felt pity, her voice was mellifluous, as gentle as a song caught on a breeze. That's what it was now.

"Finally." She opened her arms.

"Finally what?" I mumbled, my body pressed into her giant breasts—breasts that must have skipped a generation in my family. No, that wasn't true. They hadn't missed Maria. Just *me*.

"You kicked him out."

"What?" She couldn't have known. There was no way, enhanced mother's intuition or not.

She *tsk-tsked*. "It's about time."

"How on earth—"

She covered my lips with a perfectly manicured finger. "Shh. No need to explain to Ma-ma. I understand."

I had planned on taking her aside and having a nice peaceful discussion on the state of my marriage, or lack of. Now my defenses were raised. How did she know? I had even slipped my wedding band back on.

"What was it? Was he cheating?"

"I thought I didn't have to explain. You *understood*. Besides, can't you whip out your crystal ball and see for yourself?"

"Posh. You know only Uncle Guido has the sight."

I wasn't so sure.

"I wouldn't be surprised at all if he was cheating. I can always spot a man with lust in his heart, and your Kevin was definitely one of those men."

"Thanks for warning me."

"Would you have listened?"

Probably not.

She set the teapot on the stove and lit the gas burner. "Does Riley know?"

"We told him tonight."

"Oh, my Riley. The poor thing must be heartbroken."

"He took it rather well, in fact." I smiled.

"What's that smile?"

"Riley. Kevin had barely walked in the door before Ry was giving him what for. Out and out told Kevin that he was staying with me, that he wasn't packing up and leaving home again." To say Kevin had been shocked would be an understatement. Come to think of it, it had taken a full five minutes to raise my jaw from the floor. Riley's statement had certainly taken the wind out of my he's-gonna-think-you're-deserting-him sails. Kevin barely had a chance to open his mouth between hello and good-bye. Not even time for pizza.

"I think it's best for the boy, don't you?"

It was six in the afternoon and my mother looked as though she had just woken up refreshed from twelve hours' sleep. Her skin was flawless, her makeup perfectly applied. Her flaxen 'do was styled with not a single hair out of place. It was disheartening, since I resembled my father, who looked like a balding bulldog.

"I'm not sure."

"You want him with you. Don't try and deny it to me."

Deny something to Celeste Madeline Chambeau Ceceri? Impossible. "I don't want him to leave. Ever. But Kevin *is* his father."

"Kevin's made his choice. Take advantage of it."

"It's not that easy."

"Posh," she said. The teapot whistled, and she turned and shut off the burner. "This isn't about a home he doesn't want to leave. Riley cares about you more than he can admit." Facing me, she raised her eyebrows, waiting for either my agreement or my denial.

I gave neither. She was the one with the intuition—let her use it.

Steam wafted from a teacup. "He's afraid to show it."

"Even if I believed that, why?"

She *tsked* again. "Oh Nina, for someone so intelligent, you're stupid."

This from my mother. "Gee, thanks, Mom."

She set two cups on the table and smiled. "I am your Mama. I'm allowed to point out the obvious."

I sighed. The subject needed to be changed. "How are the wedding plans?"

"Just splendid. Everything's in order, except of course for your dress."

Of course. Wrong subject to change to. I tried again.

"Are you sure you don't mind having Riley here tonight? I just don't trust him alone right now. Not after the trouble he's been getting into at school." I'd filled my mother in earlier on Riley's whole situation.

"Not at all. We've missed him lately." She squeezed a lemon over her cup. "It's more than likely a phase he's going through."

"I hope so."

"Where are you off to tonight?"

I lowered my head.

"Nina?" A little shrill, questioning.

"I just have a few errands to run." She definitely didn't need all the sordid stalking details. And she certainly didn't need to know about my involvement with the Sandowskis and a particular box of rat poison. "Ana's coming with me."

"That doesn't particularly reassure me, knowing her mother."

Rolling my eyes, I let that pass. There was no use in defending Aunt Rosetta anyway. My mother was beyond listening.

"Everything will be fine."

She took a delicate sip of her tea. "You're lying to me again."

I pressed a hand to my chest. "I would never!"

My mother smiled into her cup. "Just don't get yourself arrested."

My mouth dropped in shock. It was as if she knew I planned to do something illegal. Uncomfortable, I pushed back from the table. "I'll see what I can do."

I wandered into the living room, where Riley was lying across the sofa, stomach down. He'd come home from school that day as if he'd just gotten off the bus. He'd even moaned about how much homework he had. I needed to get him into the drama club; he was a fine actor. He'd been in the house for five seconds before we'd had a huge blowout that resulted in his calling me a rather choice name, and my grounding him for life. And yet he still opted to stay with me. It did my heart good.

I wrestled the clicker out of his hand and turned the TV off. "Hey, I was watching that."

"You're grounded."

He sat up. "It's not fair."

"I don't like liars, Riley. I won't tolerate being lied to."

"You tolerated it from Dad."

I narrowed my eyes.

"This is wrong, damn wrong," he moaned.

"What's wrong is your behavior. Your vice principal mentioned morning detention, starting tomorrow."

He shook his head, muttering under his breath about fairness and me ruining everything.

"And you'll be there, Ry."

"Oh yeah?" he challenged.

"Yeah. Because I'll be there too. Sitting next to you."

His blue eyes widened, then narrowed. "You're bluffing."

Sadly, I wasn't, and I wasn't the least bit looking forward to spending my morning in detention, but I would do it if necessary.

"And if that doesn't deter you from skipping, then I'll accompany you to every single one of your classes. Your dad has handcuffs, and I'm not afraid to use them."

"You wouldn't."

"I would."

He grabbed a pillow and hugged it tight. "What am I supposed to do tonight with no TV?"

"Uh, read?"

He groaned. "That's so lame."

I wasn't going to get into a debate about the merits of reading. I walked over to my father's bookshelf and pulled down a tome on the Civil War. "Here, read this."

"That thing's thicker than a dictionary!" he whined.

"You have time." I smiled wickedly, like the evil step-mother that I was.

"Just wrong," he muttered.

I found my father in the basement workshop. He smiled. "Did you know that on this day in 1519, Leonardo da Vinci died?"

"No, I didn't."

"Or that in 1885, *Good Housekeeping* was first published?"

"Sorry, nope." Dad was a history buff. He had even named his kids after Christopher Columbus's ships: the *Nina*, the *Pinta*, and the *Santa Maria*. Mom had adamantly refused to name her son "Pinta," which is how he ended up with "Peter." I'm still trying to figure out why they didn't just name him "Nino" or "Mario," but there were a lot of things I was still trying to figure out about my parents.

I'd learned to live with Dad's hobby over the years. It drove my sister Maria to the brink of homicide. Speaking of which . . .

"Mom says everything's all set for the wedding."

"Hmmph."

"Hmmph?"

"That girl shouldn't be wearing white."

My mouth dropped open.

"She should be wearing black. That man she's marrying is a bum. She should be going into mourning."

Ohh-kay. I let the subject die. It was for the best.

"I have to go. I'll be back later to pick up Riley. Beware, he's sulking."

"He's just hurting," my father said. "I'll walk you out."

I called out my good-byes to Riley and my mother. My father opened the Corolla's door for me. We stood in silence for a minute. Something was up. My father never walked me to my car.

He cleared his throat. What was left of his dark hair blew

in the breeze. Finally he looked at me, his green eyes troubled. "I'm sorry about Kevin, Nina."

Ahh. News traveled fast in the Ceceri household. My mother must have gotten to him while I talked with Riley.

"It's okay, Dad."

"I know what your mother thought of him, but I always thought him honorable."

"I think he still is, in some ways." Man, that was hard to say.

"Not in the ways that count."

I bit my lip. "I suppose you're right."

"I always am." He kissed my cheek. "There's always a silver lining, Nina."

"Always?"

"Sometimes not as clear as one would like, but always. Stay out of trouble."

"Don't I always?"

"No."

Hmmph.

The screen door squeaked. My mother appeared. "Don't forget about Tuesday."

"Tuesday?"

"I knew you didn't write it down!"

I started the engine and backed out of the driveway before the lecture began.

Sixteen

Ana brushed Passionate Purple onto her baby toe. "Doesn't Bonnie mind you using her house like this?"

I pointed my binoculars at Marty. He danced to a silent tune as he placed the tools in the back of a TBS truck.

"I told her I'll put a fountain in her backyard."

"Ahh. Nothing like a little bribery."

I growled at her. "It was a fair trade-off."

Marty closed the tailgate on the truck and hopped into the cab. His headlights flashed on. I got ready to roll.

Ana closed the cap on her polish. "I always liked Marty. I hope it's not him."

"Me too."

He'd come to work for me at seventeen, full of attitude and with a gigantic chip on his shoulder weighing him down. Raised in the inner city, Marty had survived a horrific upbringing. He'd been a straight-A student with a college scholarship until a dare landed him in jail. He'd been charged with vandalism after spray-painting a local overpass.

"How'd your meeting with the builder go today?"

"He's a lech."

"I can see where that'd make him a murder victim, not a suspect."

My Corolla bumped over a pothole, and Ana and I bobbled in our seats.

"He wants that farm, and I have the feeling he'd stop at nothing to get it," I explained.

"I hear a 'but' coming on."

"No evidence." Yet. I checked my dashboard clock. It was somewhat early still. And not dark yet. I couldn't break and enter in the daylight. I had some brains.

Marty's left blinker flashed as he turned down Knickerbocker. "Looks like he's heading back to the office."

I ground my teeth. "He knows we're behind him."

Ana straightened. "How do you know?"

"He turned his headlights on when it's still light out, he used his blinker, and he'd doing thirty-five in a fifty zone." I banged a U-ey. "I think Coby Fowler has a big mouth. He probably told everyone about me sending him out alone last night."

"So, what now?"

"Try, try again."

Nothing much had changed inside Demming's unfinished house. It was still a shell—a dark shell. The streetlight illuminated the doorway, but as I glided away from the door, it became blacker with each step.

After figuring out that Marty was onto us, I decided to ditch the surveillance for the night. He certainly wasn't going to incriminate himself while I had binoculars trained on him. So, I dropped Ana off at her condo with her reluctant promise that she'd come with me to dinner with Bridget and Tim the next night.

I felt my way along the studs as a guide. The plywood flooring beneath my feet squeaked ever so slightly under my weight. I was sweating as if I'd just run a four-minute mile. My small flashlight barely made a dent in the pitch-black room.

I paused in my trek to the stairs, flashed my light behind me, where I thought I'd heard a sound. Its thin beam cut through the darkness revealing nothing but a row of two-by-four-by-twelve studs standing guard.

Maybe I imagined it? I paused again, listening. I could hear my own harsh breathing and the night sounds floating through the holes in the walls where windows would eventually be installed.

Nerves.

I crept closer to the stairs and cursed softly when I saw that they hadn't been cased yet. Of course not. That would have meant that I'd actually have something go my way in this wretched life of mine.

Flashlight between my teeth, I crawled up the stairs in a very unladylike fashion. My mother would not have been proud. My father . . . ? Maybe. When I reached the top of the stairs, I stopped. It was tiring, this sneaking about in the night.

The wind picked up. It caused the house to shake a bit. Or maybe that was my imagination. Up on the second floor, I could hear the leaves rustling outside the framed window space above my head. Goose bumps rose along my arms. Not the good kind of goose bumps, like you get when hearing a particularly beautiful song for the first time, or the kind of goose bumps you get when you're being thoroughly and enjoyably kissed. Nuh-uh. These were the Freddy Kruger's-behind-the-next-corner-ready-to-jump-out-at-you goose bumps; the Xena's-slithering-all-over-you-while-you-sleep goose bumps.

And my thoughts were rambling again. Not good at all. I swallowed hard. My breath hitched when I thought I heard footsteps. My ears strained to catch the sound again.

Just nerves, I reminded myself. Nerves. But I aimed the flashlight down the stairs just in case. I flashed it left and right, but saw nothing out of place.

Enough stalling. I edged away from the wall, the steady rustling of the leaves outside an accompaniment to my harsh, choppy breathing. I was trying to hold my breath, to pick out any sounds that might not be made by Mother Nature, but I was only succeeding in making myself hyperventilate.

Just find it and go, Nina.

Find it. Right. I inched my way along the floor in a half crouch, half walk. The boxes were still stacked by the wall where I had seen them earlier that day during my run-in with Big & Meaty.

I held the flashlight in my mouth so I could use both hands to search the boxes. After a minute I found the box of nails. I pushed it aside, surprised at how much it weighed.

I opened the box behind it, the noise of the cardboard echoing loudly through the empty house. I cringed, even though I knew no one could hear me.

Peeking inside, I frowned. No red box tops. Orange. Screws. I looked around. Finally, shoved in the back, behind a roll of fluffy yellow insulation, I found the box with the skull and crossbones stamped on it.

Slowly, I lifted a small box out of the bigger box. In bold black letters, it read STARTZKY'S RAT POISON, GUARANTEED TO WORK. I slipped one box into my shirt, hoping I didn't come untucked.

Suddenly, I spun. I could have sworn I heard footsteps, but the room was empty. I was really losing it.

I pulled the box toward me. As the box scraped against the plywood flooring it kicked up sawdust. The sweet smell of freshly cut wood swirled around me. I inhaled, sneezed.

"God bless you," a mocking voice in the darkness said.

I jumped back, screeching. My flashlight dropped from my mouth and extinguished as it rolled away.

Someone chuckled in the darkness. I tried to pinpoint where he stood, but it was nearly impossible.

I needed a full moon.

I needed my flashlight.

A gun would have been nice too, but I hadn't thought to bring one.

Reaching out, I searched with the pads of my fingers for my flashlight.

My heart beat so loudly I was sure it could be heard across the room. Heck, down the block.

"Trespassing is illegal."

No shit. That's why I did it when no one was around. Well, when no one was supposed to be around. The man's voice was familiar but odd. It was as if I'd heard it before, but muffled or changed in some way.

I tried to listen for his breathing, to place him in the room, but my own breathing was too loud.

"You can talk, you know," he said.

Honestly, I didn't think I could. I was pretty sure my vocal cords had frozen in terror.

Where was that damn flashlight?

I willed myself to calm. I needed to be in full control of myself. I didn't know if the man was friend or foe, but I suspected foe.

I kept searching for the flashlight, my arms making wide arcs across the floor. It couldn't have gone too far. It was reassuring knowing that he probably couldn't see me in the darkness, either. Probably.

He said, "I could probably shoot you and get away with it."

Chills danced up my neck, and I shivered.

Seventeen

Foe. Definitely foe. Glad I figured that out, the amazing detective that I was proving to be.

"But it might be bad for business," he said lightly.

John Demming. I recognized the playfulness in his voice. It was the flirty voice I remembered, not the tense, strained, angered voice he used a few moments ago.

I could probably shoot you and get away with it.

He probably could, which scared the bejeebers out of me.

He kept on talking as if he had nothing better to do. I kept searching for my damn flashlight.

"I wondered why my brand-new secretary called and quit right after you left today."

Ack! He knew it was me. Well, not technically. He didn't know my name, only my face, which was equally horrible if one thought about it. I tried not to. I tried to focus on a way of getting out of this mess.

"So I have a son, eh? I've always wanted a son."

Creeping a little to the left, I continued my search.

"And you know, I might have left my wife for someone as beautiful as you . . . if I had a wife."

Definitely insane.

"The fact is I wanted to ask you out this afternoon. And

here I was, thinking I'd never see you again because you neglected to leave me your number or your name." He *tsked*. It sounded menacing in the darkness.

"But, alas, the fates were smiling on me. I happened to look out my window to see a woman creeping into one of my houses. And lo and behold, it's you."

His window? What was he talking about?

"I bet you didn't figure into your plans that I live across the street."

Uh, no. Never came up.

"And since you snuck in here, not knowing my house was the one *across* the street, that leaves me with only one question: What are you doing here?"

I inched a little bit more to the left. Where, oh where, was that flashlight? It struck me as odd that he didn't have one of his own. Did he think he knew his house designs well enough to not need one? Was he like a cat and could see in the dark? Lord, I prayed not.

"Don't make me ask again."

I took exception to his tone. He didn't have to get snippy. Taking a quick shallow breath, I said, "*No hablo Inglés.*"

He laughed. It grated on my nerves. I heard him take a step. Closer? Back? Was he leaving? Dare I hope?

"Good try, Nina."

I nearly choked. Besides the discovery that he stood about two feet directly in front of me, he knew my name. How?

Ohmygod!

Good try, Nina. Yes, he had said it. I wasn't imagining things, was I? *How* did he know my name? I wanted to ask him, but I didn't dare give away my location. Not when he was threatening to shoot me.

"So you want to know about the Sandowskis, hmm? You think something's going on over there?"

Hell, yes. How would he know I was helping the

Sandowskis if he wasn't involved in terrorizing them? Why else would he be threatening to shoot me? Why not just call the police when he saw me sneak in here?

Did he really have a gun? Would he actually shoot someone he deemed beautiful? Could he see me?

Since these weren't exactly questions I wanted answers to, I tried to scoot ever so quietly away. I put my hand down to brace my weight and it landed on the flashlight. I almost let out a cry of relief.

"I'm getting a little peeved."

Peeved. What a shame. I felt for him.

Visualizing his form and his stance, and taking stock of the direction of his voice, I made a mental image of him.

"I'm going to count to three, then I start shooting and ask the questions later."

"One."

Ohmygod, ohmygod. Was he bluffing? Did he really have a gun?

"Two."

Breathe. Breathe. Breathe.

I heard a soft metallic click. A safety on a gun?

"Thr—"

I flipped on my flashlight and aimed it in the direction of his face. He squinted at the sudden brightness. A gun was in his left hand, his finger on the trigger.

I kicked. A sweep, really, of my foot. I put as much weight as I could behind the motion, hitting my target in his knee. He pitched forward, cursing. I scrambled to my feet. I made it to the stairs without using the flashlight, but I didn't risk going down without it.

Suddenly, I heard a pop, and ducked automatically. I didn't know if the bullet came close to me or not, and I didn't want to know. All I wanted to do was to get the hell out of there.

With one hand I pressed the rat poison box to my breasts

and used the other for balance as I slid down the steps on my butt. I ignored the pain. My adrenaline was in full gear.

I heard footsteps above. Demming fired his gun again. I rolled to the side, not knowing if I was rolling in or out of the path of the bullet. It was pure instinct.

"Dammit. Stay where you are!"

Oh yeah, I've always wanted to be used as target practice.

The front door was to my left. Outside, there was a bob-cat parked on the lot next door. The streetlights gave a clear view of everything. Which meant that if I made it to the door, Demming would be able to sight me easily.

Creeping to my right, I ducked under the steps as he came down the stairs. The corner of the rat poison box jabbed me on my breast. I shifted the box and used my foot to search for something to throw. I found a chunk of wood and tossed it near the front door. Demming pivoted and fired.

Would the gunshots rouse the neighbors? Even if they didn't, Demming would call the police. He knew me, my name, my face. He'd have no trouble picking me out of a lineup, I was sure. How was I going to explain this to Kevin, my family? As soon as Demming turned left after coming off the stairs, I sprinted right and hurled myself out the back window.

Two more gunshots followed. I prayed that his bad aim was a permanent flaw.

I ran, never looking back, to my car parked on Millson. At least I had the foresight not to have parked it anywhere in the subdivision. I wished I'd had the foresight, though, to have worn gloves when I went into that house. My prints were everywhere.

I sped to the all-night gas station across the street from Sandowski's Farm. I needed to call Bridget and I'd forgotten my cell phone at home.

The pay phone sat directly under a bright streetlight. I

turned my back away from the street and deposited my fifty cents. You had to hate inflation.

No one was home at Bridget's. I called her cell phone but it switched to her voice mail after a single ring. I even tried her office number, but there was no answer there either.

If Bridget could identify the rat poison as being the same kind found near the sheep's drinking trough, we would be one step closer to putting John Demming behind bars. And after the man shot at me, behind bars was exactly where I wanted him.

How had he known my name?

I glanced back and forth down Millson like a fugitive, as if the police were about to descend on me. Which I realized I was, and which they might be.

When I reached the safety of my car I took a deep breath. The box of rat poison was on the seat next to me. I reached over and patted it like I would a small child and started the car.

Eighteen

I'd spent a sleepless night on the couch, gun in hand. Still jittery, I'd dragged Riley to Taken by Surprise with me, and swapped my Corolla for my work truck, an unmarked F-150, before I spent my morning in detention with him.

Demming could have killed me. Poof. Gone. Just like that. It wasn't just fear that had kept me up all night, but my conscience. I knew I needed to report Demming, but there was a side of me—the, uh, felonious side—that didn't want to mention why I was in Demming's house in the first place.

It was completely my word against his about his being the shooter. I could see him now telling a judge that he had the right to protect his property against burglars.

And me? What did I have to say for myself? That a box of rat poison, circumstantial evidence at best, might prove that Demming was a murderer? Not likely to get me out of jail, since it sounded so lame. After all, that poison could have belonged to anyone. Unless Demming's prints were on the box, I couldn't even prove it was his. And even if his prints were on the box, I still had no proof that he'd poisoned the sheep. So basically I had nothing. Nothing at all.

Big help I was turning out to be.

After spending forty-five minutes in detention with Riley, I nosed around the school, looking for Michael Novak, school cop. I wanted some clear answers regarding the Skinz, was determined to get some, and figured Michael was a good place to start. But he wasn't to be found.

Stopping into the office on the way out, I hoped to catch Robert MacKenna in. He was, the secretary said, and she pointed to his office. No escort this time, I noted. Did this mean I was moving up in the world?

"Mrs. Quinn!"

"Nina, please. Please, please."

He smiled. "Have a seat, Nina. How was detention?"

I yawned. "Just as boring as I remembered it."

He leaned forward. "You? In detention? I don't believe it."

"Believe it."

"When? How? Why?"

"Let's just say that my best friend and I came up with a no-fail way of cheating."

"It must have failed or you wouldn't have gotten detention."

I smiled. My cleverness never ceased to humor me. "Well, technically they could never prove we were cheating."

"Ahh, no physical evidence."

I shook my head. "Nope."

"But you were cheating?"

"Of course."

"How?"

I widened my eyes innocently.

"Paper in the shoe?"

"Please."

"Micro words on your fingernails?"

"Do I look like an amateur?"

He bit his lip. "This is going to drive me crazy."

"I think my parents still wonder about it."

"You're not going to tell me, are you?"

"Nope. Listen," I said, trying to ignore the fact that I still found him attractive. Married men were off-limits. I kept telling myself that he wasn't my type, but my hormones were telling me differently. "Who is it that hires the school resource officer? Is it you?"

Shaking his head, MacKenna stood and poured some coffee into a mug. Gesturing with the coffee pot, he offered me some, but I declined. I hated coffee, except for coffee ice cream. Go figure. "The superintendent hires the school resource officers, though I do have a say in the matter."

"Why Michael Novak?"

"He seemed qualified. He wanted the job. We had a vacancy."

"Did you put an ad in the paper?"

His eyebrows dipped into a *V*. "Not as I recall. The superintendent brought him in."

"When was this?"

"Beginning of this semester."

Interesting. Very interesting. There was a time frame shaping up in my mind. But what did it mean?

I pulled into Mrs. Smythe-Weston's driveway and cut the engine. People swarmed all over the yard, little worker bees building a hive.

I spotted Kit's bald head through the crowd and followed the shiny beacon to where he was digging a hole for a water feature.

His eyes narrowed on me, and he pulled me aside. "What's going on with you?"

"Nothing I can talk about."

"Why're you packing?"

"Can you tell?" I touched the gun at the small of my back.

"Unless you grew a hump overnight."

"I just need to work. Get my mind off things." I walked back to my truck, put my gun under the seat, making a mental note to lock it back in Kevin's nightstand as soon as possible.

The bricklayers were hard at work laying a new patio and built-in fire pit. Coby was in the bobcat, digging up the old lawn to be replaced with sod, and Jean-Claude was wheeling away the grass clumps in the recovered wheelbarrow. Deanna was staining a pergola, and Marty was painting a mural on the eastern side of a privacy fence.

I walked over to him, eyed his work.

"You like?" he asked.

"Everything you paint is beautiful."

His mocha eyes turned somber. "Nina?"

"Yeah?"

"Would it be possible for me to have the weekend off?"

Damn. I'd been hoping for a tearful confession. "Hot date?"

"What? No."

"I was joking, Marty."

"Oh."

"Something important?"

He tugged on the bandana shading his head. "Very."

"All right, then. I'll see you on Monday."

I spent the rest of the morning elbow deep in mulch and peonies. Working soothed my nerves, though I couldn't help but wonder when the police would show up to cart me off.

Maybe Demming hadn't called them? Could a girl get that lucky? I'd pegged him as a man who liked attention, and shooting at an intruder was a perfect opportunity to get his face in the news. Of course, he might be a tad bit embarrassed that a girl outwitted him.

But I still couldn't come up with an explanation of how he knew my name. It didn't make sense. I hadn't told anyone connected with him my name.

I dropped my hand shovel. Holy Moises Alou.

I *knew* Demming had looked familiar! And now I knew

why. I had seen him before yesterday. He had been with Chanson at his office; the shorter man on his way out.

And what was it that Chanson had said to him? *It would all be over soon.*

I had nearly let Chanson off scot-free to focus on Demming. They must be in this together, which is how Demming had known my name, I suddenly realized.

Maybe Demming *had* recognized me during my pretend house hunt, and not from any TV spot featuring Taken by Surprise. He must have remembered that he'd seen me in Chanson's office. One phone call to Chanson would be all he needed to get a name to go with my face. Dammit all.

What, exactly, did I do with this information? Should I go to Kevin? My inner voice said yes, but I thought no. Better to wait and get more information so I didn't look like a screw-up when I went to him with all this.

But that was just my pride, I realized, groaning.

I decided I'd run things by Bridget and Tim at dinner, see what they thought. I'd bring the rat poison with me, see if it was the same kind that had poisoned the sheep. I sighed, looked at my watch. It was closing in on two o'clock now.

Kit shouldered up to me. "Go home. Get some rest. I can take care of things here."

I yawned. "You sure?"

"Positive."

I didn't need to be asked twice.

Back at home, I replayed the message I received from Pesky Pests telling me when they would be in the office. Playing phone tag was wearing thin. Xena still roamed free. Riley claimed to have seen her slithering past my bedroom door, but I was inclined to not believe him, because one, he would like nothing better than to scare me to death, and two, the thought of Xena in—or near—my room scared me to death.

I was really hoping that she had slithered right out of the

house and made a nice home for herself in one of Mr. Cabrera's rose beds.

I changed out of my grimy jeans into shorts and a T-shirt. I knew I ought to go talk to Chanson. And I still hadn't heard from Dave Mein.

I slumped down on the couch, yawned. My eyelids dropped. Blessedly, I dreamed of nothing at all.

Nineteen

"Wipe the drool off your lips before we sit down," I said to Ana as we walked toward the table for four where Bridget and Tim were sitting.

Ana smiled, talked through her teeth. "It's so not fair."

"What?"

"That men get better with age."

I didn't have time to voice my agreement before we reached the table. Tim stood, gave us both hugs, kissed our cheeks. Ana's face flushed crimson.

Tim was one of those guys who just got better-looking. His boyish baby fat had long since faded into hard planes, smooth lines, and mouthwatering masculinity.

Not that I noticed.

I kissed Bridget's cheek before sitting across from her, leaving Ana to sit across from Tim. She'd thank me later, I was sure.

The skirt of my black all-occasion dress bunched around my knees, and I gave it a good hard tug as Ana went on and on about how good it was to see the two of them again.

"Boy or girl?" she asked.

Bridget smiled. "Don't know. We want it to be a surprise."

Tim sipped a foamy beer, then said, "*You* want it to be a surprise. I'm all for knowing."

Color tinged Bridget's ears. "Yes, well. I want it to be a surprise. So little in life is."

A sensed a smidge of tension between the two, so I searched for a change of subject but couldn't find one. Asking about family was out, asking about work was way out, and apparently asking about the baby was a touchy subject. I signaled the waiter and ordered white wine.

Tim plucked at his napkin. "Bridget said Kevin had to work tonight?"

Really, I had no idea if he was working or not. "Yes. Yes he is."

"How's he doing?" Bridget asked. "You never did say much about him the other day."

The waiter set down my wine. I gulped it down, and looked to Ana for help. She was giving Tim big moon eyes.

I held in a big sigh as I said, "He's great. Loves his work."

"Does he get along with his new partner?" Bridget asked.

Ana's head snapped up as if just hearing what we were discussing. She smiled. "Oh, they're like this," she said, crossing her fingers.

I choked on the wine and Ana thumped me on the back.

Tim's eyebrows rose in question, but he didn't comment. "Well, that's good." He pushed a hand through his dark blond hair. "It's always nice to have someone watching your back."

I blinked. For a second there I thought he said "washing your back." Ha! The wine must have gone straight to my head.

Ana apparently hadn't picked up on the whole baby-tension thing because she said, eyeing Bridget's large stomach, "Have you had an ultrasound, Bridget? Just to make sure it's not twins?"

Bridget laughed. "I get that all the time. And yes, I had one. Two, as a matter of fact."

Tim pulled out his wallet, took out a black-and-white grainy image. "Want to look?"

"Sure." Ana snatched the picture. Inwardly, I groaned as she made as much skin-to-skin contact with Tim as possible.

I took a look at the ultrasound picture. I had no earthly idea what I was looking at. I oohed and ahhed for good measure.

The waiter came, took our orders and disappeared again. Bridget and Tim kept sharing tense glances. We chitchatted about this, that, and the other.

I took a deep breath, deciding it was time I told them about what I'd learned so far. Lowering my voice, I told them about my run-in with Demming (leaving out the shooting part), the rat poison out in my car, and the connection I'd made between Demming and Chanson.

Bridget looked interested in the information, but Tim's expression had turned into a scowl. The corners of his lips tightened. "We actually wanted to talk to you about that, Nina."

Bridget lumbered to her feet, wouldn't look at me. "I need to use the little girls' room."

Ana looked between Tim and me, and apparently sensing conflict in the air, jumped up. "Me too. The wine—"

I glared at her for abandoning me. She shrugged and scurried away, like the rat that she was.

Tim stared at the bread basket as he said, "We want you to stop investigating, Nina."

This wasn't a surprise. "Why?"

"It's not your job, you have no investigative experience whatsoever, it's dangerous, and frankly, it's none of your business. Bridget shouldn't have said anything to you at all."

Hmmph. I kept my Clue-playing abilities to myself. I didn't think he'd appreciate them.

"I'm sorry," he said, "if that sounds harsh. That's just the way it is."

"Your mother okayed it."

Guilt nudged at my conscience. I still hadn't had a chance to help Mrs. Sandowski with Joe's gardens. It was going to the top of my priority list.

"Frankly, she's depressed since Dad's death, and can hardly be called on to make a decision like that."

"Frankly," I said, mocking, "I've been getting results. Demming with Chanson, the rat poison . . ."

He took a sip of his beer. "Stay out of it, Nina."

His adamancy confused me. Why was he so gung ho I stop looking into what's been going on? With wine fortification, I said, "I think you should take this evidence to the police."

"No."

I looked to the ladies' room door. Still firmly closed. What was going on in there? "It's getting too dangerous for them to be left out."

"I can't be sure their pockets aren't lined."

"You can trust Kevin. He'll do a thorough investigation."

Did I just say the words "trust" and "Kevin" in the same sentence? Had I gone mad?

His shoulders stiffened, his muscles bunching under his Polo shirt. His dark eyes narrowed. "You already called them?"

"What? Them who?"

"The police."

"No."

He motioned with his chin. "Then why are they here?"

I turned around in my seat and saw Kevin headed straight toward me, a uniformed officer dogging his heels.

Uh-oh.

Kevin stopped in front of our table, arms crossed, looking formidable and a bit scary. He and Tim shook hands, murmured "haven't seen you in a while" greetings. The officer with him had his hat in one hand—his other hand rested on his hip. Ginger was nowhere to be seen, and I was beyond grateful.

I smiled. Kevin didn't. I swallowed. "Here for dinner?" I asked. A girl could hope.

"No."

"Oh." My gaze snapped to his, and I saw how serious he was. I jumped to my feet. "It's not about Riley, is it?" He was supposed to be spending the weekend with Kevin. But if Kevin was here, where was Ry? With those Skinz?

"Riley's fine. Watching videos."

My knees wobbled a bit with relief, and a bit of fear. If not here about Riley . . . "Then what?"

"It's about John Demming, Nina."

Twenty

"Demming?" I asked, my voice choked. I should have been expecting this. Hell, I *had been* expecting this all day, but I'd finally let my guard down. What would my parents say when they heard that I'd broken into a house? Been arrested, as my mom predicted?

"Why don't we go outside?" Kevin said, angling his head toward the patrons openly staring at us.

I made my apologies to Tim, and asked him to send Ana out when she returned.

"I'll call you tomorrow, Nina, to finish this conversation."

Weakly, I smiled. Little did he know that by tomorrow I'd probably be in the local lock-up and calling *him* to represent me.

Damp night air settled on my shoulders as we rounded the corner of the restaurant. I spotted a black and white blocking my Corolla.

"I want answers, Nina."

I tried for innocent. "To what?"

The officer—Jaredo, by the tag on his uniform—stood by my car door. Did he think I'd bolt? Guilty heat crept into my cheeks. I had to confess the thought crossed my mind.

"There's been a murder."

His words sucked the breath right out of my lungs. A

murder? What? Whoa! I thought Kevin said he was here about John Demming. Breaking and entering. Nothing that would warrant capital punishment. "A murder!?"

"John Demming was found dead this morning."

"John Demming?" I parroted, confused.

"Been dead about ten hours as close as the medical examiner could tell. Happened around eleven last night."

I could feel the color draining from my face. Eleven? He had to have been killed soon after I pitched myself out the window of his unfinished house. My heart raced, my palms dampened. A million questions surged through my mind, but only one screamed to be answered.

"Why are you here, Kevin, telling me this?"

"We'd like to know why your prints were found all over the crime scene."

My legs went weak. My prints. The crime scene. I sat on the bumper of the patrol car. This wasn't happening. "How'd he die?" I managed to say.

"Gunshot to the head."

"No!" I shook my head. "It's just not possible."

"What isn't?"

"He was alive. He was shooting at me!"

Kevin's eyes widened. Officer Jaredo stood stock still, guarding my car.

Kevin put his hand on my shoulder. "Tell me what happened."

"Why?"

"Because you're a suspect, Nina. That's what suspects do. They tell the police what happened."

I shrugged out of his grasp. "Well, you don't have to be so condescending about it."

He let out a tired, "Nina."

"Could it have been suicide?" I asked. Maybe Demming felt such overwhelming guilt for his role in terrorizing the Sandowskis that he couldn't live with himself any longer.

"No."

Ohmygod, ohmygod.

My thoughts spun. None of this made sense. I looked at Kevin. Did he really think me capable of killing someone?

Lord, how did I get myself into this mess? "You really think I'm a suspect?"

His eyes were a light green. Not muddy like mine, but emerald clear. I looked for any sign that he thought I could murder someone, but he gave none. This Kevin I didn't know, the detective. I knew the man, not the officer.

"I need you to tell me what happened. We can do it here or at the station, Nina."

The hem of my all-occasion dress rode up as my knees shook. I held tightly onto the bumper so I wouldn't slide off. "Here's just peachy."

"You said Demming shot at you. When? Where? Why?"

Why hadn't I kept my big mouth closed? I promised Mrs. Sandowski I wouldn't involve the police. She'd have to understand that I needed to talk to prove my innocence. She'd understand . . . wouldn't she?

"Nina."

Rubbing my temples, I tried to think of how to phrase my answer. "He thought I was an intruder," I finally answered. There. That wasn't a lie.

"Why?"

"Because I was in a house he was building."

"Why were you there?"

"I had . . . forgotten something." True enough, I reasoned.

Kevin tipped his head to the side. "Which would be what?" His patience was threadbare if his tone was any indication.

"My . . ." My what? My box of rat poison that I needed to prove Demming a sheep murderer? "My backpack," I blurted.

Kevin sighed. "And why was your backpack there?"

Think fast, Nina. "Because I was there earlier that day

looking at houses. I forgot it. Didn't remember where I put it until later that night. I went back to get it."

"Why were you looking at houses?"

Glancing down, I stared at my fingers wishing they had an alibi written on them. "I was thinking of moving. I think you know why," I added just so he wouldn't pursue that particular line of questioning.

Thankfully, he didn't.

"Why did Demming think you were an intruder?" His voice betrayed none of his emotions.

"I don't know," I lied.

"Did you tell him why you were there?"

"I didn't know it was him. I went in, found my backpack, and then all of a sudden a man was standing there threatening to shoot me. I panicked."

"What did you do?"

"I kicked him in the knee and took off. He fired. A couple times."

Kevin nodded. "Did you ever think about asking his permission to enter the house?"

"I didn't think it would be a big deal. The house was open. There weren't even any doors. Besides, I didn't know he lived across the street."

"How *did* you know he lived across the street?"

I clenched my teeth. "He made a point of telling me."

"When was this happening exactly?"

"Last night. Ten o'clock-ish. Exactly," I mocked.

His big form loomed over me as he took a step forward. I decided not to be intimidated and stayed where I was.

"Does this have anything to do with the Sandowskis?"

"Why would you think that?"

He rubbed his chin. "Does it?"

"I don't think so." I swallowed over the guilt lodged in my throat.

He glared at me, probably wondering if I could be

trusted. I smiled weakly, hoping he wouldn't notice my chattering teeth.

"You have any idea who would want to harm John Demming?" he asked.

I immediately thought of Chanson but kept quiet. I didn't think Kevin would believe me if I told him my thoughts on the matter.

"I can't think of anyone," I answered softly. "Can you?"

"We're looking into it."

Ana came storming out of the restaurant wearing a look that would scare a convicted felon—and had many times. "What's going on?"

Reluctantly, Kevin filled her in. His voice echoed in my head as he repeated the story. Even the second time around it sounded unbelievable.

Ana's lips turned downward into a tight frown. "I think you should go now. She's exhausted. Look at her."

Kevin's gaze swept over my face. "Needless to say," he said, "don't leave town."

"Wouldn't dream of it."

Jaredo opened the driver's side of the cruiser and levered himself in. Kevin reached for the door handle, but stopped, his hand on the metal. "Oh, Nina, one more thing."

I groaned. "What?"

"I'll be over later, and I'll want the truth. The whole truth."

"Do you have to be so dramatic?" Ana snapped, hands on hips.

"Meaning?" I asked.

"I don't think you are involved in Demming's murder, but you know more than you're saying."

"Why would you think that?"

"Despite what you'd like me to believe, there's no way you'd move out of your Aunt Chi-Chi's house. I want to know the real reason you went back to Demming's house, and it better not be a lie this time."

Ana and I watched the police car drive away.

"What have you gotten yourself into?" she said.

"Damned if I know."

Twenty-one

My weak knees brought me to the ground. Leaning my head against the door of my car, I forced myself to stop shaking. Demming. Dead. I just couldn't believe it. All those Ws tumbled through my head. Who, why, when, weird. Good riddance. Okay, "good riddance" didn't start with W, but it was still floating around in there.

Ana settled herself beside me.

"Do you think he'll arrest me?"

Her jaw twitched. "No, no, not at all."

"You're such a crappy liar."

Footsteps crunched on the loose gravel of the restaurant's parking lot.

Ana peered over the trunk. "Bridget and Tim."

I pushed Ana's head down, out of sight. I assumed Bridget and Tim would learn of Demming's death soon, but I didn't want them to hear it from me. And I certainly didn't want to hear them tell me one more time to stop looking into this mess.

I frowned.

It struck me as odd that they wanted me to stop at all. As far as they knew, I hadn't been placed in any danger, so their argument on that score was unfounded. Chanson had given me a bit to work with—not a lot, but some. Not to mention the information Dave Mein had. He was bound to call sometime. If he didn't I'd be forced to track him down and hurt him.

Tim and Bridget walked in silence toward their Jeep, a foot of space separating them.

Ana peeped over the car again. "They don't look very lovey-dovey."

As Tim opened Bridget's door, he said to her, "Do you think she'll stay out of it?"

"I don't know."

Anger laced Tim's tone. "Bridget, you brought her into this. Now get her to stop."

"And how do you expect me to do that?"

Tim walked around the car, pulled open his door. "Find a way. Or I will."

"Hmmmph," I said, as his door slammed closed.

Bridget levered herself into her seat, and as they pulled out of the parking lot I imagined it would be a long ride home.

"Seems you're getting on Tim's nerves."

Nothing like pointing out the obvious. "I guess so." I flicked a pebble. "Why do you think that is?"

She smiled. "You're irritating?"

"Har-har."

She stood, letting out a yelp. Her hair had been taken hostage by the Corolla's rust spots. After rubbing her scalp for a moment, she said, "Why do you think?"

Gravel bits stuck to my rear. I swiped them off. "I don't know." My gaze followed the route Tim and Bridget's car had taken. I had an odd feeling in the pit of my stomach, one I couldn't quite name. Something like cresting a roller coaster's highest hill with a hangover.

Tim's attitude hit me the wrong way. He should be doing everything possible to learn the truth about what's going on with his family, but instead he was throwing up roadblocks right and left.

"Nina?"

"Hmmm?"

"You have a funny look on your face."

"Just thinking."

"Well, stop. You look like you're gonna hurl."

I nodded. I felt that way too. I couldn't stop thinking about Tim. And how, with his being out of work, money would solve most of his problems. Money he could get if his mom sold her farm.

Shaking my head, I told myself it just wasn't possible. Not Tim. No way.

He couldn't have anything to do with this. Demming was behind it.

Dead Demming.

Oh.

That certainly put a twist in my thinking.

Chanson was the only one left.

My annoying inner voice whispered Tim's name. Mentally, I whipped out a roll of heavy-duty duct tape to silence it.

Ana stomped on my toe.

"Yow!"

Wagging a finger at me, she said, "You haven't stopped thinking. And if you upchuck on me, you'll be sorry."

I believed her. And I supposed she was right. I was thinking too much. I needed to get my mind off suspicions I couldn't quite put into words.

And I knew just how to do it.

Digging my cell phone out of my backpack, I flipped it open. To Ana, I said, "You up for a little investigating?"

"What kind? Is this about the hoes?"

I checked my watch. It was just past seven. Kit and the crew were due to finish the Smythe–Weston job around eight, and as far as I knew, they were on schedule.

I held up my finger as I made a quick call to Kit, who was

still at the office. It didn't take long to set my plan in motion. Flipping the phone closed, I said to Ana, "I think we should split up." I told her what I had in mind. "Two birds and all that."

Her dark eyebrows arched. "Wouldn't that be two birds with two stones?"

I rolled my eyes. "Semantics. Kit's going to send Marty home now. He'll head back to the office to drop off the truck before heading home. Or I should say that's what he's *supposed* to do. Jean-Claude's still at the site. They're wrapping up now, so he'll be there another half hour or so. Which do you want?"

"I'll take Jean-Claude. He lives closer, and really, I want to get to bed sometime tonight."

I found a receipt at the bottom of my backpack and scribbled down Mrs. Smythe-Weston's address. "Call me immediately if anything comes up."

Ana hopped in her tiny SUV in search of Jean-Claude. I turned my Corolla toward Taken by Surprise, thoughts of Tim, Demming, and Chanson still hovering foremost in my mind. I hoped tracking Marty would be just the thing to clear my head.

After a block, that whole distraction thing hadn't kicked in yet. Demming had to have been in on the Sandowski terrorist plot. The presence of the rat poison implicated him, and now his mysterious death. If the poison didn't prove anything, his shooting at me certainly proved he had something to hide.

Yet he was dead. And that left me with what, exactly? A box of rat poison, Kevin's and Dave Mein's tight lips, and a whole lot of suspicions about a certain politician.

And Tim's strange behavior.

Turning up the radio, I tried not to think of anything at all. I was giving myself a headache going back and forth between all the conjectures I had lined up in my mind.

As I turned onto Jaybird, two floodlights illuminated Marty's trusty early seventies Impala sitting alone in the TBS lot. Parked closer to the garage on the other side of the lot were Deanna's hatchback and Kit's Hummer. There was no sign of Marty yet, or the TBS truck he was assigned. I flipped on my blinker and swung into the Mighty Tots lot next door.

My cell phone chirped, scaring the bejeebers out of me. I fumbled around my backpack until I found it, read the familiar number on the caller ID screen.

Wearily, I answered.

"Nina? It's Bridget. I just wanted to apologize. I know Tim came off a little strong tonight."

"It's okay," I said, keeping an eye out for Marty's truck. "I'm so sorry about dinner."

"We really need to talk about this more. Do you think we could get together? It's early still, not even eight yet. We're at Tim's mom's, so it wouldn't take any time at all for me to meet you somewhere. And anywhere's fine, but we could meet for ice cream. I've been having a craving for pistachio. Although any kind will do."

It wasn't like Bridget to ramble, so I knew she had to be really distraught, and I felt for her, but there was no way I could deal with any of the Sandowskis tonight. I needed some space.

"Sounds great, but I can't. I have to work, paperwork, most of the night."

"Oh. That's too bad."

I could hear Tim's voice in the background and had the feeling he was behind this call.

"Maybe tomorrow?" she said.

I sighed. "Maybe. Give me a call in the morning—early. Saturday's a busy day for me, but I'll see what I can do." I'd planned to canvass Vista View, see if I could scare up a clue about Chanson tomorrow if I had the chance, but I supposed that could wait.

"Okay. Well, then. Good night."

Feeling slightly guilty, I stuffed the phone back into my backpack. Maybe getting together with Bridget would be a good idea. I could test the waters with my suspicions about Tim and see how she took to them.

I slumped in my seat as a TBS truck neared, then slowed as it turned into the TBS lot, its utility trailer clattering as it bumped over the curb. Marty hopped out, strode up the walkway, and unlocked the office door. Inside, a light turned on.

Using tactics I'd once seen on an Army Special Ops documentary, I crept through the Mighty Tots parking lot, making use of several large Bradford pear trees to hide behind as I made my way closer to the TBS office. My pumps snagged a clump of crab grass and I went flying, face first, air whooshing from my lungs.

Breathing hurt, so I took small gulps of air as I pulled myself up, sat on the damp grass. No real harm done, except getting the wind knocked out of me—and my ego. Since no one was around to see my little tumble I'd just keep this incident to myself.

I tugged off my heels, flinging them as far as I could. Good riddance. Wishing I'd worn pants, I crawled across the grass, hiding behind a large electrical transformer.

After a few minutes, Marty came out of the office and paused to lock the door behind him.

Instead of driving the TBS truck into the garage as he was supposed to do, he worked quickly to unhitch the trailer.

Confusion rippled through me. He was supposed to unhitch the trailer *in* the garage. What was he doing?

Dread built in my stomach as he unlocked the trunk of

his Impala. I felt downright nauseated as he unloaded tools from his TBS truck and put them into the trunk of his car.

I watched in complete sadness as he put a scythe into his trunk and two metal rakes into the trailer. The trailer he obviously intended on taking with him. I just didn't understand it. He was entering his second year of college, fighting the statistics. Why screw it all up now?

The utility trailer was already almost full, filled with rakes, shovels, and a rototiller, but Marty made several trips to and from the garage, adding more equipment to his spoils.

I needed to put a stop to this. Now.

When he took the path that wound around the office, heading toward the storage barn, I scampered over to his car for a better look. Just to be sure.

Unfortunately, along with the tools I'd just seen him put in, some of the missing equipment was in his trunk too. And his bumper looked like it had just recently been fitted with a trailer hitch.

"Oh, Marty."

What would I say to him? How would he react? That thought gave me pause. Did I really want to confront him out here? Alone? He didn't strike me as the violent type, but then again, with his wholesome good looks, he didn't look like a rake robber, either.

I heard the cracking of wheels and panicked as Marty came around the corner pushing a spreader. I looked around, but there was no place to hide.

My gaze darted back to the pear trees. A good fifty yards. Panicked, I couldn't move, didn't even think to run until it was too late. The rhythmic sounds of the spreader came closer. Having no other choice, I eyed the trunk. It'd be a tight fit. But desperate times and all that.

I climbed in, cursing as my dress caught on a pair of snippers, and tore. I scrambled into the dark shadows in the far reaches of the cavernous trunk, out of the fading sunlight.

Trying to keep as still as possible, I listened as Marty wrestled the spreader onto the trailer. A few dozen curse words later, he apparently got the job done. He slammed the trailer gate closed.

I jumped at the sound, banging my head. I borrowed some of Marty's colorful adjectives. Hope he didn't mind.

Marty's trunk stank of loam and oil. I've smelled better, but I could think of worse, so I counted my blessings.

The roar of Marty's Taken by Surprise truck startled me, and I banged my head yet again. Sheesh, you'd think I was on edge or something. But I also recognized that this might be my only chance to make a run for it. It would take him a few minutes to park the truck in the garage on the other side of the lot.

Carefully, I tried to find some leverage. Just as I leaned forward, I realized that Marty was *backing* the truck into the garage. I was in plain view. I ducked backward, my dress ripping yet again.

Breathing hard, I struggled to think of what to do. How did I get myself into these things?

A few quick moments later, Marty's footsteps neared. Whistling filled the silent night. Hmmph. Glad he was so chipper, the pickax pilferer. Without warning, he slammed the trunk closed.

Blackness engulfed me.

The teeth of a hand cultivator bit into my bare leg as I wiggled, and I held back a yelp as the engine turned and caught.

Faint sounds of Barry Manilow floated in from the back seat. Barry Manilow?! Marty just didn't fit the thief bill. Nothing about his stealing from me made any sense whatsoever.

I fought back rising panic as Marty hitched his car to the trailer and drove off.

After a few stops and starts, we spent a lot of time at a high rate of speed. I passed the time by lip-synching to the music. We'd gone through "Mandy," "Weekend in New England," "Copacabana" (twice), and "Could This Be Magic" before the car slowed.

Marty lived in downtown Cincinnati, so I assumed that's where we were headed, though I'd made a lot of assumptions lately that had turned out like crap.

The car slowed to a stop and started again a moment later. Stop sign? Red light?

An interminable amount of time later, the car rolled to a halt. A door creaked opened, and the car rocked as it was slammed closed.

I held my breath as I waited.

And waited.

And waited.

What had possessed me to get into this trunk? This was precisely why I should mind my own business and let the police handle criminal matters. When faced with two choices, I always picked the wrong one.

If I'd just confronted Marty in the TBS parking lot—and not been chick-chick-chicken—I'd probably be safe at home right now, and not cuddling with a flat-nose shovel.

What if Marty didn't open the trunk tonight? What then? Why hadn't I thought of *that*? I patted my pockets, hoping I had my cell, but I didn't.

Of course.

I pushed on the back seat but it wouldn't budge.

I wasn't claustrophobic by nature, but without Barry's soothing voice, I felt those first stirrings of anxiety.

An image of a coffin jumped into my thoughts. My breaths came fast and shallow.

The air evaporated.

Could I die in here? Was there enough oxygen to sustain a hysterical woman?

I needed to get out. Now.

I kicked. I screamed. I clawed.

Using the flat nosed shovel, I banged on the trunk.

A second later, it popped open. An overhead streetlight illuminated several sets of heads as they peered in at me, but I recognized only one.

I scrambled over the tools, threw myself into Marty's arms.

His eyes widened as he caught me. "Nina?"

Locking my legs around him, I held on tight, still fighting panic.

One of the kids said, "Dang, man. What you doin' with a white girl in your trunk?"

Latching my arms around Marty's neck, I took deep gulps of the night air. My heart pounded in my ears.

Another kid, a born smart-ass, quipped, "You're s'posed to kill 'em first."

This got a huge laugh from the group of preteens gathered around the car. White teeth flashed bright against their dark skin.

"Knock it off," Marty told them, prying my legs from around his waist and setting me on the ground. Small bits of *something* dug into my bare feet. My knees wobbled.

He glanced between the trunk and the utility trailer, a guilty look on his face. "I can explain," he said.

Maybe he could, but I was in no mood to hear it. My hands were still shaking. Deep gulps of the night air didn't seem to be helping the tremors.

Compassion and sincerity shone bright in his eyes. He blinked innocently. "Please?"

"Really, Marty, I'm in no mood."

"What if I begged?"

Finally, finally, I stopped shaking. I groaned. "All right.

You can explain while you drive me back to the office." I just wanted to go home, and right now he was the fastest way I was getting there.

"You're the best, Nina."

"Yeah, yeah. Spare me."

Apprehension swept across his young features. "You're not going to tell Ana, are you?"

"Ana's the least of your worries." And that was saying a lot. I folded myself into the passenger seat, pressed the PLAY button on the Barry CD, and leaned my head against the cracked headrest. "This better be good, Marty."

Twenty-two

"A restoration project?" Ana's voice echoed across the line.

I pressed my cell to my ear with my shoulder as I started down Jaybird, heading home. It was near eleven and I was bone tired. "You should have seen it. It was beautiful."

Marty had driven by the old lot turned neighborhood garden before taking me back to the office. He'd explained that no one in the area had tools of their own, so he'd borrowed some of mine, with the intention of returning them all.

"Did he happen to mention why he didn't just ask for the tools?"

"Embarrassed. Young male pride is a powerful thing. He'd told his Boy Scout troop that he'd take care of all the details, but when it came down to it, he was broke. Spent all his money on uniforms for the kids, so they'd feel like a real troop."

"Gullible. That's what you are."

I stopped at a light. "Am not."

"I bet you volunteered something. What? To sponsor the troop?"

Actually, I'd volunteered Taken by Surprise to oversee any project the young scouts wanted to take on in the inner city, but I wasn't about to own up to it just so Ana could say she was right. Instead I said, "How'd it go with Jean-Claude?"

"Oh, he went straight home after dropping off the truck."

"What's that I hear in your voice?" Sounded a bit like giddiness.

"Static? Your battery dying?"

I checked it. "Yep. So talk fast."

"Well, I followed him home, hid in the bushes and peeked in his front window."

"And?"

"His brother caught me."

"No!"

"Yes." She giggled. "We have a date next week."

"Leave it to you."

"What?"

"Leave it to you!"

"Nina? I can't hear you!"

I shouted a final good-bye and snapped my phone closed. I couldn't wait to get home to bed. I was too tired to let intruders and runaway reptiles stop me from getting a good night's sleep.

I turned on the radio, then shut it off again. I was too filled with nervous energy to be calmed by music. Just after turning right onto Mockingbird, a pair of headlights appeared in my rearview mirror, the car moving quickly, trying to pass.

The hairs rose on the back of my neck and I shivered. I flipped on the heater. I slowed and pulled the wheel slightly to the right, giving the car more room.

I let out a small cry as the car came too close. I jerked hard to the left to correct, cutting the driver off.

The car was a compact with tinted windows. White. Small. A small white car. What had Mr. Cabrera said that day? A small white car with a skulker . . . Could it be the same?

The car eased back and I sped up. He was tailgating me. I thought of slamming on my brakes, but realized that there was no air bag in my ancient Corolla, and going through the windshield just didn't appeal to me.

Pressing my foot to the floor, I could feel my nerves jumping. A trickle of sweat ran down my temple. It tickled, but I didn't dare take my hands off the wheel to wipe it away.

Who could it be? Chanson? Someone he hired? Tim? A strange lunatic just out for cheap thrills?

Tim *had* known I was at the office—thanks to Bridget's phone call. Had he been lying in wait?

My tires squealed as I whipped around a corner. The white car stayed right behind me.

As far as I knew, Tim didn't drive a white car. But that didn't mean anything. He could have borrowed it, bought a cheap junker, stolen it.

My car bumped over some train tracks at a crossing on Knickerbocker. My transmission, I was sure, was going to fall out, but amazingly the car still ran.

My speedometer read 55. The speed limit posted on the side of the road said 35.

There was a stoplight ahead. It flashed from green to yellow and finally red. I slowed ever so slightly, checked for cars, then ran the red light. I was just chalking up the violations.

I slowed at another intersection. Suddenly, I flew forward, my chest ramming into the steering wheel as I was hit from behind. I glanced up and saw the car backing up. Leaving?

Reaching out, I fumbled for my phone, punched in 9-1-1 before realizing the battery was dead.

As I heard an engine rev, I panicked. He wasn't leaving; he was gathering speed to hit me again!

My bare foot stomped on the gas pedal and my tires

screeched. I fishtailed but managed to gain control of the car. I needed to lose the lunatic. I could think of only one sure way to get him to leave me alone. I banged a U-ey, making a wide arc around my pursuer as I headed toward the police station.

As I passed by the car, I saw nothing. The tinted windows blocked any view of a face. I didn't have time to dwell on who it might be in the car—I just wanted to get to safety at this point.

My sweat-dampened dress stuck to me. My hands turned clammy as I gripped the wheel. The car made a U-turn too, closed in on me. It was so close I couldn't see the head-lights—or had he broken them when he crashed into me a few minutes ago?

I lurched forward as he hit me again. I didn't slow as I ran yet another red light at the intersection I had crossed through only moments before. I just prayed that no one else was coming.

I heard a loud *thunk* as I went over a pothole. In my side mirror, I saw my hubcap roll away.

My Corolla felt sluggish as I stepped on the gas. The white car was still behind me, but it too had slowed. When I looked ahead, two red lights, side by side, were blinking.

My heart skidded to a stop.

Blink, blink.

"Oh-no. Oh-no." A shiver swept down my spine. I let up on the gas. My luck had just run out.

The railroad gates lowered. I heard the train's whistle in the distance. If I didn't get out of there I was a goner.

Making a sudden decision, I stepped on the gas. Pressing the pedal to the floorboard, I hoped to get around the gates in time.

My car wobbled.

The pothole must have given me a flat! No, no! This wasn't happening.

I would not allow something so trivial as a flat tire to be my downfall. I rode the rim, hoping to make it over the tracks. It was my only hope.

Crossing over the safety line, I sped up only to skid to a stop before I reached the tracks when I saw the headlights of the train coming right at me.

I checked my rearview mirror. Big mistake. I screamed, my voice garbled and choked, as the white car rammed me from behind. My car jerked forward. I felt my front tires bump over the first railroad track.

I pressed the gas pedal. My tires spun, permeating the air with the smell of burning rubber.

The train's engineer must have seen me, because the whistle blew continuously. The train's brakes screeched. My ears hurt.

I threw the car into reverse and stepped on the accelerator. I was fighting a losing battle. The white car pushed me into the path of the train, nudging me farther onto the tracks.

The brakes on the train were deafening. I looked to my left and the lights on the train blinded me. It was maybe a few hundred feet away. Horrible screeching filled the air. Sparks flew everywhere.

I threw the door open, scrambled out. Dove forward, somersaulting away from the tracks. I hit my head on the pavement, but my hiney took the brunt of my rolling fall.

I heard the sickening crunch of metal on metal and glass shattering. My vision blurred and white spots danced in my eyes as the brakes screamed. Then I heard nothing at all.

Twenty-three

"Stop scratching."

"But it itches," I said with a hint of a whine in my voice. Okay, maybe more than a hint. All right, all right. I was whining.

"But it won't heal if you keep scratching it," Analise said, brushing my hand away from the big gash arcing across my forehead.

I growled. If I was itchy then I wanted to scratch! Infection be damned. When Ana slipped into the kitchen to get me water, I pressed my face against my pillow and rubbed.

"I hear that," she said.

"I itch!"

She tossed a wet washcloth onto the couch. "Press that to it."

"You're not supposed to get stitches wet."

"You're not supposed to scratch them either!"

I pouted. "You're cranky."

She threw her hands in the air. "And you're a fine one to talk!"

I made a lousy patient. I hated being cooped up. The hospital had kept me there for a whole day, for observation. Apparently I observed well, because they let me go late Saturday night. Thanks to a few pain pills, I had slept that night, and all of Sunday away too. Now Monday morning was nearly over, and had seemed impossibly long.

"Kevin's still waiting to talk to you."

I had put off talking to him. He'd made an appearance with Riley at the hospital, but he hadn't said much to me other than pleasantries. The doctors said to take as much time as I needed before talking to the police, and I had done just that.

Unclenching my jaw, I forced myself to relax. I didn't remember much about the crash. I must have passed out when the train hit the car. But I remembered with startling clarity all the details leading up to the accident.

Luckily, I wasn't seriously hurt. I had vaulted far enough off the tracks to avoid serious injury from flying debris. It could have been, as everyone who'd entered my hospital room told me, a lot worse. I broke my pinkie finger (I still don't know how), bruised my tailbone, and I had a cut that needed six stitches along my forehead from flying glass. My Corolla, sorry to report, was mortally wounded in the attack. There were no funeral plans at this time.

"You can't keep putting him off," Ana said, breaking into my thoughts. "He needs to investigate the accident. Someone tried to kill you."

As if I needed to be reminded. Everyone, from my mother (who tried desperately to find a way to pin this on Ana) to Mr. Cabrera, had been telling me so. To add to my pain, Mr. Cabrera had brought Ursula Krauss with him to visit me. I'd spent thirty torturous minutes with her clucking over me.

"Just a few more hours, Ana?"

"I'm afraid not," Kevin said from the doorway.

I jumped, not having heard him come in.

"I'll be in the kitchen." Ana brushed past Kevin without saying a word to him.

I pretended a great interest in the weaving on the throw blanket my mother had brought me.

"I know you're tired, Nina. I'll try to make this as fast as possible. The obvious question is, Do you remember any more about who might have done this to you?" Kevin's voice was soft, kind. I almost didn't recognize it. He stood next to the couch, a small notebook in one hand, a pen in the other. His wide shoulders were hunched just a bit as if he were very tired. He wore his standard on-duty outfit. A long-sleeved button-up shirt, a loose necktie that didn't match his shirt, a suit coat, and jeans. Pressed jeans. If you asked me, pressed jeans were unnatural. Talk about anal. But then again, no one asked my opinion.

"No."

"Did you get a *look* at who did this?"

I scratched at my stitches.

"That will make it worse," Kevin said.

I swore under my breath and dropped my hand. "A small white car. Tinted windows. I didn't see a plate. It was too dark to make out the driver." My tone said, *Now go away*.

He made no move to leave.

Damn.

He made some marks in his notebook. I knew he wasn't writing anything down. The notebook was for show. He had an amazing memory and rarely needed notes. "Can you tell me when you first noticed that someone was tailing you?"

"I was on Mockingbird, coming home from work. Didn't think anything of it. Traffic wasn't heavy, but there was nothing unusual in having a car a few lengths behind me."

"Then?" Kevin asked.

"Then I looked up again and the car was on top of me. I thought he was going to pass. He almost sideswiped me. I cut him off. It was stupid, but I wanted to see who it was."

I studied my fingernails. They were short, stubby, cracked. My pinkie finger was swathed in a bandage that somehow connected to my ring finger and wrist for support. It looked ridiculous.

"I sped up. He sped up."

"He?"

"I assume. I couldn't see anything."

"Why didn't you pull into a well-lit parking lot?"

I gave him an "Oh, please" look. "You've been on Knickerbocker. You tell me where I could have pulled over."

"Cranky," he muttered.

I growled. "I was heading to the police station when the train's gates came down. I tried to go around, but the train was too close. Then the white car bumped me onto the tracks. I got stuck. The rest you know."

Kevin's eyesbrows furrowed into a deep *V*. When he did that, he almost looked like he had a unibrow, with an odd resemblance to Bert from *Sesame Street*. The unibrow, the oblong face, the short spiky hair. I bit back a laugh and wondered exactly how much pain medicine I was taking.

"Is that all?" I asked.

"No."

"We need to finish our conversation from Friday night, about Demming."

"Now?"

"Why not?"

"I'm tired."

"Nina."

"Kevin."

His eyes softened. "All right. I'll come back tomorrow." He gazed down at me. "Stay out of trouble."

I bit back my usual "Don't I always" comeback. It just didn't ring true anymore.

He stood by the door. "I just wanted to say that I'm—"

Ana stuck her head in the room. "Almost lunchtime." She looked at Kevin. "You staying?"

"No," he said, not looking at me. "I was just leaving." He closed the front door on his way out.

Not a second later, a soft knock sounded.

Ana tugged open the door and Bridget's head poked in. "Are we interrupting?" Tim stood behind her.

"Not at all," Ana said, guiding them in.

Tim produced a bouquet of daisies with a flourish. "Straight from my mom's field. She sends her best."

I managed a halfhearted thank-you, but couldn't manage to look Tim in the eyes. Suddenly, I wished Kevin had stayed. I couldn't deal with this anymore. The police needed to be told. Everything. Including my suspicions about Tim.

Ana hooked a thumb over her shoulder. "I'll be in the kitchen."

Bridget said, "Mom's worried about you. Feels responsible."

I shook my head, ignored the ache. "Nonsense."

Tears clouded Bridget's eyes. "I'm feeling responsible too."

Words lodged in my throat, but I forced them out. "This could have nothing to do with any of you."

"Did stuff like this happen to you often before you started investigating my dad's death?" Tim asked.

Oh, all the time. I still couldn't look at him, never mind answer him.

"Look, Nina," Bridget said, perching on the edge of the couch, "you need to stop looking into this mess." Gruffness edged her voice.

Tim nodded, hovering over us. "It's obvious you ruffled some feathers."

I bit back an accusation. "I'm fine."

Bridget gasped. "You were almost killed by a train!" Not many ways to argue with that. "Nina!" She took hold of my hand. "You've got to stop. This is too dangerous." She stood, paced, froze.

I didn't think they'd leave unless I agreed. "Fine, fine. I'll stop," I lied.

Bridget sighed, long and heavy. "Thank heavens. I can't even tell you how worried we were about you."

I put on a brave smile. "Sorry I couldn't be of more help."

Tim said, "All that matters is that you're okay." He turned to Bridget. "We should go. Let Nina rest."

My gaze shot to Bridget. "Can I talk to you for a minute? Alone?"

Tim looked none too pleased by the prospect, but didn't protest. "I'll wait in the car."

Locking her arms, Bridget lowered herself onto the couch beside me. "What is it, Nina?"

Unsure how to say what I was thinking, I worried my lip. Finally, I said, "It's about Tim."

"Tim?"

Pots clanged in the kitchen. Ana was supposed to be making soup, but I figured she was eavesdropping for sure.

Bridget waited expectantly. Geez, this wasn't going to be easy. "He was awfully adamant I stop investigating."

"He's worried. About his mom, me, you."

"Is he?"

Her pale eyebrows snapped together. "What's that supposed to mean?"

I sat straighter, came right out with it. "It means he's a man with a motive. He needs money—"

Without effort, Bridget surged to her feet. Two angry spots of color dotted her cheeks. "How dare you? How could you even *think* such a thing? There isn't a more decent man around."

"Bridget—"

She put up her hand, palm out, the other resting on her extended belly. "No. I don't want to hear any more. I'm disgusted with you." Pivoting, she headed for the door, jerked it open and slammed it behind her.

Ana stuck her head in the room. "Yikes."

I stared at the still shaking door. "That didn't go so well."

The corner of Ana's lip hitched up in a half smile. "You don't say."

Even with Bridget's stinging rebuke still buzzing in my ears, I couldn't rid my suspicions of Tim altogether—although they had been somewhat tempered by Bridget's reaction.

I picked up the cordless phone, punched in the office number. The voice of Queen Elizabeth rang in my ear. "Taken by Surprise, this is Tam."

"Tam, it's Nina."

She gasped. "Holy hell, how are you?"

"Fine, fine. Thanks for the gift."

The gang had all pitched in and bought me a pillow to sit on, the smart-asses they were.

We chitchatted for a few minutes before she mentioned that all the missing tools had turned up over the weekend. I acted all surprised, but she didn't buy it for a moment.

"You're not going to tell who it was, are you?"

"Who was what?"

She tried prying for a few more minutes before giving in. After answering a battery of questions about the accident, I got to the reason I called. "I have a huge favor to ask you."

"Anything."

I leaned back against the sofa cushions. "It's illegal."

She laughed. "Never stopped me before. What do you want me to do?"

Sometimes having felons on the payroll was a good thing. Like when one of them used to be a professional hacker.

"I'd like you to look into an Internet account. E-mails, web traffic, that sort of thing. And bank records if you can get them too."

Rustling echoed over the line. "Give me the addresses and I'll get right to it."

I gave her Bridget and Tim's full names, then rattled off

Bridget's e-mail address. "I don't know if that's the only account. Her husband might have e-mail of his own. He's the one I really want to know about."

"If he's got one, I'll find it. Anything in particular I'm looking for?"

I couldn't say. "Just anything that strikes you as odd."

"That's many, many things, Nina."

Smiling, I said, "I appreciate this, Tam, more than you can know."

"Just get better soon. We miss you around here."

After hanging up, I stared up at the ceiling unable to shake the feeling that the police needed to be called ASAP. But I decided I'd wait to see what Tam learned before going to Kevin.

That much I owed Bridget.

I just prayed that Tam found nothing. Nothing at all.

Twenty-four

By mid-afternoon, after doing my best to swallow scorched soup, I was not only starving but also going stir-crazy. I wasn't one to be kept prone for so long.

Ana had issued death threats, though, if I tried to escape, so I was housebound. At least for the time being.

Peeking out the window, I saw Mr. Cabrera watering his petunias. They were large petunias, bright purple that circled his maple tree in his front yard. By the look of the small river than ran into the street, he'd been working on that spot for some time. I wondered if it had anything to do with his unfettered view of the front of my house.

A van rumbled into my driveway. I squinted and made out Riley in the front seat with his newest friend—the Skinz with the metal spiked dog collar. As I watched, they both got out of the van and walked toward the front porch. I dropped to the floor so they wouldn't notice me spying.

Mr. Cabrera, ever so casually, turned his hose to water the grass near my porch. I smiled at his blatant nosiness. A man after my own heart.

On my hands and knees, I listened.

Ry and Spike must have been sitting on the porch swing, or somewhere close by, because their voices easily carried in through the window.

"I don't know, man."

That was Riley. He sounded strange. Sort of cocky, yet afraid. I didn't know what to make of it.

"You need one."

One what? What was Spike talking about?

"When can I get one?" Riley asked.

Lifting my head, I peeped out the window. Spike was sitting on the swing, and Riley was leaning against the porch column, his arms crossed. Spike was smoking. I wanted to go out and snatch the cigarette out of his mouth, warn him about the risk of cancer, but I also wanted to hear what they were talking about.

"Tomorrow," Spike said.

"When?"

Spike scratched his chin. "Let's say two."

Let's not, I wanted to shout out the window.

"Man, if I cut class again, I'm dead."

Damn right! *That's the way to tell him, Ry.*

"You gonna let that woman tell you what to do?"

Hmmph. I took exception to the way he said "woman"— as if I were the lowest form of scum.

"You're not the one who's gonna have her handcuffed to you if you skip."

"She's lying."

I shook my head. Don't fall for it, Ry. I really didn't want to relive my high school days, but I would—to make a point.

"I don't know," Riley said again. "She came to detention."

Spike stood. "Look, I thought you were cool, but maybe I was wrong."

Go away, I silently urged.

He took a step off the porch.

I cringed as Riley said, "Wait!"

Oh, so close!

"Where?" Riley asked.

I whimpered as I tried to recall algebraic formulas. Tagging along with Riley in class didn't mean I had to do the work too, did it?

Spike grinned. "Here."

Riley looked panicked. "No way."

"Your mom won't even be home."

"Still . . ."

"Look," Spike said, the sun glinting off his collar, "you in or you out?"

Riley shifted foot to foot. "In. Two o'clock. Here."

"Yeah."

"And you'll bring it with you?"

"If you've got the cash," Spike said.

"I have it."

"Then I'll bring a selection. We're good to go."

Riley walked with the kid to his van. Ana came in from the kitchen and saw me sitting on the floor under a window.

"What are you doing off the couch? The doctor said to rest."

I had to grin. No mention of why I was on the floor—only that I was up and around.

"I needed a change of scenery."

She folded her arms across her chest, tapped her foot. "Lie the other way on the sofa."

I placed my hands on the floor to lever myself out of a sitting position. The door flew open.

Riley looked down at me. "What are you doing?"

"Looking for a contact?"

"You don't wear contacts."

"No wonder I can't find it."

"Don't mind her," Ana said. "She's taking some strong medicine."

Riley stared. I wanted to believe that he found my stitches fascinating, but I adhered to my commandment not to delude myself. Ana helped me up.

Riley looked at Ana. "Any sign of Xena yet?"

Ana shook her head.

A mischievous gleam appeared in his blue eyes. "She's probably getting hungry by now." He eyed my bare feet. "She might mistake toes for mice." And with that he ran up the stairs to his room.

The little bugger.

Twenty-five

I'd made a deal with the devil.

I needed to speak with Chanson, and he'd made it quite clear that the only way he'd speak to me again was if I agreed to a TBS makeover as a gift for his wife.

Which explained why I was—technically, on my day off—on my way to meet with the congressman at his quasi mansion in Vista View.

The early-morning sun was annoyingly bright as I wrestled with Mr. Cabrera's steering wheel. Since my car was at the giant Toyota factory in the sky, and my TBS truck was at TBS, I'd had to suck up to Mr. Cabrera to get him to loan me his for a bit.

It hadn't taken much to convince him to let me borrow the car, seeing as how he was deliriously happy with Mrs. Krauss, and my unsubtle reminder that I had played matchmaker had paved the way.

Well, that, and I had to promise to return the car with a full tank of gas.

So here I was. Cruising down Liberty driving a tank.

And the car was a tank, make no mistake about that. What I found particularly charming, though, was Mr. Cabrera's attempt to make the car look homey. The bench seat had a faded yellow afghan thrown over it. A little sprig of greenery sat on the cracked dashboard and two entwined hearts made from grapevine hung from the rearview mirror.

Amazingly my headache had vanished after a good night's sleep. The pain in my, uh, rear didn't feel nearly as bad as it had yesterday, but my face looked like I'd run smack-dab into . . . well, a train.

Somehow I'd managed to talk Ana into going back to work. Her mothering was killing me. Well, it was either the mothering or the soup—I wasn't sure which, but I knew both needed to go.

With a wince, I thought of the case of Almond Joys I received bright and early this morning along with a sweet letter from Robert MacKenna wishing me well. I wasn't even going to go down that road. I'd write a polite thank-you note, eat the chocolate, and that would be the end of that.

I hoped.

I rolled past the construction workers who were still hard at work on the Vista View gatehouse. Following the directions the congressman gave me, I drove down the beautifully landscaped streets, wondering who had done the work.

Trees dotted the sidewalks and canopied the street. The lawns were exceptionally well-kept, and flowers, everything from geraniums to petunias, were bright and cheery.

The tank clipped the curb as I pulled to a stop in front of Chanson's house. The LeMans continued to rumble even after I removed the key from the ignition, and slammed the door closed.

If I could absolutely rule out Chanson as a suspect, then I knew my suspicions about Tim might very well be true.

With my Polaroid, measuring wheel, sketch pad, and pencil, I headed up to the house.

It was a lot like the man himself—somewhat feminine, its stucco painted a soft pink, its trim a light turquoise. The Floridian colors somehow worked with this particular house.

Chanson pulled open the door as I climbed the tiled steps, his smile fading as I came nearer.

He clucked at me, much as Mrs. Krauss would have.

I fought back a growl.

"Ms. Quinn, you must really try to avoid collisions with locomotives. Your poor complexion."

I ponied up my own fake sincerity to match his. "I'm touched you care."

He smiled, led me into the house.

The decor had obviously been done by an interior designer, keeping with the South Beach style. An open floor plan, bright pastels, and colorful floor tile.

He escorted me through the double doors opening into the backyard. Remarkably, considering how squished these houses were to one another, there was complete privacy.

A tall line of conifers rimmed the perimeter of the yard. A small in-ground pool hogged most of the space, but there were pockets of land just begging for a little TLC.

Why I was really there nagged at me while I took a few pictures, sketched a little bit. We made small talk about what he was looking for (something romantic), how much he was willing to spend (a lot—which I planned to charge, except for my own labor), and his wife's tastes (tropical).

Finally, when I had a good vision in mind of what he wanted—a Caribbean honeymoon (which was enough to make my stomach protest)—I turned to face him, hoping that facing him straight on wouldn't send him running in fear.

Truthfully, I had scared myself when I looked in the mirror that morning.

I didn't have a lot of time to beat around the bush, with Riley's meeting with Spike just a few hours away, so I cut to the chase.

"I saw you and John Demming together that day I was in your office. You told him that everything 'would soon be taken care of,' or words to that effect, and told him not to worry. You were talking about Sandowski's Farm, right?"

He pulled out a patio chair, offered it to me. Reluctantly, I sat.

Chanson lowered himself into the chair across from me, steepled his hands under his chin. "Yes."

I was so shocked that he admitted it, I think I gasped.

He laughed.

I guessed that proved I did gasp.

"You're surprised?"

"Frankly, yes."

The pool filter kicked on, filling the air with a soft humming. "I have nothing to hide."

I sincerely doubted that. "That's easy enough to say with Demming dead. No one to corroborate your story."

"I don't know what you're trying to say, Ms. Quinn, but I don't think I like it." Even angry, he still looked peaceful, serene.

Tapping my pencil on my sketch pad, I said, "Do you deny being behind the acts plaguing the Sandowski family?"

His eyebrows dipped quizzically. Man, he was good. I almost believed that he didn't know what I was talking about. "Acts?"

"The sheep, the dog, the fire, Joe's death?"

"I don't have a clue as to what you are referring. I think I told you that the last time we spoke."

"Sure."

"I really don't," he said, leaning forward. "Has someone been harassing the family?"

My inner self told me to tell him. I opened my mouth and shut it again. He was behind this. I was sure of it.

Wasn't I?

Those nagging suspicions about Tim resurfaced with a resounding *whoosh*. "Why would you have had that conversation with Demming the other day if you're innocent?"

"He's a concerned constituent.

My inner self believed him, and I was inclined to agree, which surprised the hell out of me considering I hardly ever agreed with anything my inner self had to say. With a start, I realized I had subconsciously judged the congressman before I even showed up today. I'd come here for confirmation of my theories and to get a few answers to lingering questions.

"Demming didn't call you, asking about me? Trying to put my name to my face? He saw me in the outer room the other day . . ."

"He may have seen you, but he never called me asking who you were."

Taking a deep breath, I tried to work my way through that information. It didn't make sense. If Chanson didn't tell him who I was, then who did?

Again, Tim's name popped into my head. I'd told Bridget about my meeting with Demming. It seemed a reasonable leap that she'd share that bit of information with her husband. And if Tim and Demming were in cahoots, it would have been a simple phone call from Tim to the developer to rat me out.

And he'd known about my working late last Friday night. Had it been him in that white car? Something Bridget said also came back to me, about Joe's cremation. Had he really wanted to be cremated, or had Tim just said that to cover up his crime?

My stomach turned just thinking about Tim being involved with all this. And some of it just didn't make sense. Like why was Demming dead?

Chanson leaned back in his chair, folded his hands under his chin. "Since you seem to think I'm evil incarnate, I'll tell you everything I know about the Sandowskis."

"Please do." Maybe some of it would make sense to me,

because as of that moment I was lost, with too many questions and not enough answers.

"My investors and I made a second offer. Six point five million. I'm a businessman, Ms. Quinn. I know a good deal when I see one."

"But?"

He shrugged. I couldn't believe Mr. Perfect could pull off such a common gesture. "Still said no."

"Mrs. Sandowski said she hasn't seen you since the initial offer."

"The offer was in writing, as was the refusal."

It was enough to make my head pound. "So what did you mean when you told Demming that everything would be taken care of?"

"Just what I meant."

Wearily, I muttered, "Do I have to beg?"

Tossing his head back, he laughed. "I really like you, Nina Quinn," he said.

"I'm touched. Truly."

He smiled. "Initial paperwork is being completed for the county to seize the property."

Outrage tinged my words as I shot forward, gripping the patio table. "You can do that?"

"Eminent Domain. Ever heard of it?"

Unfortunately. I frowned.

"Anything's possible with the government, Ms. Quinn. Mrs. Sandowski will be compensated—the current market rate for that house and land."

"Which is?"

"About a million dollars."

Instead of six million. "That's crazy!"

"The county doesn't place much weight on exact location in the market analysis."

"It's got to be illegal."

"I assure you it's not."

"Does Mrs. Sandowski know?" She couldn't possibly.

"Of course. She had to have been notified."

I shook my head in frustration. "Mrs. Sandowski said nothing about it."

"The county would have sent papers to her. But I did have my secretary draw up a renewal of my offer to buy her land, mentioning Eminent Domain procedures as a possibility if she chose to stay. She could still sell to me instead of going through the courts to battle the state government."

"Why?" I asked. "Why not wait and buy the land after the eminent domain is executed?"

"Red tape," he said. "It would have been easier to buy the land ourselves as investors and then sell, or even better— donate—some of the land to the town in order to connect Liberty Avenue to Millson."

"Leaving you the rest of the land." Land worth a small fortune, land he could turn around and sell, part and parcel to the John Demmings of Freedom, Ohio.

"Exactly."

His words rang true. I saw no hint of deception in his face, and more important, my eyebrows hadn't so much as twitched. Why hadn't Mrs. Sandowski mentioned this to me? She had to have known. Why lie?

"Does that hurt?" he asked, rubbing a finger over his own forehead.

I gently touched the gash over my left eyebrow. My stitches looked hideous, like small spiders nesting. But I was grateful to be alive. Somewhat. "Not so much anymore. They itch."

"Well, don't scratch. They'll become infected."

Twenty-six

My cat clock meowed eleven times. Eleven A.M. Riley was due to meet the Skinz leader at two. I didn't dare call Kevin to tell him about the meeting because he'd only laugh and tell me I was being paranoid. But something was going down, and I planned on being there when it did.

What was Riley buying? Guns? I shuddered at the thought.

I sat atop the kitchen counter, staring at the swinging cat tail on the clock. I had called the school, and Riley *was* in class . . . As far as they knew. I asked to talk to Michael Novak, but he couldn't be found. Something big was going on—I could feel it in my bones, even my broken pinkie. Was Kevin blind to that fact?

The doorbell rang and I abandoned my perch to answer it.

Dave Mein stood on the porch, clutching a handful of pitiful-looking carnations. He thrust them forward. "Jesus, Bo-bina. I heard about your accident."

"Glad a train wreck could spur you into action."

It was such a beautiful day, I motioned him to the porch swing.

"Not the guilt, Bo-bina. I can't take it." He clutched his heart, gave me big puppy-dog eyes.

"Sit," I said. I set the carnations down next to me.

The swing swayed and creaked as we parked ourselves. "I should have come sooner. I know I should have." He winced as he took in my face, but I tried not to take it personally. "But I was scared I'd lose my job."

"Is this about Joe's death?"

He nodded, dragging a hand down his face, over the stubble. "There's a lot of pressure to keep things quiet. Lawsuits and shit. The town is scared spitless."

"Why?"

"The day of the . . . incident, Alan Kwellen and I made the run to the farm." The swing groaned loudly under our weight. "Old Joe had been dead for some time. An hour, maybe two. Looked like hell, his color all messed up. I honestly thought it was the cancer. Mrs. Sandowski had told us all about his illness when we arrived. We thought it was just a simple transport."

Mr. Cabrera suddenly felt the need to deweedicate his front yard of clover. I gave the old man a wave.

"Understandable. Why all the hush-hush though?"

"I screwed up. Didn't take a good look around."

"Why would you, when you thought it was natural causes?"

Thick hands rested in his lap. "Old people with terminal illnesses sometimes like to wrap it up early."

"Suicide?"

He nodded. The phone rang inside the house. "You gonna get that?" he asked.

"The machine's on."

As we swung, Dave explained that if the thermos were found and proven to contain cyanide, Dave, along with the department, could be sued.

"I take full responsibility, but it's out of my hands. I've got strict orders to keep my mouth shut, Bo-bina. Or risk losing my job."

I imagined him out of work, his three kids not having enough to eat. "I won't say anything." I remembered what Bridget has said about the analysis she and Tim had done being useless. As it stood, with the thermos missing, there would be no repercussions. "It's not likely that thermos is going to turn up."

"You don't think?"

I shook my head. If Tim was behind the incidents at his family's farm, he'd have tracked that thermos down before it could have been analyzed, made sure no one could trace it back to him.

Just to be absolutely sure, I asked, "So you don't think Chanson could be involved in a cover-up?"

"Chanson? No, not at all." He pressed a noisy kiss to my cheek. "Thanks, Nina. And sorry I didn't come sooner."

"Better late than never, Dave."

I sighed, thinking about Tim and how I was going to deal with the information I'd been given. And could only come up with one answer.

Kevin.

I saw Dave off and wandered back inside.

I picked up the kitchen phone, punched in a familiar number. The blinking light on the answering machine teased me. Another hang-up?

"Freedom PD."

I asked to be put through to Kevin.

"He's not here, Nina. Out in the field."

"For how long?" The uneasy feeling that time was running out had settled low in my stomach.

"All day as far as I know."

"If he checks in, will you have him call me?"

"Will do."

Nagging questions twisted my insides. I called Bridget at

home. A busy signal buzzed my ear. I tried her office number but no one answered and her cell phone immediately clicked over to voice mail. I left a message asking her to get back to me.

I pushed the button on the answering machine. It was Chanson. "Ms. Quinn, I thought of something after you left and was just able to confirm it through my secretary. The second offer on the Sandowski land and the eminent domain paperwork had been sent to the Sandowski attorney." There was a question in his tone. "Perhaps Mrs. Sandowski does not know of them? In which case she needs to fire her lawyer and contact me as soon as possible if she's reconsidered selling. I hope the information helps."

Help? Help? No. It only served to confuse me more. Was Tim Mrs. Sandowski's attorney? If he was, wouldn't he want his mom to know about the eminent domain? Wouldn't that push her to accept a lucrative offer?

I jumped when the phone rang. I was on edge. My nerves were shot. Grabbing the phone on the second ring, I answered with a terse hello. I berated myself for forgetting to buy a phone with a Caller ID window. What was I paying the phone company an extra eight dollars a month for?

"Nina?"

It was a woman. A very upset woman. "Yes. Who's this?"

"Mrs. Sandowski—Timmy's mom?"

"What's wrong?" It was clear she was crying.

"I'm at the hospital."

"Oh no! What's happened?"

"Someone shot out my kitchen window," she said on a sob. "Didn't hit me, but the broken glass cut me up some."

I stood in stunned silence for a minute. "Are you okay?" I clunked my head against the wall. *Obviously not, Nina, if she's in the hospital.*

"I can't get hold of Timmy or Bridget," she cried. "Their home phone is busy—he's probably on the computer. I can't think of anyone else to call. Can you go there?"

I eyed the clock warily. Twenty past eleven. Plenty of time to check in on Tim and still see what Riley was up to. "I'll head there now."

"Thanks, Nina. For everything."

Humbly, I swallowed any response to that and hung up. I didn't think she'd be thanking me after my suspicions about Tim came to light.

I grabbed my backpack and headed for the door. The phone rang as I reached for the knob. I hesitated, wondering if I should answer it.

Then I saw her.

Coiled by the couch, Xena appeared to be looking at me. Staring. I swallowed. What had Riley said about toes? I looked down. My Keds were safely tied, protecting my tootsies.

I really hoped it was Pesky Pests calling to say they were on their way, but I didn't dare cross Xena's path to answer it.

The answering machine kicked on. I stood frozen in the doorway as Tam left a message.

"Nina, it's Tam. I need you to call me right away. I definitely found some odd information—even for my standards. Get back to me as soon as possible."

Xena slithered sideways. There was no way I was going back in there. I'd just have to call Tam from the car.

Twenty-seven

It took me about five minutes to realize that calling from the car was impossible. My phone had been smashed beneath the train. My leather backpack had survived the wreck relatively unscathed, but the phone would chirp no more . . .

Tam would have to wait.

The LeMans rattled as I drove like a madwoman toward the heart of downtown Cincinnati. I kept reminding myself that I had to keep an open mind about Tim. I'd found no evidence at all linking him to his father's death—or Demming's either. It was just a feeling I had. A sickening one. One I would push aside for now. Mrs. Sandowski needed me to find Tim or Bridget for her. It was the least I could do.

But I couldn't help but hope it was Bridget who answered the door when I got there, despite the fact that she's probably at work.

Taking the Vine Street exit off 75, I turned east, heading toward Bridget's house. I passed the left-hand turn for the zoo and Children's Hospital and kept going.

I pulled into the driveway in front of the old wooden garage and cut the engine. Mr. Cabrera's car shook for a minute, then quieted.

I ran as fast as my tailbone would allow up the front steps

and knocked on the door of the Victorian. I crossed my arms in front of me, fighting a chill, despite the warmth in the air. I rang the bell. No answer.

After knocking for five long minutes, I walked around the back of the house, through the ankle-high grass and weeds. The patio doors were locked. I peered in the rear windows, saw the computer unmanned. No one was home.

I walked back around to the driveway, not wanting to believe what I was thinking. Tim couldn't possibly have had anything to do with what was going on. I was sure of it.

But it seemed to me I'd been sure of a lot of things lately that weren't true.

I turned to get into the LeMans when a shaft of sunlight coming out of the garage caught my eye—sunlight glinting off the rear bumper of the car inside. I'd seen it a few days ago, but hadn't thought much of it. Not until I'd almost been run off the road.

One of the garage doors was unhinged, the wood cracked. I tugged on the handle and the door lifted with a groan. It hung at an unsafe angle above my head. Dust filled the sunlit air of the stale-smelling garage. I could see a bumper and an almost flat tire partially covered by a battered tarp.

I picked my way over typical garage debris. Rakes and shovels and such.

The back of my neck felt electrically charged. I stood in front of the covered car, somehow knowing what I would find beneath the cover and yet not wanting to know for certain.

Do it, my inner voice urged.

I was too upset to defy it, so I grabbed a corner of the tarp and pulled.

It was black. The car was black. I slumped in relief, leaning on its trunk. It was a small car with tinted windows. But it was small and black, not white.

How could I have not trusted Tim? He would never try to hurt me. Or his father—or mother for that matter. I laughed at the absurdity of it. Someone else had to be behind everything. If not Chanson, then another developer. One the police would have to flush out, because I couldn't deal with this anymore.

I checked my watch. 1:04. Riley. I needed to leave.

Rushing to replace the tarp, I pulled it over the back of the car, where I was standing, and moved to cover the front. I nearly tripped in my haste. I wanted to be out of there before Tim and Bridget came home and found me snooping in their garage. How would I ever explain this?

I tossed the other end of the tarp across the windshield.

Suddenly, I froze.

I had crossed in front of the car where I saw that the front end was smashed. The grille was dented, the headlights broken.

I let out an involuntary cry and covered my mouth.

This wasn't happening.

I pinched myself and yelped, my voice echoing through the garage. Apparently, this *was* happening.

Looking at the right side of the car, I saw that the quickie paint job hadn't covered the damage inflicted by ramming my car. The front right fender was severely dented and scraped as well, white paint showing through the thin layer of black.

I didn't bother covering up the rest of the car. Backtracking out of the garage, I pushed the door shut and ran to the LeMans.

It was Tim. The whole time, it had been Tim. What a fool I had been to think otherwise, when my instincts had known all along! I reversed out of the driveway. I needed to find Riley, and then I was going straight to the police station.

Had Tim really killed his father, shot at his mother? Killed Demming?

Oh God. Oh God. He had.

I banged my head against the back of the seat. I was so incredibly, stupidly blind.

Demming must have contacted Tim, convinced him to help get his parents to sell. Tim was Demming's partner in crime. But why kill Demming?

And Chanson's offer? And the Eminent Domain? If Chanson had sent those offers to Tim, if Tim was acting as his mother's lawyer . . . It made sense. He simply hadn't told his mother of them, hoping she'd sell before they became an issue.

But I wasn't sure. Couldn't be sure until I knew for a fact Tim was his mother's lawyer.

Eying the street, I spotted a pay phone in a Walgreen's lot and pulled in. It took some time and many quarters, but I finally got hold of Mrs. Sandowski in the ER.

I didn't have time to beat around the bush. "Is Tim your lawyer?"

"What?"

"Is Tim your lawyer?" I asked, louder.

"Actually, no. Bridget is. Do you want to talk to Timmy? He's here. I got ahold of him after I called you. I called you back but you'd already left."

I sucked in a deep breath, fighting a sudden wave of nausea. The knuckles on my hand were white from gripping the metal cord. "No."

Twenty-eight

I parked in Mr. Cabrera's driveway, tossed him the keys as he pretended to weed his garden, and ran up the steps to the house two at a time.

It was 1:45. Riley was due any minute.

The wooden porch steps creaked as I bounded up them. First things first: Call Kevin, I told myself. I had tried to get ahold of him after I spoke to Mrs. Sandowski, but he was still out in the field. It was just like him to disappear when I needed him most.

I threw open my front door and froze mid-step, nearly tumbling face forward onto the floor.

Bridget was sitting on the couch, pointing a gun at my chest.

"Bridget?" I had to ask to be sure. Her stomach was now flat, not even a love handle. The possibility of an evil twin popped into my mind. Hey, it happened in soap operas.

Her hand shook as she motioned behind me. "Close the door, Nina."

I closed it.

"Please sit."

I sat.

Ever so obedient, that's me. Nina Colette Obedient Ceceri Quinn.

I'd been fighting with myself the whole way home. That there must have been some mistake, that there was no way Bridget could be involved in any of this. I'd known her forever. Then some. But the woman I was looking at now was not the little girl who'd shared her purple grapes with me in kindergarten.

A hunted wild look had taken root in her red-rimmed, tear-stained eyes. "I didn't want it to come to this. I told you to back out of it."

My throat tightened, my stomach hurt. Moisture stung my eyes. Who was this woman? Where was the Bridget I knew? Loved?

She sniffled. "But now, now you know too much."

"I don't understand, Bridget."

With the back of her hand, she wiped her leaking nose. "No one does, Nina. Not you. Not Tim. Not anyone."

I inhaled. My pulse pounded, causing blood to rush through my ears. I cleared my throat of its sudden frog, managed to say through a choked voice, "What have you done?"

My stomach turned, twisted. Farmer Joe. Oh dear God. I wrapped my hands around my middle, held on tight.

A tear slipped down her cheek. "What I needed to do."

Tears pooled in my eyes. I couldn't wrap my brain around what was happening. "Why?"

"I was going to lose him." Her lower lip trembled. "After all we'd been through, he was going to leave me."

"Tim?"

She nodded. Her finger still rested on the trigger of the gun. "He wanted a baby. A baby I couldn't give him." Swiping at her eyes, she rocked back and forth. "I had to do something."

I struggled to find something to say, to keep her talking, to *understand*. "Why didn't you and Tim adopt?"

"You know why."

Tim. Bridget had once mentioned how Tim wanted his own child, to carry on the Sandowski bloodline.

A dull ache pulsed inside my head. This was just too hard to comprehend . . . beyond all reasoning. "So you faked a pregnancy?"

"I had to!"

I leaned forward. "But Bridget, didn't Tim notice? How could he not?"

Color drained from her face. "He doesn't touch me anymore, Nina."

"But what about doctor's appointments? That ultrasound picture?"

She brushed the tears from her cheeks. They were quickly replaced. "I made sure he was out of town the days I had appointments, and that picture was easy enough to download."

A tight throat made it hard to talk. "Where were you planning to get a baby?"

Her rocking was making me dizzy. "Private adoption. Black market. Online listings to buy babies."

Realization hit me hard. "But you needed money."

Fresh tears streamed down her face. "Yes."

"Money you could have gotten if Tim's parents had sold their land?"

Rocking, she nodded, the gun still aimed my way. "I had time, almost eight months. I figured they'd sell soon enough. Who wouldn't?"

I couldn't fault her reasoning on that score. I'd thought the same thing.

"But months went by, Nina. And nothing. Nothing at all. They turned down offers left and right. Millions!"

In my head, I could see Bridget calculating how many babies that money would buy. Nausea roiled.

"I had to do something, something fast. Chanson sent me, as the Sandowski attorney, an offer for three and a half million. Dutifully, I sent him the refusal, just as I sent all the others refusals as well. But desperation was setting in."

I had a million questions, but I didn't want to interrupt her. She seemed intent on letting it all out.

"I came up with a plan. I went to Demming, made a deal with him. If I got Tim's parents to sell, he'd make sure I was compensated. I thought they'd sell quickly if they knew the lengths the buyers were willing to go to get the land. So I organized the phone calls, the letters—"

"You broke in here." I thought back to the day Mr. Cabrera had seen the skulker at my house. It would have been easy to mistake Bridget for a man if she wore deceiving clothing. With her height and build, and absence of a pregnant tummy, I could see it easily.

"Your door was unlocked. Not very safe."

I pressed the heels of my hands into my eyes. This just wasn't happening. I looked up. "Why kill Joe, Bridget?"

"The county sent me a letter about the eminent domain."

"I—" I struggled to voice my horror.

"My time was running out, Nina. The threats weren't working. If anything, it made Tim's parents more stubborn. Something drastic needed to be done. And Joe was dying, slowly, every day. It broke all our hearts to see him that way. Ending his life was an act of kindness. I told him I brought some herbal tea that would make him feel better. He was happy, Nina. Grateful."

Oh God. Oh dear God. My hand felt clammy as I pressed it to my lips, keeping my horror in.

"And the thermos?"

"Easy enough to follow the lab tech and lift the thermos from the backseat when he made a stop." She shook her head. "It was ridiculously easy. Tim would probably be able to get many convictions overturned if he knew just how easy it was."

Tim. I covered my mouth. Mentally, I sent him a huge apology and scolded myself for not going to the police sooner. I wasn't a detective, far from it, and what in the world made me think I could *help*? Seemed all I'd done was make things worse.

It took effort, but I pushed aside my past with Bridget, focused on numbing myself. "And Demming? Why kill him when you needed his money?"

"When Joe died, I'd come up with a plan to frame Demming for the death. I'd been slowly framing him all along. Leaving the rat poison at his constructions sites, using pay phones near his house, his business . . . I'd warned him about not meeting with you, but you ended up fooling him anyway, as it turns out. He wasn't pleased you duped him. After you told me you were going back there, I gave him the heads-up, and I waited nearby. It was the perfect time to get rid of him."

Still reeling from the fact that she had set me up, I said, "Still, with him dead, you wouldn't get the money."

"No, but Chanson's six and a half million was still on the table, and I figured that with everything that had happened, Tim's mom wouldn't hesitate to sell to the congressman. That, and Joe's case would be closed—Demming pinned for the murder."

The mantel clock ticked. I didn't think I could become more repulsed, but then all the pieces fell into place in my head.

"You wanted Demming to kill me."

She shook her head. "No, but it was a risk I was willing to take."

"Did you plan on me taking the rap for his death?"

"Actually, I thought the suspicion would fall on the congressman, where everything would be swept under the rug, and we'd all live happily ever after."

Except Joe. And Demming.

My brain had gone numb with all this information. "And the night you tried to force me off the road?"

"It was a warning."

"I don't think the train thought so."

Her eyebrows dipped. "You're here, aren't you?"

I didn't want to remind her that she was holding a gun on me. "And Tim's mom this morning?"

"Even after all that had happened, culminating in your little accident, she didn't want to sell the farm. So I upped the ante."

"But to shoot at her?"

"I shot the window. Not her. She wasn't hurt."

"She's at the hospital. Tim's with her."

Bridget jumped to her feet, panic etching her features. "She wasn't supposed to get hurt."

Oh, that made it okay.

"Is she all right?"

I couldn't reconcile this Bridget, the one who actually cared about her mother-in-law's well-being with the Bridget who would kill a man to cover her rear. Confusion laced my tone. "Flying glass."

Anger pierced her gaze. She lifted her arm, leveling the gun. "You were supposed to stop investigating! Stop nosing into things. But no. You had to go and hack into my computer records! Imagine my surprise when I tried to sign on but someone was using my account. Knowing how nosy you are, and your inane suspicions about Tim, it didn't take much for me to figure out you were behind it. If you had just stayed out of this, everything would be okay!"

Computer records? Suddenly, I wished that I had returned Tam's call right away. It hit me like a knock upside the head what she had found. The baby search. If I had known sooner . . .

She looked around, tears streaming. "It's time."

I swallowed. "For what?"

Big ice blue eyes blinked at me. "Life's just been too tough for you lately. Oh yes, I know all about Kevin. You just can't bear to live without him."

So she was going to make my death look like a suicide. I dropped my head, vowing to myself that I would never again fall victim to a sob story of any kind, even when I'd known the person a lifetime. I caught movement out of the corner of my eye. Xena slithered out from under the couch.

My gaze jumped up to Bridget's. Apparently she hadn't noticed the boa coiled near her ankles. Looking down, I noticed Xena looked quite intimidating for a snake that had been on the lam for over a week. Thick, fat. Hideous. I shuddered.

Using the gun, she motioned me to my feet. "Up."

"I could scream, you know," I pointed out.

"You wouldn't."

Opening my mouth wide, I hollered. It was loud, blood-curdling, and felt really, really good.

Bridget pointed the gun in my face, her finger resting on the trigger. I stopped screaming. Her hand was shaking so hard, I was afraid she'd shoot by accident.

"Don't do that again."

Ohh-kay.

"Let's go."

"Where?" I asked, taking a step back, away from Xena as she wound her way toward me.

"Bathroom, I guess. Wouldn't want to make a mess."

Outside, a car door slammed. A surge of fear flooded through me. Riley! I'd totally forgotten about Riley.

Terror took over. He couldn't come in here. With her frame of mind, I wouldn't put it past Bridget to shoot first, ask questions later.

Thankfully, she didn't appear to have heard the door. I went in the direction she motioned. The longer I could keep Bridget away from Riley, the better.

Bridget was out and out crying. "I don't want to do this, really I don't. But I can't lose Tim. I can't. He's all I have."

Grabbing my arm, she took a step, her foot landing on Xena.

Bridget shrieked.

Xena straightened, struck out. I shoved Bridget hard and she toppled onto the couch. I took off running, hitting the stairs two at a time. A gunshot echoed. I prayed Riley had enough sense not to come in after hearing it.

I ran to my bedroom, closed the door, and locked it. My hands were shaking as I felt under my mattress for the key to Kevin's nightstand. Latching onto it, I pulled it out. Bridget pounded at the door. A few seconds later, she shot at the lock. Miraculously, it held.

Shoving the key into the lock, I opened the drawer, reached inside for Kevin's gun.

Another shot rang out. I ducked as wood splintered. I could hear Bridget's sobs through the door.

The ammunition was in a small combination safe in the drawer. My bandaged hand kept slipping off the dial before I finally got it open.

Another shot. My door swung open.

Bridget stepped into the room, nearly doubled over, she was crying so hard. "I don't want to do this. Please know that."

As she raised her arm, I reared back and chucked Kevin's gun at her head just as a shot rang out behind her. Bridget crumpled to the floor.

My heart hammered somewhere near my carotid artery as I spotted Riley standing in the doorway, a pistol hanging off the end of his forefinger.

His blue eyes stared at me in shock. "I'm sorry. I didn't know what else to do."

I jumped up and kicked both guns away from Bridget's prone body. Then I held out my hand for Riley's pistol. He handed it over. I put my arm around him, felt him shaking. I kissed his forehead.

Bridget moaned on the floor, holding her bleeding head.

Footsteps sounded on the stairs. I turned in time to see Kevin round the corner into the hall with what seemed like the whole police force behind him.

I handed the pistol over to Kevin. He tucked it in his waistband and took Riley in his arms. He looked from Bridget to his son, a panicked question in his eyes.

"She wasn't shot," I said.

Riley's eyes widened. "But I fired . . ."

Kevin checked the gun's ammo. "Blanks."

"Thank God," I murmured.

Bridget sat up as EMTs pushed passed us. She had an oozing gun-sized welt on her forehead, and blood trickled from her nose.

"Who shot the snake?" I heard someone yell up the stairs.

"Xena?" Riley barreled down the steps.

"Bridget must've shot her," I said to no one in particular as I followed him down.

A uniformed officer held Xena out. She hung limply, an ugly wound marring her smooth skin. "I think it's too late."

Riley gulped air.

My heart broke for him. I had to do something. "Give her to me." I held out my arms.

The officer alternately stared at the limp reptile in his hands and at me.

"Give her to me. We've got to get her to the vet's."

"Nina, there's no point . . ." Kevin put his hand on my shoulder. I shrugged it away. If Riley cared enough about me to shoot someone to protect me, then I could damn well make sure to do my best to save the pet he loved.

"Give. Her. To. Me. *Now*."

The officer handed her to me. She was limp, her thick body seeming lifeless. She was softer than I imagined. I had been thinking sandpaper where she was more rose petals.

I handed her to Riley. "Go get in Mr. Cabrera's car."

"You can't leave, Nina."

I turned to Kevin. Tears burned the inside of my eyelids. "She needs a doctor." My voice was thick, syrupy. It came from a place deep in my soul.

"Let me drive," he finally said.

"No. I'll do it."

"Nina, you're shaking."

Even as he said it, I felt the trembling. I looked up at him, saw something soft in his eyes I couldn't quite name. "Okay."

Mr. Cabrera was on the porch when we stepped out, Kevin's arm around me, holding me up.

"I gave the keys to the boy," he said, pointing to Riley, who was already in the LeMans.

"I appreciate it," I said.

"I didn't know whether or not to call the police when I heard the scream. But I did. I wasn't interfering or anything, but that scream was mighty loud. Then when I looked in the window I saw that woman with a gun . . . I wasn't being nosey, mind you, I was just looking out for your safety."

I kissed his weathered cheek. "Thanks."

Twenty-nine

Hours later, I sat on the front porch swing with Kevin.

"A what?" I said to him, though to my ears my own voice sounded more like a screech.

"An undercover officer," he repeated.

My jaw dropped. "You used your own son as an undercover officer?"

The swing creaked as it rocked back and forth. Police technicians roamed through my house, my yard. My mother was inside, directing traffic.

While Riley and I'd be staying with my parents tonight, Xena would be staying with the vet, who assured us that she was going to recover from a graze wound. Seems when she was lying limp in that officer's arms, she was just playing dead, lying in wait until we were in the car, where she tried to make one of my Keds her dinner. So much for them being snake-proof.

For once, I wasn't dreading staying under the roof with my mother hovering over me. Sometimes a girl needed her mom.

Maybe a boy, too, which made my heart ache for Riley, for what he was going through. If we were closer . . .

I shook my head, pushing that thought aside. There was

no changing the past, and I wondered what our future would bring. Especially now.

A fingernail moon glowed above. A slash of light cut across Kevin's face. "Well, not technically an officer, more an informant."

I hit him in the chest. Twice. "What were you thinking?"

He winced. "I was thinking that we needed the Skinz off the streets. There was only one way to do it. Riley. As the son of a cop, a kid who wants to rebel against his parents . . . he was perfect. Especially after we split up."

"You used your own son as an undercover officer?" I had to repeat myself because I just couldn't believe it.

"Nina, he was never in any danger. He was properly trained and being watched every minute. He knew what he was doing."

Mr. Cabrera's front light flipped off. No doubt so he could gawk through the window without being seen. "How is a fifteen-year-old properly trained?"

"Boys younger than that fight wars in other countries."

I glared at him. "I can't believe you. And I can't believe you didn't tell me."

"I told you to stay out of it. You wouldn't listen."

I poked him in the chest again. "I was scared for him! Why didn't you tell me?"

"I couldn't tell anybody. Only a handful knew."

"Mike Novak."

"He was placed in the school to keep an eye on the Skinz."

"So he's not a school resource officer."

Kevin laughed. "Far from it."

"What about Riley's vice principal?" Crickets chirped their soothing nighttime songs. Too bad I was too jumbled inside to benefit from the lullabies. "Did he know?"

"No. Only a select few within the force knew, and the school superintendent."

"Candy?"

"No. And she started asking questions after you went to see her, so we had to get her out of town in a hurry. A seminar in Phoenix."

"Did you at least catch the kids?"

"Yes. It was one of their guns that Riley tried using on Bridget Sandowski. We were down the block, out of sight, waiting for the buy to go down. Riley had just made the purchase outside the house when he heard the first gunshot. The Skinz leader took off, but we caught him."

Bile rose in my throat. Bridget was in the hospital—in the psych wing—under police protection. If deemed competent, she'd be transferred to jail immediately. By the looks of it, though, she could be heading straight to Fairview, a state-run psychiatric hospital, for further treatment.

It was hard to believe. Even harder to believe that I really hadn't known her at all, despite being her friend for over twenty years.

"Did you talk to Tim?"

"He's with Bridget. He had no idea."

I felt guilty I'd had suspicions of him at all. I owed him such a huge "I'm sorry." "What about Mrs. Sandowski?" I asked.

"She's in shock, but I think she'll be okay." A mosquito landed on Kevin's arm, but I didn't swat it away. "She honestly loves the land, the house. It's all bittersweet now, isn't it?"

"How so?"

"You haven't heard?"

"What?"

"Yesterday Sandowski's Farm was declared a historical landmark. No one will be buying it. Mrs. Sandowski had hired an outside lawyer to do the paperwork without telling her family, in case it fell through." He scratched his arm.

So *that* was what Mrs. Sandowski had meant by having a feeling that things would be over soon. Good for her.

Kevin gave the swing a good push. "You should have told *me* what was going on with the Sandowskis."

"I was angry at you. I had also made a promise to Mrs. Sandowski." I paused. "And I didn't think I could trust you."

"As an officer you can always trust me."

My feet scraped the porch's planks, stopping the swing. "But as a husband?"

"I'm a louse."

I looked down at my wedding band, then back up at him. "Honorable," I mumbled.

"Hmm?" he said.

"Nothing."

Almost twenty-four hours later, life had calmed a bit. I'd spent all morning and most of the afternoon at the police station recounting everything I knew over and over again. The media was having a field day, and Tam had called to say that the phone had been ringing off the hook at TBS with potential clients. What a crazy world.

"That blood's never going to come out."

My mother stood over the spot Kevin dripped blood from the day I attacked him with the hockey stick, but I kept quiet, not wanting to shatter that whole "My daughter the hero" image she now had of me.

I stared at the rust-colored stains on the rug. "I'm going to get a new carpet as soon as I find time to shop."

"Good. This color is dated."

Fighting back a yawn, I rolled my eyes. I supposed focusing on the rug instead of all that had happened in this room was easier for both of us. Bridget had meant a lot to my mom too.

A sudden lump in my throat accompanied the quick sting of tears in my eyes. I sucked in a deep breath. There was a pain, a sharp ache in my chest, that had nothing to do with any physical injuries and had everything to do with Bridget.

I still didn't completely understand why she had done the things she'd done. But I hadn't been through the hell she'd been through, either. Who knew how they'd react in her situation? If my mind were to just snap, all common sense fleeing, all sense of right and wrong vanishing . . .

Mom tucked a lock of my hair behind my ear. "Sleep at our house again tonight," she offered, for the fifth time.

"I think it's best if Riley and I stay here from now on. It *is* our home." I pulled a pillow out of its case. "Besides, I don't think Riley would leave Xena." Back from the vet and safely ensconced in her cage (that now had a very heavy slab of granite on its top), Xena was doing fine. She'd have a scar where the bullet grazed her skin, but other than that, she'd be back to her normal self in no time. *Goody*, I silently mocked. Had I really held her? I must've been in shock. I'd washed my hands at least a hundred times since.

Mom sat on the edge of the bed. "How's Riley holding up?"

"Quite well, considering. Analise found a therapist for him to talk to, someone she knows through work."

"You think he needs it?"

I remembered the look in his eye when he handed me the pistol. "He needs it."

He was feeling the weight of his actions, even though he harmed no one. I think it was the realization that he could have—and most likely would have had there been bullets in the gun—killed someone that now haunted him.

I grabbed another pillow and relieved it of its case.

"Don't tell me you're going to sleep in this room?"

Nudging her off the bed, I pulled the sheets off and threw them in the hamper, my bandaged hand making it quite a chore. "I am."

"Why don't you wait a few days? Sleep on the couch."

"I have to do it."

"I don't understand."

I looked at her. "I don't quite understand it myself."

She half frowned, half smiled. Sighed. "I should have known you'd do anything to get out of that fitting yesterday."

I looked at her and grinned. "What fitting?"

Sleep wouldn't come. I kept hearing creaks and noises I couldn't place and it was freaking me out, though I knew no one was creeping around, thanks to my new alarm system.

Technically, I shouldn't be sleeping at all (not that I was). I'd promised Ana I'd wait up for her call to hear about the Big Date with Jean-Claude's brother Michel. I figured I'd hear the phone ring if I happened to drift off.

So far, no drifting and no ringing.

I pulled the sheet up over my chin, then pushed it down, unable to find that balance between too hot and too cold. The clock glowed 11:25.

The bed creaked as I thrust my foot out from under the covers to hang over the edge of the mattress. I should have been exhausted after the day—heck, the week—I'd had, but my eyes were open wide. I rolled onto my side, staring at the cold, empty expanse of space to my right. Where Kevin should be.

I'd finally taken off my wedding band for good, stashing it in my underwear drawer. Out of sight and all that. My hand felt light. Awkward.

I lifted my nightshirt to my face and inhaled. It smelled of Kevin. It should, as technically it was his shirt. It was no big deal to sleep in it, I deluded myself, breaking a cardinal commandment.

Baby steps, I told myself.

Tossing onto my back, I stared at the ceiling. The plaster was still swirled. Nothing had changed since the last time I looked at it, two minutes ago. Giving up hope of sleep, I jumped up and grabbed my robe.

Down in the kitchen, I pulled a roll of cookie dough from

the fridge, peeled back the wrapping, and started eating it, banana-style. I climbed up on the counter and swung my legs, trying not to think about how pitiful I must look.

A second later, Riley came down, darkness circling his eyes, a scowl tugging on his lips.

"Can't sleep?"

He shook his head.

I offered up the cookie dough—a big sacrifice, in my opinion. "Want some?"

His eyebrows darted up in a "no way, no how" look. Crossing over to the fridge, he removed the orange juice carton from the top shelf. He raised it to his lips.

My eyes narrowed in warning.

He took a swig, replaced the carton, and turned to give me a sly "what're you going to do about it" smile. It would have been charming if he weren't purposely making me suffer.

Okay, I admit it—it was still charming.

He levered himself up beside me on the counter. My gaze took in his sullen face, sweeping over his angry, troubled eyes, his still chubby cheeks, his pinched lips, and I realized, maybe for the first time, that he was *mine*. My son.

My father's words came back to me. *There's always a silver lining, Nina. Sometimes not as clear as one would like, but always.*

I smiled.

"What?" he said.

"Nothing."

"Then why are you smiling?"

I pushed off the counter, headed for the stairs, cookie dough in hand. I had been thinking that as far as silver linings go, Riley wasn't too shabby. Not that I'd tell him so, and have him get all defensive on me.

Pausing on the second stair, I turned to him. "I was just thinking about your hair."

He patted the stripes. "What about it?"

"Have you ever thought of going silver? You'd look good in silver."

"Uh, Nina?"

"Yeah?"

"You still taking that medication?"

"No, Riley," I murmured. "I'm just starting to see things a whole lot clearer now."

Take Your Garden by Surprise
by Nina Quinn

To all landscapers, amateur and professional, poison ivy is a pain in the rear—sometimes literally, as my cousin Ana almost discovered.

Poison ivy grows anywhere and everywhere, is often misidentified, and is a beast to get rid of, but it *can* be controlled in various ways. For those less brave, remember the adage, "Leaves of three, leave them be." For you wannabe pros, here are some tips to get rid of that pesky poison ivy.

Before you start, the first thing to know is that the leaves themselves don't cause the allergic reaction—it's the oil, called urushiol, on the leaves, stem, and roots, that makes us miserable. Do not touch anything—anything—after coming in direct contact with poison ivy until after you wash.

All right, if you're set on getting rid of that problematic vine, first and foremost, you can dig the sucker up. Wait until the roots are good and wet, arm yourself appropriately (heavy duty gloves, a hoe, poison ivy preventative lotion, and thick paper or plastic trash bags), and dig the vine out at the root and drop it in the bag, being careful to come in as little contact with the plant as possible.

Sound like too much work? Try cutting the vine back with a pair of clippers at its base. Any branches or leaves left behind need to be gathered up (again, appropriately arm yourself) and thrown away—to the curb, not the compost pile. Continue to cut it back as new sprouts, well, sprout.

If such close contact with the plant gives you the heebies, bring in the big guns—herbicides. Best used in the spring and fall, a few doses of glyphosate or triclopyr, either sprayed or brushed onto the leaves and stem of the poison ivy, will usually kill the vine—and any other shrubs or brush around it, so be careful what you're aiming for.

Or, you can mix and match. Cut the vine back and blast any new sprouts with the herbicide. You might need to repeat the treatment once or twice, but it is highly effective. Please never use salt as an herbicide—it's highly toxic for years after use to all vegetation later planted in that spot, and it can leach into groundwater.

If you're out and out lazy and don't mind a little unsigh liness, a tarp thrown over the poison ivy growth w smother it over time. To pretty things up, you can add a ni layer of mulch and a birdbath on top of the covering.

If the poison ivy is in a little-used area, out of danger accidental brushing up against, and isn't causing any pr lems, I suggest you leave it be. Honest to goodness, it's tually quite valuable to our wildlife. Its pretty berries the creepy-crawlies hiding on its vines are a great sourc food for birds, and its leaves provide a 24-hour buffe various forms of four-legged critters, such as deer goats. Yes, goats—should you have any wandering by.

Above all, *never* burn poison ivy! The urushiol oi causes the rash can become airborne and might be inh causing a rash on your lungs that can be deadly. Mowi vines isn't a good idea either. It just spreads what trying to avoid.

Again, be sure not to touch anything after dealin poison ivy. The allergenic oil can stay present for ye many surfaces, including shoes and garden tools. A always, always wash everything, including yourself and your clothes, that comes in contact with poison ivy.

If all else fails, call in the professionals. It's what we're here for. Until then, be careful when you're playing (or spying) in the bushes.

Best wishes for happy gardening,
Nina Quinn

nt-
ill
ce

of
ob-
ac-
and
e of
for
and

that
aled,
g the
ou're

g with
ars on
lways,